THE WOMAN UNDER THE BRIDGE

A JAY DELP MYSTERY THRILLER

DOUGLAS PRATT

MANTA
PRESS

For Ashlee

1

A breeze rippled over the water, raising goosebumps on his arm. Jake let the rod fall loosely in his hands and, with a swift flick of his wrist, sent the lure soaring into the night sky. The line released a soft whizzing sound as it flew, only to be followed by a single thump as it reached its destination in the tranquil waters of Biloxi Bay. The bright lights from the casinos glowed and spilled across the surface, creating a kaleidoscope of colors that shimmered along each wave. Even with the roar of vehicles passing over the bridge above them, all was still in this moment.

Troy steered the boat as Jake cast his line out over the side. The gentle waves rocked the vessel, and the moonlight reflected off of the glassy surface. A salty breeze caressed their faces, carrying with it the warm scent of the nearby shoreline and a faint hum from the cars traveling across the Biloxi Bay Bridge.

"Do you remember that time we almost got arrested for trespassing?" Jake asked.

"Of course," Troy said, a smirk on his face. "You've always been good at talking your way out of trouble."

Jake laughed. "Yeah. It was the only way I survived high school."

Troy chuckled. "It's a gift. But we were lucky that night. I thought we'd end up in jail."

They fell into a comfortable silence, the only sounds the gentle rocking of the boat and the occasional splash of a fish breaking the surface.

Troy watched as Jake's expression changed from ease to seriousness. A heavy weight settled in his stomach, the unease growing with each passing second.

"Hey, Troy," Jake said with some trepidation, his gaze fixed on the waves washing against the shore. "There's something I need to talk to you about. It's about Sarah."

Troy expected what was coming, and he wasn't sure if he was ready for it. Troy's chest tightened as Jake spoke, his words hung in the air.

"She looked... bad. Like she's been going through some rough stuff."

A rush of emotions came over Troy—sympathy for Sarah, fear that her troubles would come to haunt them, and an underlying sense of dread that this was all somehow connected to them. He swallowed hard. "What does it have to do with us?" he asked, his voice trembling slightly.

Jake didn't answer right away. He stared out at the water, the occasional splash of a fish breaking the surface the only sound between them. Finally, he sighed. "I don't know. I just wanted to talk about it, I guess. It's been weighing on me."

Troy shivered despite the warmth of the night. Something deep inside him sensed this would not end well.

Suddenly, a tug on his line alerted Jake. His knees went

weak, and he fell backward as the weight of whatever was on the hook pulled hard against him.

Troy, behind him in the boat, roared, "You got a big one!"

But as Jake reeled in his catch, he knew something was wrong. The tension on the line seemed too heavy, not flapping like a fish's tail should. More like the pull of a pail at the end of a rope after being plunged into a well.

He squinted into the black waters, and what lay beneath the surface made him sick to his stomach. A pale, lifeless human hand floated up out of the cold, dark depths toward him.

Troy's eyes widened, and his jaw dropped as he saw Jake's catch. Floating face down in the murky water, the woman was a ghostly figure with pallid skin stretched across her slender frame and long, matted hair. As they peered closer, they realized her disheveled and torn tank top exposed more of her than intended.

"What the fuck?" Troy mumbled.

Jake's pulse throbbed like a bomb in his chest as he stared at the harrowing scene before him. "We need to call the police," he gasped, his voice squeezed out of a stricken throat.

Troy nodded, his face drained of all color. "I'll get the phone," he muttered, scrambling in his pocket for his Android. "What the hell happened here?" he croaked, a haunted whisper echoing in the hushed atmosphere.

As Troy dialed 911, Jake clenched the wheel and steered the boat closer to the body. The gentle lapping of waves against the hull was the only sound in the eerie stillness as Jake leaned over the edge. He barely brought himself to reach out and touch her shoulder, his lungs so tight with fear, he thought he would faint. What if she was still alive?

His fingers grazed her skin, and a chill ran through him as he realized she was gone. He stumbled back on unsteady legs, his head spinning from the sudden crushing weight of death.

"Watch it," Troy warned as the boat tipped from side to side.

"How could this happen?" Jake's voice trembled as he gazed in shock at the devastation before him. His mind raced with confusion and fear, unable to comprehend what had caused such a tragedy. "Who could do something like this?" he whispered, powerless against the wave of emotions that had overcome him.

Troy put his phone away, his face grim. "The police are on their way. They'll sort it out."

"What did they say?"

"It was only the operator," Troy replied. "She said to stay here. The cops would be here as soon as they could."

"It's after midnight," Jake snapped. "Do they have a boat in the water?"

Troy squinted at the shore, just seventy-five feet away. He didn't think the police would need anything more than a dinghy or a small rowboat for them.

But Jake's unease lingered in the air. He couldn't shake the realization that the girl lying inches from them was already dead. His mind raced with questions that had no answers. Who was this woman? The cities along the Mississippi Gulf Coast connected like one extended town, and he wondered if he'd ever encountered her before. A sour taste rose in his throat as he struggled to contain the fear building up inside him. He had to swallow hard to keep down the bile threatening to overflow.

As they waited for the police to arrive, Jake and Troy huddled on the boat under the bridge, muscles taut and senses alert. The rhythmic crashing of waves against the hull seemed an eerie backdrop to their restless waiting. The weight of her body hung over them like a dark cloud, and they sat there in silence until the sound of approaching sirens shattered the stillness.

2

———

Thick raindrops laced with sea salt slashed across the windshield. Jay grumbled as he switched his wipers on and off. It was typical coastal weather—fierce, sudden thunderstorms that sent torrents of water pelting against the already humid air. He endured the deluge from dark clouds that brought the temperature up a few degrees when he lives in Panama City or West Palm Beach. In these cities, heavy cumulus clouds blew in suddenly from offshore, dropped a short downpour, and moved on.

He remembered the streets of Ocean Springs like the back of his hand, and he didn't need to slow down. The navy-blue Jeep Wrangler was a blur as it sped through the city and around the bends. Jay slammed on the brakes just in time to avoid being run off the road by a dually truck—probably a local boy heading home from the bar.

He soon recognized the white house as the Jeep pulled up into Terry Delp's drive, its engine still purring from its eventful journey. His knuckles grew white as he clutched the steering wheel tightly as he turned off the vehicle, anxiously taking in every detail of his surroundings. A clap of thunder rolled across the dark, shrouded sky, casting an eerie light on drenched streets.

Beside him stood an old, twisted metal mailbox. Its jagged edges and distorted form reminded Jay of the night some twenty-five years earlier when, with the help of Zima and Southern Comfort, he drunkenly side-swiped the box while attempting to drive into his parents' driveway. He remembered his father's angry red face, lit up by the headlights. The stinging pain on his right shoulder still lingered from when Terry Delp pressed his burning cigarette against it.

Before he took another breath, Jay watched his brother, wearing a tattered leather jacket over his head, appear at the door.

"Jay!" Sam exclaimed as he dashed through the rain to greet Jay. "What happened to tomorrow?" he added, still struggling to put his thoughts together.

"Change of plans," Jay replied with a sigh as they ran to the cover of the carport. "I drove all the way up from West Palm."

Sam nodded and gave Jay a pat on the back. "It's good to have you home, brother."

Jay's lips twitched slightly, attempting to form a smile, but his weariness from the long journey stopped him. Doubt crept into his mind. Had he made the right choice? The title of Chief of the Ocean Springs Police Department sounded impressive enough, but he wondered if it was worth giving up on his progress at the Palm Beach County Sheriff's Department, where he had become Chief of Detectives just last year. He was here for his father now, who had once barely tolerated his sons before dementia set in. Was this a wise decision?

Jay stepped over the threshold, and a wave of stale cigarette smoke smacked him in the face. His nose wrinkled as he tried to breathe without inhaling too deeply. The air was thick with it, and he knew his clothes would smell like it for hours after he left this place. The television screen blared some network cop show.

"Dad, it's Jay," he stated, trying to make him listen.

Terry rotated his head and squinted at Jay. "Who are you?" he grumbled.

"It's me, Jay. Your son," Jay uttered.

Terry snorted. "I don't have a son named Jay," he barked, turning his attention back to the TV.

"It's good to see you, too, Father," Jay replied in a sarcastic tone.

"There's beer in the kitchen," Sam told him.

Jay gave a half-grin. "I wouldn't turn one down," he admitted as he made his way to the fridge, where he pulled out a six-pack of Dogfish Ale.

Sam watched Jay and smiled, chuckling softly. "Old habits, old friends."

"Quiet down," Terry's voice snapped like a whip, and Sam quickly motioned for Jay to follow him outside.

The rain had lessened to a soft pitter-patter on the roof as they stepped onto the porch. Sam sank down into a wicker chair next to the front window, resting his elbows on its armrests. He nervously eyed the light spilling from inside the house. "I'm glad you're back," he said through gritted teeth, averting his gaze away from Jay's.

Jay spun around, frustration radiating off him in waves. "It's not just on your shoulders, Sam," he declared vehemently. "Dad is even more unmanageable than before."

Sam heaved a massive sigh, his heart heavy. "He's always been difficult," he muttered. "Now with his memory gone... the other day, he thought Danielle was Mom!"

A deep growl escaped Jay's throat as he inhaled sharply. "That must have been tough," he snarled.

"Danielle handled it perfectly until Dad realized what was happening," Sam finally responded, his voice barely over a whisper. "But the worst part was when he mistook Julia for Sandra."

"Shit," Jay cursed, shaking his head in disbelief. "How old is Julia now?"

"The same age as Sandra was when she passed," Sam replied hollowly. "Somehow, Danielle is one of the only people who can get through to him."

Jay pursed his lips and nodded in understanding. "We have to find someone to stay here with him during the day," he pointed out matter-of-factly.

"Danielle has already found us a few candidates to interview," Sam informed him, desperation palpable in his tone. "But I know you'll want some time to settle into your new job."

"Eh, I'm flexible," Jay spat. "After all, I think I have an 'in' with the city councilman..."

Chuckling, Sam shook his head as a smirk spread across his face. "Yeah, until he gets voted out for hiring his older brother."

"Let's hope it doesn't come to that," Jay remarked.

Sam's shoulders lifted with mirth. "I'm not worried. The mayor and the council decided on you unanimously."

"I'll try not to screw it up," Jay assured Sam, taking a sip of his beer.

"Your bosses in Palm County and Panama City raved about you," Sam told him. "It was almost gratuitous. If I didn't know you better, I'd believe you were RoboCop."

Jay laughed. "Oh, I'm sure at least one of my wives referred to me as that," he said, adding, "I doubt she meant it in a good way."

"I'm guessing that was Katie," Sam stated. "She was a bit of a bitch."

"Eh, we were both young and dumb," Jay acknowledged.

"Doesn't mean she wasn't a bitch," Sam retorted. "She left you for that dickhead on the billboards."

"He didn't have those signs at the time," Jay pointed out. "He built that law firm from the ground up."

"You don't sound bitter about it at all," Sam remarked, looking astonished.

"I'm not," Jay told his brother, and when Sam narrowed his eyes, he added, "Really, I'm not. Katie and I weren't going to last. Long before she met Clayton, we were on the outs."

"You two talk at all?" Sam asked.

"Naw," Jay said, allowing his drawl to stretch the syllable out. "It's been a bit."

"Well, you haven't lived here in a decade," Sam reminded him. "Certainly not since you joined the Corps."

Jay shrugged. "Hard to settle after that."

Sam nodded. Jay didn't think he understood what time in the Marine Corps did to a man. They had changed him irrevocably. Jay wasn't the same man he had been when he got on the bus to Parris Island. First, he'd only been eighteen. Even Sam, who had never left South Mississippi, could say he was the same man now that he had been at eighteen. But Jay's change was deeper. His years in Recon had taken him into Afghanistan, Iran, and several other countries that required a certain force to prevail. He'd killed people in every one of those places. Jay had watched—up close and personal—men's heads explode after he put a round through them. The first time Jay saw that pink mist in the crosshair of his rifle, he would never be the innocent kid from Ocean Springs again.

Those kills didn't keep him up at night. He'd only performed his duty, and duty wasn't something to feel guilty about. Even the men he'd killed since leaving the Corps had been in the line of duty.

None of that was a subject he could talk to Sam about. His brother would never understand. Jay didn't always grasp it himself. A thousand-yard shot on a windy day was a challenge, and the first time Jay hit his target, he felt a level of elation he didn't comprehend. He'd just killed a man, yet he could have just scored a touchdown from the dopamine punch his brain got.

"It's raining out here," Terry Delp barked from the screen door. "You boys might need to go find Sandra. I think she went down to the water to fish out some crawdads."

Sam shot Jay a concerned expression.

"Dad, I'll look for her in a minute," Jay called back.

"Thanks, Jaybird," Terry replied.

Jay bristled at the old nickname. He hadn't heard his father use it since before he could remember.

No, he corrected. He remembered when Terry Delp last called his son that. Jay couldn't recall the exact date, but it was before his sister died.

Terry added, "Tell her not to stay out in the rain."

"Okay, Dad," Jay responded. He watched his father turn and walk inside, letting the screen door slam shut.

"Sad, isn't it?" Sam remarked.

"Yeah," Jay admitted. "I wasn't ready for that."

"He'll be back to himself in a few minutes," Sam explained. "Although, sometimes that's worse. The other week, he thought Mama was at Winn-Dixie. I watched him realize she was dead. His face twisted in agony."

"Geez, she's been gone a long time," Jay said.

"In that moment, she'd just been there and went to the store. It would be the same as you telling me Danielle died in a car accident tonight. I ate dinner with her two hours ago. To him, it's the same thing."

"Damn, that sucks. Even for him."

Jay regretted saying the last part as it left his mouth. But Sam nodded in agreement.

"In some ways, this is better, but in others, it's so much worse," Sam considered. "He can be the dad he was before Sandra drowned, and then it's like a roller coaster ride to him after Mama died. I'm only there on the outside, but it's emotional still."

"Just like now," Jay suggested. "He's convinced Sandra is down at the bayou."

"He does that a lot, and it's not that she's just down at the water," Sam explained. "He thinks it's that day."

"Oh," Jay muttered.

"Yeah," Sam continued. "It's usually earlier in the afternoon, at least before the police came by. Sometimes it's like he's talking to that officer that delivered the news. It can be a bit much."

"Sam, I'm sorry. You should have told me about all this."

His brother only shrugged. "What good would it do?" he asked. "You were too far away to do anything."

"I'd have come back," Jay emphasized. "Helped you more."

Sam shook his head. "No regrets, brother. There wasn't a job for you here then. What, were you going to be the guy set up at the causeway to ticket travelers?"

"I could have done something."

Sam shrugged. "You're here now."

Jay lifted the last of his beer in a toast to his brother. "I am. Thanks, Sammy."

Sam clinked the neck of his bottle against Jay's. "Glad to have my little brother home," Sam told him.

A shrill tone erupted from Sam's pocket, and the man's face contorted with that surprise people get when their phones ring at odd times. Sam set the beer bottle on the table and stuck his hand into his pocket. He gave the screen a questioning look before answering.

"Hello?"

There was a pause, and Jay swallowed the rest of his bottle.

"Dang, where?" Sam asked.

Another pause.

"I'm with Jay—er, Chief Delp now. I'll bring him along." Sam disconnected the phone.

"What's that about?" Jay asked.

"Looks like you get to clock in early," Sam told him.

"What do you mean?"

"Ocean Springs PD just responded to a body in the water."

3

———

The downpour hadn't slacked up at all. In fact, Jay noted the rainfall had only increased. His weather gear was packed in a bag somewhere, still in the back of his Jeep. Luckily, he found his father's fishing equipment, and while it was worn in patches, it seemed to protect him from the rain.

Well, not really. He was far from dry; however, he was only slightly moist as opposed to drenched.

Sam stood next to Jay in his Frogg Toggs raincoat. He wasn't staying much drier than Jay, but at least his jacket didn't have a three-inch slice down the backside. When Jay went to put on the gear, he wondered who had stabbed his father in the back to produce such a perfect gash.

The Delp brothers hunkered down on the beach behind the Ocean Springs Yacht Club. The surf splashing in at their feet seemed not quite as brown tonight. Unfortunately, there was nothing pretty or clear about the water in the Mississippi Sound. The barrier islands along the Mississippi coast protected the shoreline, but they also prevented the muddy runoff spilling out of the rivers from the Mississippi River in

Louisiana to Pascagoula from escaping. It left Biloxi Bay somewhere closer to the color of a watered-down Yoo Hoo. But at night, it looked less nasty. After leaving the waters around South Florida, Jay wondered how he ever swam in this sludge as a kid.

Jay buried his balled fists deep into his pockets. It was a pointless endeavor, and after a couple of minutes, Jay would pull them out and dump the rainwater from them. Still, it seemed like if one had to stand on a rainy seashore waiting for a boat to ferry him out to a dead body, hands-in-pocket was the desired look.

Sam shifted from foot to foot with anxious energy. Jay doubted his brother had ever seen a corpse outside of a funeral. At the very least, he'd never laid eyes on a victim who had expired from something other than natural causes. At present, Jay didn't know the exact causes of death. However, history suggested a floater didn't succumb to old age.

On the ride over, Sam relayed the little bits of information he'd gotten from the caller on the other end. Jay learned the person on the call was Rick Lawson, one of Jay's officers. In lieu of a chief, the calls upstream ended up with Sam, who had been the councilman overseeing the department operations in the interim since Chief Ward retired.

According to Lawson, two fishermen hooked the corpse under the bridge. The local boys called 911 and waited for Lawson to show up. The officer, sensing foul play, immediately contacted Sam.

"Any ID on the victim?" Jay asked in the car.

"I don't know," Sam admitted.

Jay only nodded. They drove the five minutes to the yacht club in silence. Jay wondered what the odds were of having a body float up on day one of his new job.

But it wasn't his first day. Not technically. He was supposed to get to town tomorrow and start on Tuesday. That didn't seem likely. Jay was never a man to shirk his responsibilities, and while he hadn't clocked in yet, he had accepted the Chief of Police position in Ocean Springs. That made it his duty to protect and serve the community from the moment he agreed to take the job.

The only sounds Jay could hear were the rushing rainfall and the surf pounding against the sand. Occasional flashes of electricity streaked across the bay. Hobie and dinghy sailboats littered the beach, and the lightning illuminated the masts with eerie flickers. A red and green glow penetrated the sheets of rain. The vessel headed straight toward the pair.

Jay wished he'd thought to grab a good flashlight, but again, his tactical light remained stuffed in a bag in his Jeep. He did not know where his father might keep one and if it even had batteries. For a second, Jay wondered how the boat operator could make out the brothers in all this rain. Then he turned to stare at the yacht club towering behind him. The driver would use the building as his guidepost.

As the white hull came into view, Jay noted two individuals in the vessel. Both wore heavy ponchos that, like Jay's own gear, only abated a few raindrops. Gusts billowed the material up like a cape flapping in the wind. A bright spotlight lit up, blinding Jay until he raised his hand to shield his eyes.

The fiberglass bottom grunted as the driver slowed the engine and allowed the boat's momentum to carry it up onto the sand. He'd done so with the deftness of a lifelong boater.

Jay didn't wait on Sam. He trudged through the ankle-deep water as the muddy surf lapped up his legs. No point in pretending to stay dry. Jay put both palms on the bow and pushed up onto the watercraft he now recognized as a Grady-White. He turned to extend a hand to his brother, who accepted the assist and allowed Jay to hoist him up onto the boat.

"Mr. Delp?" the passenger asked as he stepped toward the two brothers.

"Yeah," Sam said. "This is the new chief, Jay Delp."

"Chief, I'm Rick Lawson," the behemoth of a man greeted. His hand jutted out from his slicker to Jay, who shook it.

"Jay Delp. You see the body?" Jay appraised Lawson quickly. In the rain poncho, it was hard to determine if the big, black officer was all muscle or all fat. Or more likely, Jay concluded, a combination of the two. When Lawson clasped Jay's palm, he apparently decided it was more of the former.

"Yeah. It's not pretty," Lawson stated.

Jay gave the driver a quick glance. The other man was smaller and a little younger than Lawson. "Jay Delp," he introduced himself to the captain over the sound of the pelting rain.

The man shouted something in return, but the wind carried the words away. Jay must have furrowed his brow in confusion because Lawson said, "That's Tim. Tim Lamb."

Jay nodded. Now would have to be the best time to do a meet-and-greet with some of his staff.

"Want to fill us in?" Jay asked as Lamb reversed the throttle. He was shifting between the two 400-horsepower Yamaha outboards hanging off the stern. The powerful engines rocked the boat from side to side for a few seconds before the hull inched out of the channel it created in the mud and sand.

"Two local boys were out fishing for some specks when

they snagged the corpse," Lawson explained as Lamb spun the helm, rotating the bow toward the bridge.

"They catch any?" Jay wondered, referring to what the locals called speckled trout.

Lawson shrugged, having obviously not asked that. He continued, "They're still out there with Dr. Harley."

"He's the medical examiner," Sam explained before Jay had to ask.

"The victim?" Jay asked.

Lawson shook his head. To what, Jay wasn't sure. "African-American female. Early twenties. We haven't ID'd her yet."

Jay gave a terse nod. "Cause of death?" he asked Lawson.

Again, the big officer gave a head shake. No surprise to Jay. If they'd seen a bullet hole in her, the officer could be confident enough to make a reasonable assessment. However, with nothing so obvious, a good investigator didn't waste time speculating—at least not out loud.

Jay assumed everyone made some assumptions. Without having examined the corpse yet, he still guessed there was some foul play. That might include suicide, given the location of the victim's body under the causeway. One thing he'd learned in his years of working deaths was that there were far more jumpers than any police force publicized. The reason was simple: no point giving anyone an idea—as if no person considered leaping off a bridge. Even considering that, television and movies made it seem like someone throwing themselves off the bridge was a weekly occurrence.

"She looks bad, though," Lawson acknowledged. "Her clothes are ripped to shreds. Could have been scavengers, or she got caught on something."

"What do you think?" Jay asked.

"Someone killed her after doing some terrible things to her." Lawson gave a visible shiver that had nothing to do with the weather.

Jay lifted his gaze. "How long has she been in the water?"

"Can't say," Lawson admitted. "At least a day, given how many crabs got to her."

Hoping the hood hid his face, Jay grimaced. Dead bodies weren't altogether as gruesome as some thought, but what time did to them made them so. He'd been the first to arrive at more than a few scenes where the body was already in the midst of decay. On land, the maggots and blow flies arrived first to attack the rotting flesh. In the sea, it was the crabs, especially in the shallower waters. The result was never pretty.

Lamb held a steady pace, keeping the hull from pounding through the waves. The arching bridge rose above them as they plowed forward. Lightning illuminated the concrete in rapid flashes.

Jay lowered his head, trying in vain to shield his face from the pelting drops. Ahead, a bright LED light created a bubble of white in the dark sheets of rain. Two boats were tied together. One was a flat-bottomed fishing boat that Jay deemed far too small to be on the water in this weather. The other was a matching Grady-White center-console vessel with "Police" stenciled on the side.

Lamb slowed his approach, pulling back on the throttles until the Grady-White only pushed ahead at a crawl. The change in speed opened the craft to the sea's assault, and Jay had to compensate for the pitch by shifting his weight from his right leg to his left. Beside him, Sam seemed to follow suit. Neither brother even registered they were doing it, a common occurrence for a boater.

"Rick, be ready to toss them a line!" Lamb shouted.

"Can I help?" Jay asked.

"Grab the stern line," he ordered Jay, then a flash in his eyes signaled he just realized he was bossing his new boss around. Unfazed, Jay shuffled aft to find the rope.

Sam stepped near the ship's wheel as he tried to get out of Jay and Lawson's way. He grabbed the stainless-steel bar on the side of the helm to steady his stance. Lamb shifted one engine forward while pulling the other into reverse. With perfect timing, the quick thrusts in opposite directions spun the Grady-White's aft around to the other police boat. Lamb slid both throttles into neutral as the hulls kissed the fenders on both watercrafts.

"Tie us off!" Lamb shouted.

Jay threw the stern line across to a man on the other vessel. The officer—at least Jay assumed that's what he was—appeared the youngest of them all. His hood hung off his back, so the twenty-something kid was drenched. Rainwater matted his hair down, and he swiped the spray from his face before tying off the rope.

Rick Lawson reached across to the younger man and caught his grip. The two pulled the boats closer before both re-tied the lines.

"This is JD!" Lawson shouted as he motioned to him. "JD, meet the new chief."

JD's eyes widened with some apprehension. He hadn't planned on encountering his new boss out here. As happened in nearly every workplace, self-doubt overcame the young officer. Had he done everything correctly? Would the new boss judge his every action?

"Jay Delp." Jay reached toward JD. They shook hands before Jay moved across the gunwales and into the other vessel.

Another man leaned over a shape, and it took a second

before Jay's eyes adjusted to the bright spotlight. When they did, he recognized the form of a human. What remained of a human, Jay mentally amended. He stepped toward the body and squatted beside it. The other man lifted his gaze to Jay with some annoyance.

"You are?" the man asked.

"Jay Delp. I'm the new chief."

"Oh, I thought you weren't here till later this week," he said curtly.

"Figured I'd clock in early," Jay quipped.

"Hmmph."

"You are?" Jay repeated the same question.

The man, whom Jay already believed to be Dr. Harley, returned Jay's stare with some surprise. "I'm—uh—Dr. James Harley." He used the title "Doctor" with the sort of expectation that it deserved respect.

"ME?" Jay asked, knowing the answer.

"Of course," Harley snapped.

"What's the cause of death?"

Harley glared at the chief. "Can't say until I get her to the morgue."

"I don't suppose you have a time of death?" Jay asked.

"I can't give you that until I get her to the morgue," Harley repeated with more annoyance. "The water plays havoc with body temperature, you know?"

Jay did know, but it never hurt to ask questions. How the person responded was as important as what they responded. In this case, James Harley craved control. He didn't want to offer someone an opinion on the spot. This reasoning differed greatly from Lawson's reasons for not committing. Jay guessed Harley wanted to parse the information flow to increase his importance. Jay also figured that the medical examiner believed himself to be the smartest person in any room. It was intuition on Jay's part, and until he confirmed his suspicions, he'd let Harley run this play out.

With his elbows on his knees, Jay remained on his haunches, studying the girl on the floor of the Grady-White. The victim was African-American, just like Lawson told him. Jay estimated she'd been in her early twenties. The tank top she wore only stayed together thanks to three strips of fabric. The ripped material exposed her breasts and torso. Visible wounds over her chest and stomach indicated some postmortem gnawing by the bay's blue crab denizens.

Jay squinted to study several slices through the skin. Because the water had washed away any blood, Jay could not tell if the girl sustained those injuries while alive or after she died. What they suggested was someone else had made those marks. With nothing but his gut to substantiate it, he theorized they'd been carved into her while she was still breathing. That indicated someone had tortured this poor woman.

Jay didn't like the implications that came with that realization.

4

───────

The coffee tasted weak, and Jay worried its efficacy was hindered by that. The generic brand was the only thing his dad had in the house. When he examined the best-use date stamped on the foil bag, he noted it had passed a year earlier. That didn't surprise him. He'd never seen his father drink coffee. The man started every single morning with a can of Coca-Cola and finished the day with another. The second one had always stayed topped off with Old Charter 8 Year or, if that wasn't available, Seagram's 7. But Terry never drank coffee.

This bag must have been a holdover from someone else. It would do until Jay made it by the store to pick up something with a little more punch. He considered grabbing a new coffee maker, too, since Jay wasn't too sure the last time anyone had cleaned the one. However, his years in the service and on the force meant he'd drunk his fair share of terrible coffee. He'd only balked once when he went to pour some at a sheriff's substation, only to see a palmetto bug backstroke out of the coffee pot and into his cup.

For now, he sipped what he considered nothing more

than hot brown water and hoped that whatever caffeine was in it would light his fuse today. He'd been out on the bay until about two in the morning. While he had been on the clock, he also felt he couldn't come in late on his first official day.

The Ocean Springs Police Department was housed in a newer construction on Highway 90 near the Walmart. The red brick building stared at the road with a crisscross design that made Jay think of a headband.

Jay grinned as he pulled into the "Reserved for the Chief" parking spot. The Jeep's soft top was still up since it had been raining last night. Jay would try to wash his baby before heading home, then he could drop the roof after that. For now, he'd leave the windows cracked open.

Jay's Tecovas boots clunked against the tile floor as he entered the building. A wave of frigid air hit him when he stepped inside. Shivers ran through him, and he made a note to raise the temperature.

"Good morning," a woman greeted him from behind a receptionist desk encased in bulletproof glass. She was in her fifties—Jay guessed pushing toward sixty. Her hair, colored a golden brown, didn't move when she moved. Hairspray held the strands together in a way Jay hadn't seen since his high school days. "How can I help you?" she asked, punctuating the question with a nicotine-laced cough.

"I'm Jay Delp," he told her. "I think I'm starting my job today."

Her eyebrows stretched upward as far as they could. Given that they'd been filled with Botox or whatever age-defying techniques were popular now, it wasn't a big stretch.

"You're the new chief!" she exclaimed as she pushed away from the desk and came around the glass divider. She grabbed Jay's hand with both of hers and shook it. "I'm

Jennifer. Jennifer Kelly." She said it the same way James Bond introduced himself. "I work the front desk."

"Ms. Kelly," Jay replied. "That must make you the woman in charge."

She beamed at him. "I try to keep things running smooth up here," she told him.

"It's nice to meet you," he responded.

"Oh, I adore your boots," she gushed. Her expression twisted into a coy look. "I do love a boy in boots."

Jay smiled back, ignoring the somewhat inappropriate comment. Now that she was up close, he had no choice but to inhale the lingering aroma of cigarettes. As often happened when he encountered a heavy smoker, he wondered if he had smelled that bad when he used to smoke. It also made him grateful that he'd long ago quit the habit.

"Do you mind pointing me toward my office?" he asked.

"You're upstairs on the right," she explained. "The elevator is to the left."

Jay tilted his head in appreciation. "Thank you, Ms. Kelly."

"Oh, call me Jennifer," she trilled.

"Jennifer," he repeated, testing the name in his mouth.

"Nice to meet you, boss," she told him.

"You too," Jay replied, adding, "Jennifer."

She continued smiling and standing in the corridor as he marched down the tiled hallway. The elevator dinged as he approached it. Jay froze for a second, curious if it was automatic. He laughed to himself as the doors opened and a woman in her thirties stepped out.

"Excuse me," she apologized, sidestepping out of his way.

"Hello," Jay said. "I'm Jay Delp."

"Oh," she blurted out. "The new chief?"

"That would be me," he replied, figuring today would have a lot of those introductions. "And you are?"

"I'm Shannon Towns."

"Judging from your uniform, you must be one of my officers," he suggested.

"Yes, sir—Chief."

"How long have you been with the department?"

"Four years," she told him. Before Jay could respond, Towns added, "I didn't join until my kids went to junior high."

"Good. How old are they now?"

"Sixteen and fifteen. And at minimum, they understand if they get caught doing anything, I'm going to learn about it."

Jay laughed. "That wouldn't have slowed me down much at that age."

Towns nodded. "I'm not sure it does them, either."

"As long as you keep them alive," he said.

"That's the goal, right? Do you have any kids?"

Jay shook his head. "No, I've never settled down."

Shannon Towns furrowed her brow. "Weren't you married to Rebecca Thomas?"

Jay flushed. "Yes, we were."

"Becs and I ran track together. She was a year or so behind me in high school. I see her down on Government Street sometimes."

"I haven't seen Becca in twenty years," Jay admitted. "Other than on social media, though I don't think that counts."

"If that did, I'd be in at least two throuples."

"Praise be for small mercies."

"Amen," Shannon agreed. "It's nice to meet you, Chief. I have to run and take a prisoner over to court."

"You do that by yourself?"

She shrugged. "It's Carson Walker. He's about seventy."

Jay raised an eyebrow. "What did he do?"

"He peed behind a car over by the beach."

"Oh?"

"The old guy's harmless, but he's also a cranky bastard. I've known him since I was a kid."

Jay nodded as he tried to search through his memory bank for a Carson Walker. He came up empty, but then he couldn't remember Shannon Towns, who must have graduated before he left for the Corps. Jay had long joked that the only person he remembered from high school was Becca, but that wasn't true. He remembered at least three other people from his already small graduating class. The years must have vanquished the rest from his memory.

In fact, he hadn't considered that when he accepted the job. There had to be childhood friends still floating around the area. It was more than likely he'd cross paths with a few of them.

"When you get back, why don't you pop in for a minute?" Jay suggested.

"Sure thing, Chief."

Jay repressed a smile. He liked how she called him "Chief." It was the deference, and he thought it came across as respectful instead of cynical. Ranks and titles weren't something he was unfamiliar with. In the Corps, it only seemed to matter when looking up at the senior officers. Within his unit, it mattered less—except for Colonel Shaw's. She might not have expected it, but he never recalled referring to her by anything other than Colonel.

After boarding the elevator, he pressed the button

marked "2." When the doors slid shut, he noticed a hint of ammonia mixed with a floral perfume. The elevator groaned with what sounded like a wheezing effort as it rose to the next floor. For a newer building, the sound didn't strike Jay as comforting. He would take the stairs after this. It was, after all, only one flight up.

The doors opened to a small office area subdivided by five-foot temporary walls that created cubicles. They didn't offer any privacy for each desk's occupant.

"Chief?" a familiar voice called.

Jay turned to see a much drier Rick Lawson at the coffee pot. "Get you a cup, Chief?" Lawson offered.

A quick look at the tumbler in his hand reminded Jay that anything the department made had to be an improvement on what Terry Delp kept in his pantry—assuming there were no bugs doing laps in his mug.

"I'd love about six," Jay responded, shaking the cup in his hand. "This is utter garbage."

"Can't promise this stuff is much better," Lawson told him. "How do you like it?"

"I like it black with some cream waved over it."

Lawson nodded. "I'll bring it to you."

"Thanks, Rick," he replied, testing the man's first name. It fit him. Or, rather, it fit how Jay saw him. "How about I just take it, and you can point me to my desk?"

Lawson chuckled as he poured coffee into a Styrofoam cup. With the bottle of cream in his hand, he made a quick motion with his wrist, splashing a drop into the brew.

"Come on, sir." Lawson gestured with his cup as he handed the other to Jay.

"We need to examine new sizes," Jay suggested when he took the six-ounce container.

"I'd pump this straight into my veins, so you won't get

any complaints from me about that. Might save me some man-hours going back and forth."

Jay smiled in agreement as he trailed behind the officer.

"You're right here," Lawson told him, pointing at the door of the corner office. Glass walls separated the room from the bullpen. There were automatic shades that could be lowered for privacy, along with only two high-back chairs opposite the desk. Neither seat appeared too comfortable.

He moved around the oak desk to the swivel chair. Jay cocked his head to stare at what he could best describe as a stool with a back. A rather uncomfortable thing that had a manufacture date before Jay joined the Marines.

Lawson laughed. "Chief Ward stole the other one."

Jay glanced up at the muscular black man. He had a mirthful smile that brought a matching one to Jay's face. "I suppose we could press charges," Jay suggested.

"You can try," Lawson quipped.

"The town council might frown on that," Jay conceded.

"No doubt," Lawson agreed. "Let me get back to work."

"Wait, Rick," Jay said, stopping him. "Sit for a minute."

Rick Lawson shrugged and settled in the chair on the right. He squirmed for a second, confirming to Jay that the seats were less than inviting.

"That chair looks awful," Jay stated.

Lawson froze and stared at him for a moment.

Jay sat in the rickety desk chair and pointed out, "I didn't buy them. Otherwise, we'd all have one as nice as this piece of crap."

Lawson chuckled. "Right. No, it's not comfortable."

"I wouldn't have expected to see you this early," Jay told him. "You had to be here later than me last night."

"I'm heading home in a bit," Lawson said, adding, "If that's okay."

Jay smiled. "You strike me as a straight shooter."

Lawson inclined his head. "I guess so. Try to be, at least."

"Tell me about the department," Jay prodded.

Lawson blanched. "Uh, I'm not sure."

"If you could fix one thing, what would it be?"

Lawson considered the question for a second. "I don't really have anything. You mean besides bigger coffee cups?"

Jay nodded, his grin spreading. He liked Lawson right off the bat.

"I'm not too sure. Your predecessor had a habit of micromanaging. He wasn't a bad boss, mind you," Lawson added as a sudden afterthought.

"Don't worry, I won't tell him anything."

"That was it. He preferred having tight reins."

"You think that's a bad thing?"

"Not really, Chief," Lawson explained. "After all, he's the boss, right? I mean, I guess you're the boss now. But at some point, a person has to trust the people he hired. Otherwise, why hire them?"

"Agreed, Rick," Jay replied.

A knock at the door startled both Jay and Lawson. They turned to the entrance to see a man in his fifties with graying temples. The man leaned against the jamb as if he was avoiding falling into the office. Jay recognized him from his interview process. Tom Franklin.

"Mr. Mayor?" Lawson blurted out in surprise.

"Officer," the mayor greeted Lawson with the tone of someone who didn't recall Lawson's name. "Just thought I'd drop in and greet our new chief."

Lawson rose to his feet. "Yes, sir. Let me get back to work."

"Thanks, Rick," Jay said to his officer as the man left the office.

Without waiting for an offer to sit, Franklin stepped over and took the seat Lawson hadn't occupied. "Chief, it's good to have you here. Especially now."

Jay leaned forward in his chair. "Especially now?"

"I heard about the girl in the bay. Wish she'd have washed over to the Biloxi side."

"Yeah, it was fairly inconvenient of her," Jay remarked.

"Guess how much of our revenue is generated by tourism?" Franklin's eyes narrowed as if he was searching his own memory bank for the answer. When it refused to present itself, he said, "Plenty, I can tell you."

Clearly, Jay thought but didn't say.

"Tourists don't want to come to someplace where murders happen," the mayor continued.

"Of course not," Jay agreed while thinking that lots of people visit places like New York City, Miami, and Los Angeles with no concern for recent deaths.

"I know it's your first day, Chief, but we need to wrap this up before the word gets out."

Jay noticed how Franklin used his "Chief" title vastly differently from Lawson and Towns.

"Mayor, I have plenty of investigative experience to lean on," Jay assured his superior. "It's tragic, but I promise I'll do what I can to close this case as quick as we can. We still can't be certain that someone murdered this woman. It appears suspicious, and until Dr. Harley gets back with his autopsy results, I'm treating it as such."

Franklin gave a curt nod. "Good to hear, Chief. Let's keep the backlash at a minimum."

"Of course," Jay replied.

5

For someone concerned about Jay solving a murder, Tom Franklin remained in his office talking about politics. Mostly local gossip, but it was the mayor's way of sowing loyalty. That sort of manipulation had little chance of success with Jay, who'd had his sycophant glands removed when he was at Parris Island. That didn't mean he couldn't play the game. After all, he'd learned politics was nothing more than a game. That meant there was always a loser.

Once Franklin headed over to his own office, Jay got to his feet. The backrest on the old chair leaned back as he stood, sticking in the position. After planting his foot on the base, Jay pulled at the back, trying to straighten it up. It didn't budge. Jay gave up and left the dilapidated seat to stroll through the bullpen.

Rick Lawson was on the phone at a desk on the other side of the office by the coffeemaker. No wonder he wished for bigger cups. Jay watched the man hang up, stand, and walk toward him. Rick made eye contact, and Jay motioned him to come in as he leaned against his desk.

"Franklin finish up with you?" the officer asked.

"Yeah. He urged me to wrap up this investigation."

"Sounds about right," Rick replied.

"I'm guessing there aren't a lot of homicides here," Jay ventured.

"Not many. The ones we get are usually closed immediately. We already know who did the deed. Half the time, the guy is still there with the smoking gun."

"This one might not be that easy," Jay noted.

"I think I have an ID," Rick told him. "Her description matches a Jamie Rene. She's a twenty-three-year-old student at Gulf Coast."

Jay's forehead wrinkled in confusion.

"That's Gulf Coast Community College," Rick clarified.

"How sure are you?"

Rick shrugged. "Nothing confirmed. But her roommate reported that she didn't come home."

"Where did she live?"

"I only talked to the public safety officer at the school. He pulled her address for me. It's an apartment over in Gulfport."

"Do you know anything else?" Jay questioned.

"Not yet. Taylor Jackson—that's the campus safety officer—said he'd send her records over once we know this is her."

Jay nodded. "Rick, you need to rest," he advised. "Who can you put on getting the girl's information?"

"JD will be in later," Rick replied, though with some trepidation in his voice.

"Anything wrong with JD?"

"Eh, he's just young. I'm not sure he'd push back when the college doesn't respond."

"Oh?"

"Don't misunderstand me, Chief. He's a good cop. Great for traffic and such. But the kid's not much of an investigator."

"Does this department have an investigator?" Jay asked.

Rick shook his head. "Remember how I said Chief Ward liked tight reins?"

Jay nodded. "He did all that?"

"Yeah," the older officer replied. "Not that we had tons of major crimes. A few thefts and robberies. Like I said, the occasional homicide that wrapped itself up. I think he liked to stay in the field."

"We'll make do, then," Jay stated. "I met Officer Towns earlier. Who else is on the roster today?"

"Right now, me and Shannon. Tim's off till tomorrow. And like I said, JD will be in later. Probably around noon. Tomkins and Felton are on street duty."

"We seem a little strapped for bodies," Jay remarked. "When I interviewed, I thought this was a bigger department."

Rick gave a palms-up gesture. "We were. After Ward retired, several of the senior officers resigned."

"When Ward quit?" Jay asked. "Or when they hired me?"

"I can't say for sure, Chief, but I think you hit the nail on the head. We were running with a few veteran officers who'd been on the force for a bit."

"So some thought they should be in line for this job?"

Rick nodded. "You know how it is."

Jay nodded back. "I do. We need to bolster our ranks, then."

"It would help. Normally, we've been splitting the shifts pretty easily."

"Right, but when a homicide occurs, it throws off the schedule?"

"Seems so," Rick confirmed.

"Tell you what, Rick," Jay said. "Why don't you go get some rest? When Officer Towns gets back, I'll put her on getting the school's records."

"That would be a smart idea," Rick affirmed. "Shannon's got a good head on her shoulders."

"Has she done any investigative work?"

Rick glanced over his shoulder, ensuring no one lingered near the door. "I'm not certain that Ward used her to her best abilities."

"Why do you say that, Rick?"

"He didn't have the highest respect for females."

"Ah, well, I'll try to be better," Jay assured him. "Now, go home and rest."

Rick gave him an appreciative nod before leaving. Jay straightened up and marched into the bullpen. He saw the other two officers preparing to head out on the streets. Tomkins and Felton, he remembered. Jay would pull everyone's file later just to get an idea of who he was working with, but for now, he went to greet the two beat cops.

"Gentlemen," he said as he approached the pair of uniformed officers. "I'm the new guy."

"Oh, good morning, sir," the taller one responded.

Neither man was much more than twenty-one. *Rookies*, Jay thought.

"I'm Jay Delp," he introduced himself.

"The new chief?" the second one asked.

"I hope so," Jay joked. "Otherwise, I'm in the wrong place."

Both men gave a forced chuckle, and Jay regretted the dad joke.

"Why don't you guys tell me who you are?" Jay asked.

The first one blanched. "Oh, I'm sorry. I'm Drew Felton, sir."

"And I'm Grayson Tomkins. People call me Gray."

"Good to meet you. I hear you're on the streets today?"

"Yes, sir," Tomkins responded.

"I won't keep you long," Jay promised. "But real quick, what does that entail?"

"Sorry?" Felton asked.

"Are you partnered in the same cruiser? Do you have a set patrol?"

"Oh, sorry," Felton repeated. "We are in separate cars. I'm starting at the east end of the city and working my way to the center. Gray heads north and patrols everything north of 90. If any calls come in, the closest one responds. Or we both do if we need to."

Jay nodded. "That's a lot of ground for only two of you," he considered.

"It can be," Tomkins agreed.

"Great, I'll let you guys get on the road. Tell me, who is the watch commander?"

The two young officers exchanged a questioning look. "I guess you are," Felton replied.

"Okay, then," Jay said. "Before you go off duty, why don't you pop by to see me?"

"Yes, sir," the two cops said in unison.

Jay left them to their duties and strolled past the coffee pot again, stopping to pour another thimble-sized cup to carry to his office. After settling back onto the mangled metal someone called an office chair, he opened his computer. He'd need to get the passwords changed, but for now, he was signed in. He opened Google.

"Jamie Rene." Jay typed the name into the search bar and punched the enter button. Results flashed on the screen, starting with several Instagram accounts, an X account, and a LinkedIn Profile. None of them matched the face he'd seen on the young lady last night.

He dropped the cursor back into the search field and added the word "Gulfport." The findings changed. A Jamie Reneé Mckay popped up. Still not the same woman. The Gulfport Municipal Court website was the second line. Jay clicked the link.

The page opened to a court summons for Jamie Wilson Rene for a traffic ticket. She had a broken taillight and expired tags. The date was last month. She'd appeared with documentation that her tags were up to date, and the judge had dismissed the charge with only court fees.

At Jay's previous departments, it would be easy to obtain the records for Jamie's address, but a required username and password stymied him now. He needed to find out who controlled IT around here and get his computer access granted.

He returned to the Google search results, adding the middle name "Wilson." New results cropped up, and the first one, an X profile, was her. The profile picture showed a much younger face. With a quick scroll through the tweets, he found Jamie hadn't used her X profile since long before it stopped being Twitter. The last one she posted was in 2016.

Jay clicked on her image and enlarged it. He selected "Print" and then scrolled through the selection of printers for him to use. He tried the first three in succession, with no results. At least none were in the general vicinity. Jay wondered if someone on another floor had started getting this picture through their printers.

The fourth one he chose activated a printer on a desk outside his door. Good enough, Jay considered as he rose from the medieval torture device Chief Ward had left in his office and strolled out to the printer. He picked up the picture of the young African-American girl. She was only thirteen or fourteen in this photo, but she looked like someone trying to grow up too fast. Jamie was pretty, making Jay curious about what else there was to the girl. With no basis to work with, he only had her looks to judge the woman. That wasn't sufficient. Her eyes sparked with intelligence, and her smile appeared genuine. At least, that's how it appeared.

In homicide, he'd seen the darker sides of people. Once in Panama City, he arrested a man who'd raped and killed three little boys. His Facebook profile showed his friends and family members. It detailed his work as a youth pastor, where he'd found troubled kids to lure back to an anonymous apartment. Unfortunately, that was an example and not an extreme. Jay rarely trusted the public persona most individuals put on every day. It didn't matter if they were killers or victims. Everyone had a secret.

With Jamie Rene's picture in hand, Jay returned to his office. He needed a corkboard if he was going to run an investigation. Really, he needed an investigator to run an investigation, but in lieu of one, he would do it himself. At least for now.

He looked out across the bullpen. It was empty. Who was he supposed to requisition for things like a corkboard, or even a new desk chair? For a moment, he worried he stepped into a job that needed more than he could handle.

Nonsense. He'd handled far worse.

Still, he found himself alone. On the plus side, the phones weren't ringing.

As if on cue, the phone on his desk released a shrill screech. He strode to his seat and answered it.

"Chief Delp," he said awkwardly into the speaker.

"Ooh, *Chief* Delp," Sam teased.

"Sam," Jay replied.

"How's the first day?" his brother asked.

"It seems my department is sorely understaffed," he commented. "Not something I'd been told before I took the position."

"Yeah, there were several people who quit in the last couple of weeks."

"That wasn't worth mentioning to me?" Jay questioned.

"I was worried you wouldn't take the job," Sam admitted. "Truthfully, the department was already short-staffed, but the walkout just made it worse."

"Sam, I am the only person in this office right now."

"First thing on your agenda will be bringing in new blood," Sam said, his voice laced with optimism.

"After a chat with the mayor this morning, it seems his priority for me is clearing this murder. Something I'm going to struggle to do if I have to climb in a police car and ticket speeders."

"Oh, you won't be doing that," Sam assured him.

"Sam, I don't even know who to ask for a new desk chair."

"You don't have a chair?"

"I have something that once resembled a chair."

"I'll have one brought over," Sam said. "What else do you need?"

"Log-ins, protocols, bigger coffee cups."

"Bigger coffee cups?" Sam asked.

"I'm joking," Jay replied. "Kinda."

"How about lunch?"

"Let me get someone in the office first," Jay said. "Officer Towns is supposed to be back in a bit."

"Oh, Shannon?" Sam asked in a tone Jay found odd.

"What about her?" Jay asked.

"She's divorced," he commented.

"Yeah, but you aren't," Jay reminded his brother.

"Oh, it's not like that," Sam protested.

"Sam, any time someone says, 'It's not like that,' it is always like that."

"You're being an idiot, Jay," Sam argued. "I meant you might like her."

Jay was unconvinced but replied, "She's my subordinate. That would be a terrible way to start a new gig."

"True," Sam admitted, then changed the subject. "Any word on the girl? I won't lie—when I got home, I couldn't sleep. That poor thing."

"We have a possible ID. Although it's going to be difficult chasing anything down without an investigator."

"You're a terrific detective," Sam said.

"Yes, but I'm supposed to be a chief," Jay reminded him. "That takes a deal more time."

"Ward worked as the lead detective."

"Sam, when was the last gruesome murder in Ocean Springs?"

"I don't recall," Sam confessed.

"Let me say, I've seen a lot, and those never wrap up in a day or two. The mayor is already wanting it swept away."

"You'll solve it," Sam stated. "Then it will be back to normal."

Normal. What was that? Jay considered pointing out that this was still his first day, so he had no gauge of what normal was.

Someone in the bullpen whistled, and Jay's head popped up. Officer Towns emerged from the elevator with the tune of what Jay recognized as "Janie's Got a Gun."

"Sam, I got someone in the office. Call me in an hour, and I'll see about lunch."

"You got it, man," his brother responded as Jay hung up the phone.

"Hey, Chief," Towns greeted as her face appeared at his door. "You said to drop by."

"Yeah, how was your elder pee party?"

Towns cocked her head. "Pee party?"

"Yeah, sorry, I tried to run a few things through my head," Jay admitted. "None of them worked."

"Neither did that one," she told him with a wry grin. "However, he got probation and a $500 fine."

"Just for peeing?"

She shrugged.

"Why don't you sit for a bit? Let's talk."

Shannon Towns sat down in the same chair Rick Lawson used earlier. Like Rick, she fidgeted for a second before settling. More confirmation that the seats were uncomfortable. Maybe Ward had wanted to keep people from overstaying their welcome. After Jay replaced his chair, he would get a couch and some more appealing furniture.

"How's the first day, Chief?" Towns asked.

"Enlightening," Jay admitted.

Towns smiled, flashing almost perfectly straight teeth. Her right eyetooth cocked off at an angle, though it wasn't noticeable. In fact, it was the kind of imperfection that only improved her overall appearance.

"Would that be the lack of officers?" she wondered.

"It wasn't a problem I expected on day one," he told her.

"Chief, you dodged a bullet," she confided. "The five that quit needed to go."

"Indeed?"

"That's just my opinion, sir," she amended.

"It's valuable," he said. "Speaking of which, my under-standing is that the department is underusing you."

Towns lifted her eyebrows. "Uh, I don't... yeah, I'd like to do more than I have."

"What did Chief Ward have you doing?"

"Besides getting coffee? Menial jobs like taking defense-less old men to court or filing arrest reports."

"You went through the academy?"

"Yes, sir."

"You worked patrol?"

"Yes, sir."

"Then I'd like to see what you can do."

"Anything, sir."

"Rick got a potential ID on our victim last night. Can you see about getting all her information together? I'd like a bio on her before lunch."

"Yes, sir," Towns replied. "You think she was murdered?"

"Yeah. I'm sure when the ME comes back, it will be foul play," Jay explained. "I want to be ahead of it by then."

"Yes, sir," she repeated, her face breaking into a smile.

"Can you find us a corkboard, too?"

The corner of Shannon Towns's mouth turned up. "A murder board?"

Jay let his lips lift in a half-smile as he nodded.

6

The Jackson County coroner resided two cities east of Ocean Springs in Pascagoula, a town most known for the famed troubadour, Jimmy Buffett. Jay left Shannon Towns in charge of the office until he came back after lunch. He hoped Dr. Harley would brief him over the phone, but the receptionist told him that Dr. Harley was too busy to come to the telephone. He'd have a report to Jay at the end of the day.

That wouldn't work for Jay.

Rick had nailed one thing on the head: Cops solved most murders within minutes. Either someone witnessed the murder and positively identified the suspect, or the killer remained at the crime scene. Nowadays, with doorbell cameras and constant surveillance, tracking a murderer was easier.

However, in those instances when the perpetrator wasn't waiting with their victim, time became crucial. Every hour that passed increased the odds that the culprit would not get caught. In this instance, the clock was already against them. Jamie Rene had been in the bay for at least twenty-four hours. Jay needed confirmation of that, but until he got more details, he worked with that premise—one day submerged in the murky waters. That likely washed away most, if not all, usable DNA or evidence. Even if Harley found something, a halfway decent defense attorney could call it into question.

"How do we know that strand of hair wasn't in the water and tangled with the victims? My client regularly swims in the bay, just like most of the jurors here. This could have been anyone's hair."

Jay had seen worse moves by defense lawyers, which was why he liked to have the best case when he took it to the prosecution. Unfortunately, that wasn't always the situation, and now Jay counted at least three men he knew were guilty who walked at their trial. All because there wasn't sufficient evidence.

He had no desire to step on the ME's toes. Especially during his first day on the job. Jay also respected the time it took to collect the evidence and data required to convict. But Jay needed more information to get ahead of the case.

However, he already disliked Dr. Harley, and Jay was unwilling to be stalled by the coroner just because he wanted to make a power play.

Jay parked in the visitor's space and got out. The parking lot of the beige building was only half-filled. He stared out the windshield, wondering why every government structure opted for the tan bricks. Maybe it was a bulk purchase. He supposed it was better than the bright red bricks that had cropped up during the '70s and '80s.

He pushed through the glass entry doors. When the frigid air inside hit him, he realized this was likely par for the course along the coast. At least here, they kept dead bodies. Heat and corpses didn't make the best combination.

"May I help you?" a receptionist several years older than Jennifer asked. She was stationed behind a similar counter, but she wasn't protected by thick bulletproof glass.

"I'm on my way to see Dr. Harley," Jay informed her, marching past her desk.

"Pardon me, sir," she blurted after him. "I need you to sign in."

Jay stopped, turning to her. "I'm so sorry. I'm late, but that doesn't excuse my manners. Please forgive me." He turned on his Mississippi drawl. Just another friendly neighbor.

"Who are you again, sir?"

"Jay Delp," he told her as he picked up the pen next to the sign-in sheet. "I'm the new chief over in Ocean Springs."

"Oh, you have that girl that came in," she noted.

"Unfortunately," he responded. "It's pretty bad. My first day, too."

She curled her lip in disgust, making Jay curious if she'd seen the girl or had just heard about her. "We don't get a lot of murders around here," she remarked with some disdain. "I hope this isn't something regular."

"I'll try to keep it under control," Jay quipped.

The woman behind the counter either ignored the sarcasm or failed to pick up on it. "Please do," she responded.

"Harley's still on the second floor?" he asked, taking a stab and bluffing at the same time.

"Yes," she answered.

He gave her a nod and an assuring smile before walking toward the stairs. He was through the door before she turned around. Jay didn't want to give her the opportunity to realize he might not have an appointment or to announce him to Harley, who would likely refuse to see him.

After today, Jay assumed Harley would like him even less. That didn't bother him at all. He'd been disliked before, but as long as he was able to do his job, he considered it a success.

When he exited on the second floor, ammonia assaulted his nostrils. It was actually a cocktail of chemicals in the air, but the ammonia struck him first. Without knowing where Harley's office was, he strolled down the hall, checking each office.

Harley's was at the end on the right side of the corridor. The door hung ajar, and Harley's name was displayed on a plaque next to the doorway. Jay opened the gap wider with the palm of his hand. Inside, the same man he'd encountered last night sat behind a desk, his reading glasses pulled down to the tip of his nose. If Jay hadn't met the man the night before, he might have mistaken him for someone else. This doctor appeared more professional than he had last night in his storm-drenched poncho. Today, he wore an off-the-rack suit that probably came from Dillard's or Macy's. The tie around his neck was the only bit of mirth Jay noted. It was crimson red with the tusks of an elephant and the prominent "A" associated with the University of Alabama.

Jay smiled. An Alabama fan. He could work with that.

"Dr. Harley?" he asked.

Harley lifted his gaze to the door with wide eyes. "Can I help you?"

"Jay Delp," he introduced himself again. "We met last night. I probably look drier here. You do for sure."

Realization dawned on the ME's face, followed by an expression of sheer annoyance. "Oh, Chief Delp, right?" he clarified, as if Jay hadn't just identified himself.

"Yes." Jay extended a hand to the doctor. "Did you graduate from Alabama?"

Harley glanced down at his tie before his eyes went to the chief's palm, waiting to be shaken. Harley blinked twice before some part of his brain triggered the proper response. He reached forward, grasping Jay's proffered hand.

"Yes, I did," Harley responded after a beat. "Long time ago, but always a fan."

"You should be," Jay replied. "Hell of a season." Jay didn't follow football, and if he had, it would have been Mississippi State, where Sam had played a semester of college ball. His brother had never been much more than an adequate player. In Ocean Springs, Sam was an athletic god, but in the SEC or any tier-one school, he'd never have been a starter.

During practice one day, Sam twisted a knee that killed the rest of his athletic career. Jay assumed that was for the best, but he never mentioned it to Sam, knowing that Sam had fancied playing in the NFL.

"Yeah, we barely missed that championship," Harley remarked.

"Next year," Jay assured him, and the doctor nodded. "Listen, Dr. Harley, I'm sorry to pop in, but I'm in a pickle."

Harley released Jay's grip and folded his hands in front of him. "How so?"

"Do you mind if I sit?" Jay asked.

The medical examiner waved a hand at the single stool opposite his desk. His face seemed to dislike the idea, but decorum ruled. Jay slid into the seat. It was more comfortable than his office chair.

"Today's my first day, and the mayor is already breathing down my neck," Jay began. "Add that to the fact that half my department quit before I showed up. That's not a big confidence-builder, you know what I mean?"

Harley cocked his head as Jay talked. When he finished

talking, the doctor nodded with understanding. "That doesn't bode well," Harley remarked.

"I just need to get ahead of this," Jay admitted. "I'm hoping you will give me something to begin investigating."

"There's not much I can tell you yet," Harley confessed. "I have toxicology and DNA testing out. That could be a few days."

"Do you have an estimated time of death?" Jay asked. "I won't hold you to it, but it gives me a window to start with."

Harley studied him before saying, "Just an approximation, but I'd say she died at least forty-eight hours ago. Not much more, unless someone stored her in a cooler somewhere."

"Like a fridge?" Jay inquired.

"Or on ice, but I don't think so. I'll do some cellular tests to confirm she wasn't frozen."

"Frozen?" Jay repeated, though he knew what the doctor meant. It never hurt to play up the expert.

"Yeah, it's possible. We should be able to see micro-distortions in the tissue, among other things. It would be more intense than the effects of the cooler waters in the bay."

"If someone stored her in a freezer, would that skew your estimate?" Jay asked.

Harley nodded. "She had no water in her lungs," the coroner explained. "The cause of death will be severe trauma resulting from three knife wounds to her liver. She bled out fast, if that's any consolation."

It wasn't, so Jay said nothing as Harley continued, "I noted vaginal tearing, too. We swabbed, but I'm not hopeful. She'd been in the water too long."

The chief nodded.

"There were some scratches and cuts that were older. Rough guess is a week old."

"What kind of scratches?" Jay asked.

Dr. Harley jutted his right arm out toward Jay. The coroner's left hand wrapped around his forearm. "It looked like someone grasped her here, digging their fingernails into her skin. I counted four such marks that would line up with the fingers."

"Can you tell how big the hand was?"

"We don't have a thumbnail, but I'd say it was a larger hand. Probably with shorter nails."

Jay stared for a second. "A man's?" Jay asked.

"That would be inconclusive, but a safe theory."

Of course it was a safe theory. Statistically, men were more likely to commit a crime like this.

"Chief Delp, there were also ligature marks on her wrists, ankles, and neck."

"You mean she was bound and strangled?"

"Collared, I would think."

An image of Jamie Rene, restrained by her four limbs and collared, flashed through Jay's mind. His skin prickled, sending the hairs on end.

"Can you tell me anything else?" Jay asked.

Harley shook his head. "Not until we do the autopsy today. That will be this afternoon."

"Doctor, I appreciate the help," Jay said. "I'll get out of your way."

Harley nodded as if he were a king dismissing a peasant. "You should have a report tomorrow."

"Great, this is a good start," Jay replied. "Let's grab a beer and catch a game this season."

Dr. Harley almost cracked a grin. "Well, I don't drink," he countered with some condescension in his tone.

Jay half-smiled back. *Of course he doesn't*, he thought.

7

Jay parked on the curb on Government Street. He'd made it back to Ocean Springs in record time. Though, since Jay hadn't taken that trip in decades, he wasn't positive what record time was. It was half past eleven, and the popular downtown thoroughfare remained quiet. The lunch crowd started filtering out of their offices and shops. Over the next hour, traffic, both pedestrian and vehicular, would increase by thirty to forty percent. It was a Tuesday, so the weekender population was in their workplaces in Jackson, Mobile, or wherever their daily grind existed.

Sam came down the street from the opposite direction. He gave Jay a two-finger wave before pointing at a sign with an arrow aimed up the staircase beside the placard. "Rooftop Bar" stood out in colorful raised letters. Below that, an arrow pointed to the double doors, reading "Rooftop Tacos and Tequila."

Jay paused on the street, waiting for his brother to get to him.

"It's Taco Tuesday, man," Sam announced as he grabbed

Jay by the shoulder. "Come on up." Sam bounded up the stairs, leaving Jay on the sidewalk.

With a shake of his head, Jay followed Sam to the Rooftop Bar. At the top of the steep steps, Jay found an open-air bar with tables encircling the area. Sam marched over to an empty table overlooking Government Street.

As Jay took his seat opposite his brother, he admired the bar. He could see it being a popular nighttime venue. A couple of stools and two microphone stands occupied a makeshift stage. Live music fit the spot, and Jay suspected he'd be back, assuming the tacos were tasty enough for an encore. As far as he knew, it was pretty hard to ruin a taco.

"You like birria?" Sam asked.

"Love it," Jay claimed.

"They got good ones here," he declared, and Jay nodded.

"I have an office chair coming over for you," Sam told his brother after Diego, the bartender, took their drink order. Both brothers went with the official drink of Mississippi: sweet tea.

"My hindquarters will thank you, Sam," Jay replied.

Both Delp men ordered three birria tacos and an order of queso and chips.

"Tell me about Ward," Jay said to his older brother.

"What about him?"

"Was he a decent chief? He'd been here a long time, right?"

"Twenty years as chief. He had over thirty on the force."

"All that time here?" Jay inquired. He had spent only a little time in Ocean Springs since he'd left for the Corps, and as a teenager, Jay couldn't have cared less about town politics.

Sam shook his head. "I think he was in Nawlins. But he's been here longer than I've been paying attention."

Jay understood. Sam had run for councilman eight years ago. If Ward had been chief for two decades, then Sam would have been a teenager when the city hired Ward.

"Any red flags?" Jay asked.

"Not that I ever heard," Sam replied. "Why?"

Jay pursed his lips. "It's nothing. Rick Lawson mentioned he liked to micromanage."

"What does that have to do with anything?"

Jay waited as Diego appeared with the queso. Sam grabbed a tortilla chip and dunked it into the melted cheese.

"Sometimes the reason managers control every detail is that they want others staying out of their business. It diverts attention."

"That's not always the case," Sam argued.

"No, it's not. Some bosses are just bad. But I've seen managers stealing thousands and hiding it by micro-managing their staff to death."

Sam shook his head. "I don't know of anything," he said. "After all, Ward quit on his own. If he were doing something criminal, why stop?"

Jay shrugged. "I said it was probably nothing."

Sam scooped more cheese into his mouth. "Then you got this murder," he muttered, spewing flecks of corn tortillas across the table.

"Dude, say it, don't spray it," Jay barked.

Sam grinned. "Sorry, bro." Jay suspected Sam wasn't all that remorseful. Brothers never were.

"Didn't you run over to Pascagoula?" Sam asked.

"Yeah, to see the ME," Jay answered.

"Is it like in *Bones*?" Sam asked.

Jay shook his head. He did not know what *Bones* was, but he assumed it was a cop show. In which case, he wagered the fictional setting had no similarities to real life. None of them ever did.

"What did you find out?" Sam pressed.

Jay's face twisted. He wondered about the risk of telling his brother. On the one hand, he never enjoyed discussing open cases outside of the department. A lot of that had to do with leaks to local news people. Also, it was a smart policy to compartmentalize that information. On the other hand, Sam was an elected city official. Not only that, he was also the official overseeing the police force in the last month. That might not make Sam his direct report, but he was a cog in the machine that was Jay's boss.

The deciding factor for Jay was Sam's presence on the boat last night. He saw the victim firsthand. That gave his brother a vested interest in the case.

"Not much," Jay said. "Definitely murder. She'd been dead a couple of days. Harley thinks she was in the water most of that time."

"Oh, wow," Sam mumbled in a defeated tone.

Did his brother's mind just flash with the image of Jamie Rene bobbing around the bay? Was it similar to the image of a bound Jamie that struck Jay at the coroner's office? He considered it humanizing. That created the difference between them and the killer. What happened to Jamie Rene was unconscionable to the brothers. The man who held, raped, and killed Jamie had no problems with his conscience. He'd never felt the revulsion that was now coursing through Jay.

"You think it's a one-time thing?" Sam asked.

Jay lifted his eyes to his brother. "I don't know," he replied, but he was lying. Instinct urged him that this wasn't a one-off murder. There was no crime of passion. It had been deliberate. Jay didn't question that at all.

In fact, two questions lingered. Was Jamie this guy's first victim? How did he pick her out?

The first question mattered to Jay because it allowed him to develop a pattern. That information would help the investigators determine how long it would take until he struck again. Because Jay knew for certain that it would happen again.

The second question could help Jay find a connection. That was most important now if Jay wanted to stop him from finding his second—no, next—victim.

"That could have been Danielle or Julia," Sam said glumly.

"It wasn't," Jay reminded him. As a Marine and a cop, he'd seen death in the face. It wasn't something to fret about because it didn't matter. Ever. No one escaped it.

"But it what if—"

"What if you were a billionaire?" Jay interjected. "What if you never met your wife? Or what if Sandra never drowned? You waste time with silly 'what-ifs' and recriminations."

Sam stared at his brother before placing another cheese-covered tortilla chip into his mouth. Each bite crunched loud enough for Jay to hear over the sound of a motorcycle rumbling along the street below. When he swallowed, Sam said, "Recriminations? That's a big word for a redneck."

Jay chortled, nearly spewing sweet tea through his nostrils. His nasal cavities flooded before the liquid receded back into his mouth. Forced to swallow, Jay still laughed at his brother's innate ability to bridge the tragic with the humorous.

Diego, of course, had to choose the moment Jay gulped down the nostril tea to bring the birria. Sam thanked the bartender as Jay wiped a dribble of liquid from the corner of his mouth.

"Listen, Jay, this murder might be a good thing," Sam mentioned after finishing the first fried taco.

Jay was in the middle of dunking his second taco in the au jus sauce. "Au jus" seemed to be a fancy word for grease, but that didn't stop it from being delicious. "What do you mean?" Jay asked, revulsed by his brother's comment.

"Not that anyone died," Sam clarified. "But you're a new chief with what is going to be a high-profile murder around here. People will decry how unsafe Ocean Springs has become. My guess is they'll cite those new apartments near the backside of Forty Bayou. When the citizens blast their concerns on Facebook, the city council and Franklin will want to set their minds at ease. You might double your budget if you played it right."

"Double my budget?"

"Yeah, there's a price on ease. A tax hike to hire more officers. Those new men will need new squad cars and equipment. It could be a gold mine. The city would jump to secure its safety."

"That is devious, but doesn't that create its own problem?"

"How so?"

"If I get this blank check, that's great for now. But next year, what then? If I push for all this money, then it all depends on what happens. Suppose I keep crime down to nothing, right? When the time to review the budget rolls around, the question becomes, why are we paying all these taxes for the police department when crime is way down?"

"That would be a good problem to have," Sam declared.

"Except, inevitably, cuts have to happen. Those often equate to personnel. Now our force decreases and crime statistics tank. I have to go back and ask for more funds to increase manpower, and the cycle begins again. Until the council decides they need a new chief."

"You are being pessimistic, Jay," Sam scolded. "That won't happen."

"No, you're right. I could request all that money, only to have another random murder spotlight the city. It will be a question of why so many tax dollars were spent and the results didn't match. And you guys on the council search for a new chief who can clean up the mess."

Sam shook his head. "You are a glass-half-full guy, aren't you?"

"No, but I'd like to get a better lay of the land before I try to beg, borrow, and steal."

Shoving half a taco into his mouth, Sam replied with a jumble of meat-filled words, "It's how it works."

Jay recognized when his brother had something set in his mind. It wouldn't matter what Jay thought—Sam would push for a budget increase. It might be as soon as the next council meeting. After all, Sam believed in striking while the fire was hot. If Sam pushed for it, then everyone would assume Jay was behind the request.

At a loss, Jay kept his mouth shut and took another bite of birria, allowing the grease to drip down his chin before he swiped it away with the paper napkin.

"How was Dad this morning?" Sam asked.

"Still asleep when I left," Jay told him. "The nurse arrived at 6:30."

"Gee, how much sleep did you get?"

"Two and half hours."

"How are you functioning?"

"I'm built to run," Jay quipped. "Lotta years on the go

with limited rest. It's what the Corps taught me, how to never sleep and die fighting."

"You're getting older, Jaybird. That's going to catch up to you."

Jay smiled. He didn't care, because he liked the idea of growing older. "Thought I'd grab a pizza for Dad tonight. What's good around here?"

"You want Tom's," Sam answered, pointing at the building across the street. "It's over two blocks that way. And Dad only wants the meat one. All the meats."

"No veggies?"

"He spits the onions out on the pizza, so that's up to you," Sam told him.

"Got it," Jay replied. "No onions."

8

———

"Chief, you got a sec?" Shannon Towns asked as Jay came out of the stairwell into the bullpen. She sat in a cubicle in the corner nearest the coffee pot. Her little workspace had pictures of two toddlers and another of a pair of teenagers.

Towns had a can of Diet Coke on her desk, and Jay wondered at the irony of her being positioned so near the beloved coffee pot and not drinking it. Yet Rick, who seemed to thrive on it, had ended up on the other side of the cubicles.

We just need another coffeemaker in that part of the office, Jay thought. "What's up?" he asked the woman.

"Jamie Rene," Towns informed him. "I know a lot more."

"Want to do it here?" Jay questioned.

"I have most of it in your office already," she stated. Her face shifted. "Is that okay?"

"Of course," Jay assured her. "Let's go."

He stepped into the glass box that doubled as his office. Two things surprised him as he came through the door. First, a rolling whiteboard appeared. The picture he'd printed of a teenaged Jamie adorned the top of the panel. Another recent photo of the girl hung next to the much younger version. Notes scrawled under the pair of matching faces.

Before he started reading what Towns listed on the board, he stopped, staring at the new office chair behind his desk. "Hallelujah," he praised, scurrying around the desk with more excitement than a piece of furniture should cause him. He settled into the soft, comfortable chair. The cushion, a memory foam, squished under his cheeks. Jay marveled that a jagged spring wasn't stabbing his backside.

"Sam sent a new chair," he explained to Towns.

"What?" she asked, looking confused. "I got this from an empty office downstairs."

"Oh, thank you so much. I thought it came from my brother."

"No. I tried sitting in your other one, and it violated the Geneva Convention."

He chuckled. "You're right. Thanks for this." Jay leaned back, and the backrest reclined with him. "Ah, I could sleep here," he told her.

"I just want to be your favorite," she joked.

Jay smirked and straightened up. "How about Jamie? I like your board."

"We didn't have a big enough corkboard," she informed him. "I stole this from the training room."

"Until we hire some new people, we don't need it," he supposed.

"I scoured several things and created a biography for her. Jamie Wilson Rene lives—lived—on Bayview Street in Biloxi."

Jay furrowed his brow. "Is that on the back bay?"

"Yes, Bayside Apartments. They're over by Boomtown."

"The casino?"

Towns nodded. "I forget you haven't been here in a long time."

He shrugged. "When I moved away, only trees covered that area."

"In my day," she croaked in an old man's voice.

"Aren't you older than I am?" he asked pointedly.

Towns blushed. "We don't talk about such things," she scolded.

He lifted both hands in mock surrender. "Tell me about Jamie," he said.

"She works at—worked—at Blues Crab Shack. It's over on the back bay, too. I spoke to the Biloxi Police. Her roommate called them three days ago when she hadn't seen Jamie in over twenty-four hours."

"She's been missing four days?" Jay asked.

"That's what I'm assuming. Obviously, since the roommate didn't see someone grab Jamie, we don't have an exact time frame." Towns paused. A cloud passed through her eyes.

"What is it?"

"I find it weird talking about this girl being kidnapped. It's disturbing."

Jay could have gone into the same talk he'd had with Sam. However, Towns's reaction differed. Her worries weren't about what might happen, but she found what had happened upsetting. Jay trusted his brother had experienced a range of emotions from this murder, but they were reactive—the what-ifs. Towns and Jay asked a different question: "What could?"

What could happen if we didn't catch this man? What could have been done to protect Jamie? What could they do to stop another young woman from floating up in the bay?

Jay made no effort to comfort her. The moment passed before she finished her last sentence. She rolled into what else she knew about Jamie.

"Both of her parents are dead," she continued. "She grew up in Jackson and moved down here to go to school."

"Siblings?"

"A much older brother who lives in Louisville. I reached out to the Kentucky State Police to contact him."

"Good," he praised. Those were the hardest tasks, and knowing that another department would handle it eased both their minds.

"How old was she?" Jay asked.

"Oh, right," Towns said, her face flushing again. "Twenty-three."

"Have you talked with the roommate?"

She shook her head. "Not yet. I considered calling her, but it occurred to me the roommate might be a suspect."

"We should drive over there," Jay suggested. "We need to talk with her—wait, is it a female?"

"Yes."

"Don't want to get ousted on my first day for being boorish."

Towns offered a smile. "I think if you are concerned about it, then you're safe."

"One would hope. Do you know when JD is getting here?"

"Should be any moment."

"When he does, we'll put him in charge of the office."

Towns wrinkled her forehead. "You want me to come along?"

"Yes," Jay told her. "Look at what you've gathered in just a couple of hours."

"It's nothing that a Google search wouldn't spit out," she countered.

"Don't sell yourself short. That stuff is all important."

"Thank you, Chief."

Across the bullpen, the elevator dinged.

"Bet that's JD," Towns said.

"Great. Put him in charge of—" Jay paused, unable to pull something out for JD Baker to manage. "Put him in charge of whatever needs to be done."

Towns lifted half her lip in a knowing smirk. "Yes, Chief."

She turned to head into the bullpen, but she stopped when Jay said, "You're driving, by the way."

Shannon Towns twisted her head to look at Jay. "No problem," she replied.

Jay leaned back in his new seat. He considered throwing his feet on the desk, but that would imply he had leisure to rest. With a murderer roaming the cozy streets in and around Ocean Springs, it seemed there wouldn't be time to relax.

His attention turned to the whiteboard and the faces staring back at him. Jamie Rene watched him from across the office. Even if he wanted to put his feet up, his conscience wouldn't allow it. As long as those hazel eyes remained locked on him, he had to fight to find her the justice she deserved.

"Okay, Chief," Towns called from the doorway. "Ready to roll?"

Jay stood up and stared at Officer Towns. "Where did Chief Ward keep his service piece?"

"I bet he took it with him," she answered.

"Just like the chair?"

"He might've assumed he deserved it after twenty years," she considered.

"Hmm. Still might call that theft," he mused.

Towns shrugged. "We can hit the armory," she offered. "Or you can bring your own gun. You'd just have to log it."

Jay nodded. His M45 sat under the driver's seat of his Jeep. He'd prefer a department-issued weapon since that M45 had followed him from his Corps days. If he ever used it in a shooting, it might take months or years to get it back—that was, if it was ever returned to him. Plenty of evidence like that never saw the light of day, depending on the circumstances.

"Let's find something," he told her.

"Before we leave?"

"I'd rather none of us were in the field unarmed."

Towns motioned with her head for him to follow her. Jay obeyed, falling in behind her. As they crossed the bullpen, he scanned the empty desks again. JD was settled at a workstation located at the center of the cubicle maze. Jay considered telling the young officer not to respond to any media. It was only a matter of hours before the regional news sought the details. The fact that they pulled Jamie Rene out of the water in the middle of the night during a storm had slowed the local journalists' response time. That wouldn't last the day, and Jay knew he should issue a statement by the end of his shift.

He recalled Sam's suggestion to use the murder to spur the citizenry into action. Jay disliked that tactic, but he understood the sentiment. It highlighted the difference between Sam and Jay, too. Sam had left college with higher aspirations. Jay suspected there'd be a run for the mayor's office in Sam's future, and some of his brother's ideas likely fed into that. As for Jay, he hated politics enough to avoid all of that. What Jay wanted to do was help people. He liked justice, and that entwined with his belief in duty.

"Here's the locker," Towns told her new boss, waving her hand Vanna White-style over a solid metal door. She swiped a keycard over the reader and waited for the light to flash green. When she opened the door, Jay found a small closet stacked with riot guns, assault rifles, and several handguns. He stepped inside, selecting a Beretta PXP. The forty-five-caliber pistol fit in Jay's grip.

The chief checked the weapon's action, ensuring it was in properly maintained condition. He selected three loaded magazines and a hip holster. The extra magazines went into his pocket, and the fully loaded forty-five slid into the holster.

"Feel better?" Towns asked after watching him handle the weapon.

Jay smiled in answer.

"I thought you might need a cigarette after that," she quipped.

"Just proper training," he reminded her.

"Gossip around here is that you were Recon," she told him.

"That would be accurate," he confirmed.

"Word is you were a sniper," she added.

"How did you hear that?"

"I think Sam liked to rave about you," she replied.

Jay's face flushed a bit, and he turned away from her. Few things struck Jay quite like hearing his big brother had been bragging about him. It didn't seem to matter how old one got; that sibling approval still hit the right spot.

"My cruiser's out back," Towns told Jay.

"I'm on your six," he informed her. He trailed behind as she marched toward the elevator. Outside, the pair climbed into a blue and white squad car. Each side advertised "Ocean Springs Police Department" on one line and, in smaller font beneath it, "Protect and Serve."

Jay folded his arms and watched out the window as Shannon Towns pulled onto Highway 90, heading west. A couple of minutes later, Jay stared out across the bay he'd been on last night. Had the murderer thrown Jamie Rene off the side? Jay didn't think so—too much traffic.

No, he decided. Whoever dumped her had done so from a boat. Of course, almost everyone owned or had access to a boat along the coast. That was no help at all.

9

———

"How long since you've been home?" Towns asked Jay.

"Two Christmases ago," he admitted.

She threw a shady glance across the front seat at him. "Why did you run away?"

Jay rotated his head ninety degrees to stare at her.

"I don't mean it in that way," she said quickly. "I understand folks leaving. It's a small town."

"The city wasn't the problem," Jay explained.

Shannon nodded. "I get it. Family is brutal sometimes. Are you and Sam close?"

The question came out a little forced. Was she just a nervous chatterer? Jay had encountered a few people like that. They struggled with chit-chat in awkward situations. A ride along with the new boss might constitute awkward.

"We've remained close. The issue's always been my dad."

Shannon shrugged. "For me, the issue's always been my mother."

"How so?" Jay asked, hoping to shift the conversation from his family dynamics.

"Mom was a beauty queen," Towns told him. "That doesn't matter too much nowadays, but forty years ago, it made her a minor celebrity—at least along the coast. She would work grand openings for car dealerships or make appearances with the local radio stations. You know, back when they set up at different businesses. She never understood why I wouldn't follow in her footsteps."

"You didn't want to be Miss Ocean Springs?" Jay teased.

"No, it was Miss Gulf Coast. They wanted to include all the cities along 90."

"That had nothing to do with the lack of contestants?"

"In 2001, totally. When my mother did it, the competition was fierce. She was up against hundreds of girls. By the time I was sixteen, there were less than fifty from the area."

"But not for you?"

"I preferred boys over fighting with debutantes," she remarked with a coy grin.

"You might have come off better if you'd done the beauty contests."

"No kidding. I could have stayed single and skipped on that last husband."

"How many times have you been married?" Jay asked.

"Only the once," she confessed. "He was enough."

Jay shrugged. "Smart. I have three under my belt."

"Any kids, Chief?"

Jay shook his head. "Not yet."

"I thought Becs had a couple?" Towns questioned.

"She has one, but she's not mine."

"Oh, sorry," she said, her tone sympathetic. "If it's any consolation, most of the time, children are crap."

Jay gave her a comforting grin. "I'm good. It just didn't work out. Such is life."

"You're still young," she offered.

He said nothing. Instead, he looked out the windshield as they drove through unfamiliar territory.

"I used to smoke weed back here," he commented.

"We all did," Shannon informed him as she turned into a drive. A large oval sign set atop a stone pedestal read, "Bayside Apartments. 1, 2, and 3 bedrooms available. Come home to style." The two-story complex didn't scream glamorous. In fact, the architecture came closer to some newer military housing that he'd seen. A Floridian influence spilled over here, with terracotta roofing and a stucco exterior. With the Air Force base around the corner, Jay suspected that many of the tenants here were airmen.

"When we get in there, I want you to take the lead," Jay told her.

"Chief? I'm in uniform."

"So what?"

"I don't look like a detective."

"You'll just have to act like one," he explained as she pulled into a spot designated by a small sign for guests. The placard stated, "No overnight parking."

"Okay," Towns said in a shaky voice.

"Nothing to worry about, Shannon," he reassured her. "I'll be there. If I have a question, I can jump in."

"Thank you, Chief," she replied, her tone hardening.

Bayside Apartments seemed composed of single and two-story condos. Most looked like mid-scale townhouses and reminded Jay of hundreds of similar communities he'd seen in Palm County and Panama City. The front yards had been landscaped years earlier but not recently. The bushes grew without abandon, and the grass in most places was nonexistent. Cheap plastic toy trucks and tractors littered the dirt, and three kids' bicycles lay strewn about where their riders had abandoned them.

Towns exited the cruiser, and Jay stepped in behind her. They approached a larger unit, a two-story condo with some of the healthier shrubs. It was one of the few patches of grass clear of toys and trash. Did Jamie like to clean the flower bed? The dirt showed almost no weeds, but it was old soil. Nobody had mulched this garden in years.

Officer Shannon Towns stopped on the stoop. Her finger wavered over the doorbell for a few seconds before she pressed the button. Jay sensed her trepidation, and he understood it. Jay recalled his first house call after he got out of the Marines. He went with a state trooper to notify a family that the father had been killed in the rush hour traffic heading into downtown Panama City. Here he was, a grown man working on his second career, and he almost broke down when the man's widow answered the door, a two-year-old on her hip and a three-year-old holding her thigh.

Jay remembered her name even now: Angela Hopper. Her face was emblazoned on his memory like a GIF, replaying her reaction as the trooper had relayed the terrible news. Her visage had transformed from annoyance at being disturbed to terror to grief in a matter of two seconds.

The door on 3721 Bayview Drive swung back, revealing a white woman in her early twenties with reddish-brown hair. She was wearing sweatpants and an LSU sweatshirt. Her face was drooped, probably from hours of worrying. When she took in the sight of the uniformed Shannon Towns and Jay, her cheeks sagged even more.

"You found her?" she asked.

"Did Jamie Rene live here?" Towns asked.

"*Did* she live here?" the girl echoed, tears welling up in her eyes. "Is she dead?"

"Ma'am, I'm so sorry," Towns offered.

"No!" the roommate wailed. Her posture sagged forward, and Shannon caught her weight as she seemed to melt into the officer.

"I'm so sorry," Towns repeated. "Can we talk with you?"

The woman's head nodded against Towns's shoulder. She sniffed and pulled away from the cop. Her eyes were now bright red, and tears stained her cheeks.

"I'm Officer Towns and this is Chief Delp."

The woman blinked. "The chief?"

"We're from Ocean Springs," Towns explained. "Chief Delp just started."

Jay reached his hand out to Jamie's roommate, who took it without a thought. "My condolences for your loss," he offered.

"Thank you," she said between what were either gasps or hiccups. "Come in."

The pair of police followed her inside.

"I'm afraid I didn't get your name," Towns told the woman.

"Danni," she responded. "Crews."

"Ms. Crews, we need to ask you some questions," Towns explained.

"What happened to Jamie?" Danni Crews inquired.

Towns threw a gaze at Jay from the corner of her eye. If she was asking for a lifeline, he declined to offer it.

"A couple of fishermen found Jamie in the bay last night," Towns said.

"She drowned?" Crews asked.

"We don't know yet," Towns answered. That wasn't entirely true since Jay knew what killed her, but he hadn't shared that with Towns. He planned to wait until the official report came out. But then again, they hadn't confirmed her identity, though Jay had no doubts that the body they found in the bay was Jamie Rene. Unless Jamie Rene had an identical twin, then she was lying in a cadaver locker in Pascagoula right now.

"We need to establish her last known whereabouts," Towns explained.

Jay turned and took in the interior of the apartment. The occupants kept the residence clean. While the furniture appeared dated, it showed proper maintenance and cleaning. No obvious tears in the upholstery. No stained fabric. Even the vents were dust-free.

Jay's place in Florida resembled this level of tidiness, but that was another by-product of the Marine Corps. He owned little, but what he had, he kept neat. Danni Crews and Jamie Rene appeared to have the same mindset.

"When did you last see Jamie?" Towns questioned Danni.

"Friday morning," the girl reported. "She had a nine o'clock psych class. We saw each other before school. Jamie made me coffee because I had a big ethics exam."

"Do you go to Gulf Coast Community, too?" Jay interjected.

"Yes, sir."

"What's your major?" he followed up.

"Business. But I'm shifting to pre-law."

Jay nodded. "You want to be a business attorney?"

"Yeah," Danni answered.

Without moving, Jay signaled Towns with his eyes for her to continue the questioning. The officer picked up her cue without wasting a beat. "What did Jamie study?" Towns asked.

"Jamie wanted to go into social work and teaching,"

Crews replied. "She had her first student teaching job last week. Gaw, she was so excited about it."

"You saw her off to class, right?"

Danni nodded.

"Does she drive?" Jay interjected.

Danni frowned. "Yeah."

"She drove to school on Friday?"

The girl nodded.

"What kind of car does she have?" Towns asked.

"It's a 2014 Honda CRV."

"Color?"

"White."

Towns continued, "When did you suspect something was wrong?"

Danni settled on a yellow loveseat, folding her hands on her lap. If Jay asked the internet for a picture of a grieving Southern girl, he thought this might just be it. Of course, he expected Google to dress the subject like she was June Cleaver.

"She was on the schedule for Friday night, and it wasn't unusual for her to stay with Clay," Danni said.

"Who's Clay?" Towns interjected without a pause. Jay resisted the urge to offer her an approving nod.

"Clay Miller. He and Jamie are dating," Danni answered. "Were dating." Tears welled up again as she amended her comment. Towns waited several seconds for the girl to recover.

"Do you have an address for Clay?" she asked.

Danni's eyes lifted upward, as if the answer she wanted was written on the popcorn ceiling. Jay followed her gaze, noticing that even the bumps on the ceiling hadn't accumulated the cobwebs and dust flowers common on these atrocious features.

"I don't know his address," Danni said. "He lives in D'Iberville. Over on Church Avenue."

"How long have they been together?" Towns asked.

"Six or seven months," Crews answered. She ran her index finger under both eyes, wiping away any moisture.

"Did they get along?" Towns asked.

"Of course," Danni Crews stated.

The front door rattled, and Jay jerked around. His right hand dropped to the butt of the PXP. The cold metal against his palm slowed him down, though he'd pull the pistol before the door opened all the way if he needed to.

The door swung into the entryway, and a young man with dirty hands and a greasy shirt stepped inside. "What the hell is this?" he demanded. He sounded like he wanted to come across as gruff, but his voice cracked at the end when he locked eyes with Jay.

"Kyle, it's the police," Danni said. "They found Jamie."

"Good, is she okay?" he asked in an oblivious tone.

Jay cocked his head and moved his hand away from this firearm. "Someone murdered her," he answered without emotion.

"Oh, crap," Kyle blubbered. "How?"

Shannon Towns ignored the question. Instead, she asked, "Were you friends with Jamie?"

"Uh, yeah. We all hung out," he replied. "Oh, Danni, I'm sorry."

He moved over to the girl and sat on the loveseat, wrapping his arm around her shoulder.

"Who are you, sir?" Towns asked.

"This is Kyle, my boyfriend," Danni explained.

"What's your last name, Kyle?"

"Rose," he replied.

"You said you all spent time together?" Towns continued

with the careful interrogation that Jay admired. "Did that include Clay Miller?"

"Oh, yeah," Kyle said. "Clay's cool."

"When was the last time you saw Jamie, Mr. Rose?" Towns asked.

Kyle repeated Danni's action, staring at the ceiling for his answer. "I guess it was Wednesday night. We watched that movie with the scary clown."

"*Terrifier*," Danni offered.

"Right, *Terrifier*," Kyle responded.

"You guys watch a lot of horror movies?" Jay asked.

"Some."

Jay nodded, pursing his lips.

"No, man," Kyle snapped. "It's not like that."

"I never suggested it was," Jay replied.

"The hell you didn't," Kyle groaned. "You're saying we watched some psycho movies and killed Jamie."

"Mr. Rose, no one is suggesting anything," Jay stated. "We only want to catch the person responsible for murdering your friend."

Danni Crews started crying again. Kyle, now animated, pulled his arm off his girlfriend's shoulder and gestured toward the two cops.

"You need to find who did this," he demanded. "We'd never hurt Jamie."

"Mr. Rose, we understand your concerns," Towns consoled. "We just have a job to do."

Kyle Rose shook his head in disbelief. "You better catch this person."

"It's our number-one priority," Jay assured him.

"Right," Kyle said sarcastically. "I'm sure the Mississippi cops want to solve the poor black girl's murder."

Jay cocked his head at the insolence, but he held his

tongue.

"Don't, Kyle," Danni urged. "They are just trying to help."

"Lotta good it did Jamie," he retorted.

"We want to stop it from happening to anyone else," Towns stated, and Jay cringed inside. She'd almost admitted they were worried there would be more victims. Luckily, the young couple didn't notice the flub.

"Did Jamie have any weirdos show up around her?" Jay asked, hoping to steer away from Towns's comment.

"She worked in a bar. Weirdos hit on her all the time," Kyle pointed out.

"But nothing she mentioned that scared her or anything," Danni elaborated.

Jay pushed off the seat he'd been occupying. "We've got enough for now," he told them, signaling Towns to get up. "We may be in touch if something else comes up."

Danni nodded.

"If you remember anything at all, let us know," Towns said, handing her a card.

"We will," Kyle assured them as he rose to escort them out of the apartment.

Jay allowed Towns to lead the way out, and before the two were off the condominium's front step, the door slammed behind them.

10

————

Once they were in the squad car, Jay asked, "Initial thoughts?"

Shannon Towns put her hands on the wheel at ten and two and stared out the front window toward the front of 3721 Bayview Drive. "Mr. Rose seemed high-strung," she remarked.

"My opinion, too," Jay concurred.

"Danni was genuinely upset, too," Towns noted.

"Yes."

Towns turned to face him. "That might have been a sham, though?"

"Is that a question?" Jay probed.

"No," she said uncertainly.

"It could have been an act, although I don't think it was."

"Why not?"

Jay smiled. "Gut instinct."

Towns nodded. "And Kyle."

"I'm undecided so far," he admitted.

She refocused out the front window. "Where to?"

"Isn't her work close by?" Jay asked.

"Yes," Shannon answered.

"If we already crossed the bridge, let's kill two birds. Whatcha say?"

"You're the chief, Chief."

Jay lifted the left side of his mouth. "You got a way with words."

"I wanted to be a poet."

"Really?" Jay replied with surprise in his voice.

"No," Shannon Towns spat out and laughed. "I only wanted to be a cop. Or a female Michael Knight."

"Since they just came out with self-driving cars, I guess a police officer was a better choice."

Towns changed subjects. "Do you think Rose is involved? I mean, does your gut think it?"

"I am not sure. He might have just been emotional. Men that age struggle with those feelings."

"You'd expect this new generation to show more enlightenment."

"In southern Mississippi?"

"True," Towns allowed. "It's not something you see a lot of."

"You always live here?" Jay asked, changing topics.

"After high school, I traveled all the way to the University of Southern Mississippi," Towns answered. "Worked on a criminology degree, but got pregnant instead of graduating. That led me to marry far too young to a raging—well, you know. One kid turned into two kids. Then my husband, a godly Baptist pastor, had an affair with someone we went to church with. After that, I moved back to Ocean Springs and joined the department."

"You moved back?"

"Yeah. All the way from Bay St. Louis."

Jay chuckled. "That's only, what, twenty miles east?"

"Try thirty," she corrected.

"Picky, picky," Jay joked, adding. "You acted like you see Sam a lot," he ventured.

"It's a small town. We run into each other out and about."

"Are you friends with Danielle?"

"Not really," she confessed. "She kinda keeps to herself."

Jay shrugged. "She's quiet," he admitted. "I think it was culture shock for her, moving down here from Enid."

"Where is that?"

"Between Jackson and Memphis. It's a tiny bump on the interstate. It has a lake, which is the only thing it has."

"No post office?"

Jay crinkled his forehead. "I guess it has a post office. Probably a Mexican restaurant, too, but I can't say."

"Is it too liberal down here for her?" Shannon mused.

Jay chuckled. The idea that any part of Mississippi would be too liberal for the rest of the state amused him, having been all over the world. Either way, Shannon had hit it on the head. He liked his sister-in-law, even if they had nothing to discuss, but she'd always struck him as wound up a little too tight.

Sam and Danielle met at Mississippi State, and after a long courtship, the pair married and had kids. Sam had never intended to move away from Ocean Springs, and Jay suspected it had required little to convince Danielle to live somewhere with more than one fast-food option.

Unfortunately, Danielle had never blended with anyone other than Sam, and even that pairing never seemed like the best fit. Still, Jay had nothing negative to say about Danielle. She was a loving mother and spouse, and, as Sam described it, a devout daughter-in-law to Terry Delp. That alone garnered her sainthood in Jay's eyes.

"Have you eaten at this crab place?" Jay asked.

"Yeah, but it's been a bit. Guy took me on a date there. The food wasn't bad, but the company wasn't great."

"Ugh, dating," Jay moaned.

"It is the absolute worst," Shannon confessed. "I used to do the online thing, but that was depressing. Either I'd end up with guys who've been single since birth and now hate everyone or divorced men who got divorced for a reason."

Jay frowned. "I've been divorced. Three times now."

"Was it for a good reason?"

He shrugged. "At least one of us thought it was at the time."

"Fair enough," she acknowledged. "I never regretted getting married. Not leaving the day after my second son was born, I should have done that."

Jay nodded along. "I wish mine would have worked out. Mostly I don't blame anyone. It's tough being married to a Marine."

"Cops might not be much better," Shannon suggested. "I haven't been married while I was on the force, though."

"It's not much better," Jay affirmed.

"Think you'll get hitched again?" she asked.

"I wouldn't mind," he told her. "Most of marriage agreed with me. There's a nice feeling about having someone to go through life with."

"I suppose," she replied with no enthusiasm.

"Guess I haven't ruled it out," he added.

Towns turned into a gravel drive that meandered through a copse of trees. A parking lot spread out as they came through the path. A stilted building stood on the shore of the back bay. The lunch rush had ended hours ago, and the Biloxi Crab Shack seemed only to have a few customers based on the number of vehicles parked along the restaurant's side. Jay figured three of the six cars belonged to employees. Could have been all of them, but it was, at least, a slow time for the staff. Perfect for asking questions without interrupting the flow of business.

"I might have to pop over for some gumbo," Jay considered as he got out of the car.

"Lots of folks say the best around is over at Mary Mahoney's," Towns told him. "But I've never liked it. I'm not a fan of the flavor."

"Oh, I missed it," Jay said. "Plenty of places serve what they call 'gumbo' in Florida, but it's not the same."

"We have a plethora of seafood joints," Shannon informed him. "Lots have cropped up since you left town."

"I might need to catch up," Jay stated. "Start working my way around the area until I find the best."

"That sounds like a chore," she pointed out. "You could just have all the places cater lunch for your new staff."

Jay smiled. "It builds morale, doesn't it?"

She shrugged and gave a smile.

The two climbed the stairs to the upper level. The structure was new—"new" being a relative term. Jay guessed the building was a couple of years old. The Mississippi sun and salt air wreaked havoc on timber, but the wood still had the yellow tint of new lumber. Even if the owners had sealed the wood, which Jay was positive they'd done, it would age fast. He'd seen the same effect in South Florida and the panhandle.

"Table for two?" a young man with a pockmarked face asked as he approached the pair at the entrance.

"Is the manager here?" Shannon inquired.

His countenance fell in a mixture of fear and anxiety. "Uh, yes," he replied. "Would you wait here?"

"Yes, we can," Shannon confirmed, offering the boy a reassuring smile that said everything was okay.

His expression didn't show the same assurance. Given that Shannon Towns was wearing her police uniform, the kid might make all sorts of speculations about their presence. Without another word, he scurried toward the kitchen like a hungry rat searching for cheese in a maze.

"Do you want to take the lead?" Towns asked her boss.

Jay shook his head. "You did great with Danni. Keep it up."

"I messed up, though," she admitted.

Jay gave her a questioning stare.

"Didn't you hear me when I almost said we implied there would be more murders?" she asked. "As soon as the words came out, I realized how it sounded."

"You did fine," Jay assured her. "Nothing you mentioned was out of line."

"But we don't know it's not just her," Towns told him.

Jay shook his head. "We don't know anything yet."

"What do you think?" she asked.

"I don't like the possibilities," Jay admitted.

"Me either," Shannon agreed.

"Can I help you?" A large black man waddled toward them. He flashed a grin that exposed a jagged smile, missing several teeth. Jay estimated he was in his fifties. He wore a polo-style shirt, and Jay's eyes drifted for a second to his inner forearm where scars showed prominently. They were old—years old—but still looked like track marks.

"We're from Ocean Springs," Towns told him. "We need to talk with you about Jamie Rene."

His eyes widened. "Jamie? Is she okay?"

Towns shook her head in slow motion. "Unfortunately, Jamie was found dead last night."

"Oh no!" The man stepped back, grabbing the host stand for support. "What happened?"

"Do you mind if we sit down and chat?" she asked the manager.

He nodded fervently before waving his hand toward a table by the window. Jay and Shannon Towns followed him to a four-top table.

"Can I get you officers anything?" the man offered.

"No, thank you," both replied in unison.

"Sir, I'm Officer Towns and this is our chief, Jay Delp."

"Sid Collier," the man said. "I am the daytime manager here."

"Were you close to Jamie?" Shannon asked.

"She worked nights," he explained. "I didn't work with her much. She was an excellent employee, but she worked with Michael in the evenings more than me."

"Who is Michael?" Towns inquired.

"He's the GM," Sid explained. "He works the floor at night and on weekends."

"Is he here?"

"He texted earlier that he was on his way in," Sid replied. "He's usually here by now, but he's a little late today."

Jay inclined his chin to study the assistant manager. "Did he say why?"

Sid Collier turned from Shannon to the chief, fixing Jay with a perplexed gaze. "He didn't tell me."

Jay gave his head one nod as if considering that. "Let's hope that he'll get here before we leave. I'm sure we'd love to ask him some questions. You know, since he worked with her more."

Sid's face puckered. "Can I help?"

Jay signaled for Towns to continue.

"How long did Jamie work here?" Towns inquired.

Sid shook his head. "I can't say. A few years. I've been here almost three years, and she started after I did."

Towns nodded, making a note on her little scratchpad. "What did she do here?"

"She waited tables. Sometimes she might bartend, but mostly she was a server."

"How was she at her job?"

"I guess good. She had some regulars. But again, I'm not the one who worked every night with her."

"You don't know of any problems she had with other employees, do you?"

"Problems?" Sid echoed. "Did someone kill her? You just said she was found dead."

"Yes, Mr. Collier," Towns said. "We suspect she was murdered."

"Oh no," he muttered. His head bowed, and he mouthed something with his eyes closed. It took only a couple of seconds, and he lifted his face to stare at the two cops. "I'm sorry. I wanted to say a quick prayer."

"Are you religious?" Towns asked him.

Sid made a so-so gesture with his head. "I don't do the whole church thing, but I trust in a higher power."

Jay asked, "How long have you been clean?"

On cue, Sid's right hand stroked the inside of his left arm, tracing the scarred needle marks. "Four years," he confessed.

"Good for you," Towns praised.

"Can we go back?" Jay asked. "Did Jamie have any problems with anyone else?"

Sid shook his head. "Nothing that would warrant murder."

Jay doubted that. He'd seen the reasons people murdered others. It could range from a person giving another guy a strange look to someone suspecting their significant other of flirting with someone else. The pettiest he'd seen was a man who wouldn't share his Twinkies. The suspect Jay arrested proceeded to complain that there were two snack cakes in the package and his friend had no reason not to share with him.

People killed for a variety of stupid reasons.

"What about customers?" Towns asked. "You mentioned she had regulars. Were any ever a problem?"

"I can't say," Sid admitted. "Like I said, I didn't work a lot of nights. Jamie had a good rapport with our guests. I can't imagine there being an issue."

The front door opened, and a younger man in his late thirties strolled through the doors.

"Hey, Michael," the young kid who'd greeted Jay and Shannon announced across the room.

Michael waved at the kid before his eyes trained on the three seated at the table. His face paled as his brow furrowed with a look of sheer panic.

11

———————

Sid lifted his hand to wave the newcomer over. The man called Michael took two steps toward the trio. His face was aghast with fear, and he struggled for a full second to recover and return his expression to a calm demeanor.

"Sid, what's going on?" Michael queried as he approached the table. The manager's gaze shifted from Jay to Shannon. He examined her uniform, pausing at the logo on her shoulder that read "OSPD."

"Who are you guys with?" Michael asked.

"They're here about Jamie," Sid explained. "She was murdered yesterday."

Jay watched Michael's features. A strange sense of relief crossed the manager's face. "Murdered?" he repeated.

"Yes, we're with the Ocean Springs Police Department," Towns informed the manager. "You must be Michael Collins?"

Collins nodded. "Yes, I am," he replied, taking a seat next to Sid. "What happened?"

Jay interjected, "We can't give out too many details yet. However, Jamie's body was found yesterday."

"That's terrible," Collins remarked. "We all loved Jamie."

"We were just talking with Sid here about her," Towns began. "He mentioned you worked with her more than he did."

Collins nodded. "Yes, she was one of my best servers."

"Do you know how long she worked here?" Towns repeated the question she'd asked Sid Collier a few minutes earlier.

"I'm not sure," Collins confessed. "I can check her employee records, but I think it was close to two years."

"You say she was a good server?" Towns pressed.

"Oh, yes," Collins said. "She could handle the weeds. The guests adored her. Lots only wanted her to wait on them. Even the kitchen staff loved her."

"Even?" Jay questioned.

"Well, line cooks don't always mix with the front of the house."

"Why is that?" Towns inquired.

"Money, for the most part," Collins told them. "The servers might make a couple hundred bucks a night, but the cooks get paid by the hour. They don't have the same incentive to please the guests as the front of the house."

Nodding, Towns made a brief note. "And the cooks liked her?"

"Yeah, I never had a real complaint about her from them. Some of the line cooks gripe about every girl in here."

"Do you only hire female waitstaff?" Jay asked.

"Not only," Collins explained. "But it seems to work out that way."

"What about him?" Jay pointed at the pockmarked boy who greeted the officers.

"That's Jimmy. He's the busboy."

"No busgirls?" Towns asked pointedly.

Michael Collins shrugged without offering an answer.

"No one ever had a problem with Jamie?" Jay pushed with a dubious tone.

"Nothing worth killing anyone over," Collins answered.

This time, Jay responded with, "I've seen people murdered over the silliest things."

Collins narrowed his eyes. "I suppose, but I don't think we have anyone here like that."

Towns glanced up from the note she was jotting down. "When did either of you see Jamie last?"

Both managers exchanged a quick glance. Sid answered first. "If I remember right, it was Thursday afternoon when she came to work. We passed each other, really."

"Friday," Collins answered. "She worked her shift. I think she left about nine that night."

"You never see her after that?" Towns asked.

"She never showed up Saturday or Sunday," he told them.

"You didn't think that weird?" Jay questioned.

"Weird?" Collins repeated. "For Jamie, yes. In general, no."

"What do you mean?" Towns inquired.

"Jamie never pulled a no-call, no-show. She'd always call out if she wasn't going to make it. So that's a little weird, but it happens with a lot of the others."

"Would you fire her for that?" Towns asked.

Collins leaned back in his seat. "I don't know," he answered with careful consideration. "I've had servers miss shifts for a variety of reasons. This was a first for her, so I'd want to understand why before I decided."

"Hmm, every restaurant manager I worked for would fire someone for that," Towns said.

"Ten years ago, yes," Collins admitted. "Now the job pool is different. It takes forever to replace an employee today."

"You put up with more crap, huh?" Jay commented.

"Pretty much," Collins agreed.

"That's frustrating, I imagine," Towns noted.

Sid nodded, but Collins only pursed his lips.

"Did you try to call Jamie?" Towns asked. "Since that wasn't like her?"

Collins answered, "No, it was a weekend. I think I had someone text her, but they never heard from her. But like I said, it was a weekend. We were swamped, and I never slowed down until closing. By then, I forgot about it." He leaned forward, shifting his gaze to Sid. "I should have called her," he said to his assistant manager. "It never occurred to me."

"Not your fault, man," Sid assured his boss. "How could you know?"

"We're supposed to be family," Collins moaned. "We just let her get killed."

"Mr. Collins, this isn't anyone's fault except the person who murdered Jamie Rene." Shannon Towns set her pad face down as she attempted to console the manager. Jay watched the man's face as he spoke. The muscle next to his right eye twitched.

"If you want to help Jamie now," Jay added, "you can help us find anyone who might know where she went after her shift on Friday."

"Callie's working tonight, isn't she?" Collins asked Sid.

"She's in the back, rolling silverware."

"Jimmy, will you get Callie for me?" Michael Collins

called to the busboy, who was wiping down the nautical decorations adorning the walls.

"Yes, sir, Michael," Jimmy responded, hurrying through the double swinging doors leading off the dining room to what Jay supposed was the kitchen.

After a moment, the doors banged open, and a young, fair-haired girl came out. She carried a bus tub filled with silverware rolled in blue cloth napkins. Jimmy walked up behind her and took the container from her with a gleam in his eye. The blond gave him a smile before coming toward the foursome.

"Jimmy said you needed me?" she asked as she approached.

"Callie, you worked Friday night, right?" Towns asked.

The girl nodded. Her eyes drifted to Towns's uniform. "What's going on?"

"I'm sorry. Can you give me your name?" Towns asked in a motherly tone.

"Callie Wilson."

"Callie, do you know Jamie Rene?"

She nodded again.

"Unfortunately, she was murdered, and we need to track her last known whereabouts."

"No!" Callie wailed. "What do you mean?"

"I hate to tell you this," Towns added.

"She was just here," Callie said. Tears started flowing down her cheeks. "I don't understand."

"It's okay, Callie," Collins assured her, touching her forearm. Her hair flopped from side to side as she shook her head in disbelief.

"Ms. Wilson, you were here with Jamie on Friday night?" Shannon continued to use a comforting tone.

She nodded, still crying and unable to form the words.

"Do you remember what time she got off work that night?"

"We both closed," she blubbered between sobs.

Jay lifted his head to see Jimmy scamper through the double doors. It took less than five seconds for three faces to appear in the door's windows. Six eyes stared at the group.

"Why don't you sit down?" Jay suggested. He pushed his chair back, but Sid had already risen to his feet and motioned for Callie to take his seat. As she settled down, Sid dragged an empty chair from a nearby table.

"What time did you leave?" Towns asked the server.

"We left about midnight," Callie replied. "I was going downtown to meet some friends and asked her if she wanted to come. She told me she couldn't."

"Does she often go out after work?" Towns continued, adding a note. Jay read the number "12" on her pad.

"Sometimes. Depends."

"On what?" Towns pressed.

"How busy we were. How much we made. How the shift went."

"How busy were you that night?" Jay inquired.

"Slammed. We were in the weeds almost until we closed. I made good money."

"Did Jamie do well, too?"

Callie nodded. "Yeah."

"Any issues with customers?" Towns asked.

"Nothing that night," she told them. "At least, not that I knew about."

"Were there other problems?" Jay interrupted before Towns could follow up. He kicked himself for cutting her off.

"Sometimes, yes," Callie admitted.

"Like what?" Towns asked.

"Guys being guys, I guess," Callie murmured. "There's always one getting pushy."

"Callie, why didn't you tell me?" Collins blurted out.

"We do, Michael. If it's a problem."

"What do you consider a problem?" Towns asked the young woman.

"If they get handsy. Or demand to meet after work. Sometimes they might wait until we leave to talk to us. Some of these guys think that we're nice to them because we like them."

Jay nodded but held his tongue. *Let Shannon run with this. She's doing great.*

"Could someone have been waiting for her Friday night?" Towns folded her hands on the table and locked eyes on Callie.

The girl shook her head. "We walked out together. No one was in the parking lot, except Jimmy."

"Jimmy?"

Callie instantly realized what she'd implied and backtracked. "No, he was just taking the trash out. Nothing like that."

Jay noticed Towns consider that information and choose not to make note of it.

"Were there any guys causing problems? Guys being guys?"

Callie shook her head, then stopped. "I was off that day, but Lexi talked about some guy getting real handsy last Wednesday."

"Who was it?" Towns asked.

"I wasn't here," Callie repeated.

"Who is Lexi?" Towns looked to Collins.

"She's another server."

"Is she here?"

Callie answered, "Not today."

Jay's gaze scanned along the ceiling, counting six cameras angled around the dining area. He jutted a finger to one. "Do those work?"

"Yeah," Collins replied. "We keep the video for sixty days unless there's an issue we need to review."

"Mind if we look at Wednesday night?"

Collins squirmed, and Jay cast a sidelong glance at Shannon. Jay added, "We can always get a subpoena, but I'm sure you want to catch Jamie's murderer, right?"

"Of course," the manager assured the officers. "I was just worried about the implications to our customers."

"Up to you," Jay replied, knowing it wasn't. If Collins refused, he'd reach out to the restaurant owners and suggest they share the video before Jay and Towns had to get a court order.

"Yeah, let's look," Collins agreed. "It might take a minute to find the right time."

"I don't mind," Jay promised him.

"While you're examining that, I could talk with the rest of the employees," Shannon suggested. "If that's okay with you two."

Sid Collier had no intention of offering anything else without his boss's approval. Collins, however, nodded. "Of course. Whatever we can do to help."

Jay signaled to Towns with an approving bob of his head.

"Chief, you can come with me, I guess," Collins said.

"Thank you, Mr. Collins," Jay replied.

"Sid, why don't you introduce Officer... I'm sorry, what was your name?"

"Towns."

"Introduce Officer Towns to the staff."

"Would it be possible to get a copy of the schedule?" Shannon asked.

"Absolutely," Collins said as he rose to his feet.

Jay followed him, leaving the other three at the table. "How long have you worked here, Michael?" Jay asked when they entered the small office next to the bathrooms.

Collins pulled the door closed, saying, "Don't like guests to see in here."

That space could have been an old broom closet, given its size. There was a tiny, utilitarian metal desk and a filing cabinet. An older Dell PC rested on the desktop with papers scattered all around it.

"You didn't say how long you'd been here?" Jay repeated his question.

"Three and a half years. Since we opened."

Jay nodded and sat in a chair that had been in the dining room until someone had cut the upholstery with a knife. Now the vinyl fabric folded back to reveal a once-yellow foam that crumbled when Jay ran a finger over it.

"What were you worried about?" Jay asked.

Collins, who sat opposite Jay behind the computer screen, looked up in surprise. "What do you mean?"

"When you first saw us, you got anxious," Jay noted, although he was holding back. What he'd seen on Michael Collins's face was more than worry. It was fear.

"A police officer questioning my employees? That's concerning."

"Why, though?" Jay asked. "We could have been having lunch."

"This late in the afternoon? I just had a sick feeling something was wrong," he explained. "It's obvious I was right."

Jay nodded as if he understood the man.

"Here's Wednesday's footage," Collins announced. "If you want to step around here."

Jay moved to stand over Collins's shoulder. The chief stared at the screen. The image was grainy, but he suspected that resulted from the antiquated Dell monitor and not the recording.

"Is this as clear as it gets?" he asked.

"On this old piece of crap, yes," Collins confirmed.

"I will need to take a copy of this video to the station to have it analyzed," Jay told him.

Collins looked back over his shoulder at the chief.

"Don't worry," Jay assured the manager. "I'll get a subpoena to make it official. That way, you won't have to be concerned about customers getting upset with you."

Collins didn't respond, but he also didn't argue. Since Jay gave him little room to counter, Collins simply pressed play.

"I can run it at high speed," Collins suggested. "Otherwise, we'll be here all day. And you said you'll be able to go over it better at the station."

Jay almost grinned. Collins's cooperation was running out. So much for treating the people here as if they were family.

The scene on the monitor raced by like one of those Benny Hill movies Terry Delp used to watch at night after drinking a twelve-pack. To Jay, a six-pack of beer was the bare minimum required to tolerate those shows.

"Wait, what's this?" Collins stated, slowing the footage down.

Jay noted the time stamp on the video: 7:27 p.m. On the screen, he saw a very alive Jamie Rene talking with a group of four guys seated at a window table. One grainy man continued to reach for Jamie, who shooed away his advances over and over. After the fifth instance, he grabbed part of her body. She grew visibly angry and stormed off.

"I remember this," Collins remarked just as he walked on screen to talk to the four customers. There were some words, and all four men stood up with obvious glares of anger. The one guy who'd been harassing Jamie continued to berate Collins.

"You didn't mention it earlier?" Jay asked sharply.

"It slipped my mind."

"Do you know these guys?"

Collins shook his head. "I don't recognize them."

"Did they pay with a credit card?" He hadn't seen a transaction on the screen but hoped he'd missed it.

Again, Collins shook his head. "I told them to leave, and they never paid."

"Why would you let them do that?"

"I didn't want them bothering anyone else, and I wanted to get them out so they wouldn't have time to harass Jamie anymore."

"Do you have cameras outside?"

"We do," Collins said, changing the screen to show the exterior. The four men stomped across the deck past a small stage where a duo of guitar players serenaded the crowd on the patio. Jay watched the foursome climb into a Ford F-150. When they backed out, he tried to read the license plate number, but the image was just too blurry.

"What about Jamie's car? Can you see it from the cameras?"

Collins typed a command, changing the view to show a row of cars. A small white SUV sat between a muddy Jeep Cherokee and a late '90s Mazda Miata.

"The white one is hers," Collins informed.

"You're sure?" Jay asked.

"She had a dead battery the other day, and I jumped her off."

Jay nodded as he pondered that. "I'll send someone to get the footage once I obtain a court order," he told the manager.

Collins leaned back in his chair. "I don't want to hamper the investigation. If you make sure the proper documentation gets here, you can have it today."

"We'll do that," he promised Michael Collins.

12

J ay stared at the whiteboard with the newest information scrolled across the panel. Shannon Towns had developed the start of a timeline for the crime, though it was scarce still. She'd marked down when Jamie had left her home based on Danni Crews's recollection. She'd included the Friday shift on the board, leaving a question mark at midnight. That was the last time they'd found that anyone had seen Jamie.

Callie had said Jamie "couldn't" go out after work. That phrase bothered Jay. He wished he'd prodded a little more, but it hadn't started bothering him until the ride back to the station.

Couldn't. Did that mean she had other plans? The boyfriend? Clay Miller? No one was home when they visited his place after leaving the Biloxi Blues Crab Shack. There was at least a day's worth of mail sticking out of the mailbox at the little cottage-style house.

They knew little more about Miller, but Shannon was already tracking down his data. Jay found Shannon to be quite adept at investigative work. He figured she'd have Miller's next of kin by the morning.

That left Jamie's Honda. Her clothes and phone could easily be in the bottom of the bay, but dumping a car was a lot more difficult. Towns put out an area-wide alert to all the local jurisdictions. Theoretically, a CRV could be loaded onto a barge and dumped, but that would present a lot of difficulty. If the killer did that, why not leave Jamie in the vehicle? She'd probably never be found that way. If the murderer had chosen to dump the vehicle in the bayou, he'd run the risk of someone seeing him or it being discovered at low tide by a local fisherman.

No, Jay decided. The Honda CRV was somewhere. However, even without submerging it, there were hundreds, if not thousands, of places to hide it for a long time.

He rolled his neck around. Shannon still sat in her cubicle, working on something. Jay wagered it was Miller's background, but he didn't want to bother her yet. Besides, it had been a long first day, and he needed to get home to relieve the nurse sitting with his father.

Jay stood up and stretched. When the elevator dinged, his eyes scanned across the bullpen as a rail-thin man in his seventies pushed something past the cubicles. When the custodian rounded the corner, Jay saw him rolling an office chair like it was a stroller.

"I think this is for you," the wiry fellow announced, pushing the new chair through Jay's door.

"Awesome," Jay beamed. "Another one. Where did this come from?"

"Mayor sent it over," the man told him.

This armchair was leather, with electronic buttons on the side. A cord coiled at the base.

"It plugs in?"

"This baby's heated," the city worker mentioned. "Got a massage feature, too."

Bemused, Jay gave the furniture a walkaround as if it were a new car. "That's nice," he admitted.

"Your tuchus should be quite comfy."

"Thank you," Jay told him.

"I'm supposed to take the old one."

Jay turned to see the chair that Towns had tracked down for him. "No," he replied, shaking his head. "Leave that one. Someone already dragged the original ratty piece of trash downstairs."

"Whatever you say," the city employee replied. "They told me to toss it, so if you want to keep it, whelp, it's all yours."

"Thanks again," Jay said.

"My pleasure," the man replied. "I don't gotta take your old chair, then I can head out of here for the day."

With that, the older custodian picked up his pace as he made his way to the elevator. Jay pushed the new chair behind his desk next to the other one Towns brought up. Tomorrow, he'd decide which one to keep. Now, he needed to pick up pizza for himself and his dad before the nurse started into overtime.

Jay tossed Shannon a wave as he exited the bullpen, shouting from the stairwell, "Don't stay here too long!"

"No worries, Chief," she answered, leaving Jay wondering if that meant she intended to leave soon or if he shouldn't concern himself about it.

Jay marveled at the changes Ocean Springs had undergone since he'd left. The one thing he disliked was the newer police department. It had moved from near city hall in the historic downtown area to the eastern edge of its limits. If Ocean Springs were a larger town, he might find it more annoying. Still, it was a ten-minute drive back to the historic city center.

He found Tom's Extreme Pizzeria thanks to the large pizza sign with an arrow directing traffic to the little building on Robinson Street. He parked his Jeep and started inside. In front of the restaurant was a small patio with several tables for outdoor seating. Almost all were occupied as locals dropped by after work for some dinner and a few drinks. He passed a placard that read "Ocean Springs: A drinking town with an art problem." Based on the number of people already imbibing out here, he suspected that sentiment held true.

"Is that Jay Delp?" a feminine voice called behind him.

Jay turned to see two familiar faces staring at him. Mayor Franklin had his hands folded on a table with a satisfied grin. Next to him sat a tall brunette with soft curls that looked like she'd woken up with the wave in them. Her green eyes cut across the space between them, and when she smiled at him, he froze in his tracks.

"How are you?" Rebecca Thomas asked as she slid out of the booth and ran over to him. Jay caught his ex-wife in his arms as she gave him a big hug and kissed his cheek. "Good grief, it's been forever," she muttered. "Yet, somehow, you look better than ever."

"That's the diet of cheese puffs and Old Grandad," he told her.

"How was the first day?" Tom Franklin inquired.

"Busy," he answered the mayor, not wanting to go into details about the investigation. "Thanks for the chair, too. It showed up as I was leaving."

"I saw the piece of junk you had in there," Franklin remarked with some bemusement.

"It's much appreciated. What are you two doing here?"

he questioned, pulling back to take a long look at his ex-wife.

"Oh, we're planning the Christmas festivities around here," Becs told him.

"Are you working for the man himself?" Jay joked.

"She's invaluable," Franklin assured him.

"I have no doubt," Jay remarked.

"How do you know each other, Chief? I thought you hadn't been back in years."

Jay nodded. "I haven't."

"Tom, Jay and I were married," Rebecca told the mayor. "A long time ago."

"Oh, you were the one who stole young Rebecca?" Franklin mused.

Jay struggled not to dislike the mayor, but he was not succeeding.

Rebecca chimed in. "Heck, Tom, we were both young and stupid," she explained. "Jay was my first love."

"High school sweethearts?" Franklin prodded. His smile displayed a litany of lechery.

"Yes, but we didn't survive boot camp," she said. Her eyes turned to Jay's. "I mean, I didn't survive it."

"We all make youthful transgressions," the mayor conceded.

Rebecca's grin softened. "Not Jay," she corrected her boss. "He never did anything wrong. I was far too young to know what I was doing. He, on the other hand, had clear goals."

"Eh, it all worked out, right?" Jay said to his ex.

"We have to catch up," she insisted.

Jay gave a quick nod. "What are you guys working on after hours?"

"It's all about Christmas," Rebecca replied. Her green

eyes glowed, and Jay had forgotten how closely they resembled the color of a raw emerald.

"We're in August," he pointed out.

"There's lots of planning to get ahead of," Franklin noted. "We need sponsors for the parade, route schedules, and at some point, we have to discuss with our chief the police logistics for the day."

"That can be managed," Jay assured him.

"First, this nasty murder should be put to bed," Franklin groaned.

Jay cringed. He had expected the mayor to ask about Jamie Rene, but he'd hoped the man had the decency to do so in a less public setting.

"I heard all about it," Rebecca said. "It's so tragic. Things like that never happen here."

"We can't know the killing happened in Ocean Springs. Someone could have dumped her, and the current dragged her to our shores," Franklin suggested.

Jay chose not to mention that her corpse never made it all the way to the beach. It didn't matter.

"Was she really in the water for a week?" Rebecca asked Jay.

The chief shook his head. Where had she heard that? Suddenly, he realized he hadn't given a statement for the local news. But no one had called him for a quote, either. Still, his attention returned to Rebecca. It seemed most plausible that Franklin was her source of gossip.

"No, she wasn't," he answered. "A couple of days, we think. Won't be sure until the coroner gets back to us."

"Any leads?" Franklin asked.

"Nothing I can discuss yet," he replied.

That answer didn't sit well with Franklin, who narrowed his gaze at Jay. The chief wasn't bothered too much by that.

Tom Franklin portrayed a man seeking power and esteem over serving his community. That did not sit well with Jay Delp. So, the mayor could dislike Jay, and possibly he thought he could control him. That was Franklin's mistake.

Rebecca interjected, "Jay, can we get dinner sometime?"

Jay nodded, though he'd have preferred the invitation to come when their mutual boss wasn't in earshot.

"Tomorrow night?" she asked.

"You should take him over to Evergreen," Franklin suggested in a voyeuristic tone.

"Yes, let's do that," she agreed. "Are you available?" she asked Jay.

"I need to see if Sam or Danielle can check in on Dad," he replied. "But that should work."

"I saw Sam the other day at the Wynn Dixie," she told him. "Terry sounds like he's not doing well."

Jay shrugged. It was another topic he'd just as soon discuss away from the mayor. "He has good days and bad, according to Sam."

"I heard old Terry was going downhill," Franklin remarked in the off-handed manner of someone who doesn't want to be left out of an intimate conversation.

"It's all inevitable," Jay said simply. "Text me, Becs. I gotta get inside and pick up Dad's dinner."

Rebecca leaned forward and wrapped him in her arms before kissing his cheek. "It was great to see you," she gushed.

Jay noticed Franklin's half-sneer in his periphery vision. He suspected the mayor had eyes for his assistant.

While Jay and Rebecca had stayed friendly on social media, they hadn't spent over five minutes in the same place in over two decades. He wondered how different this Rebecca was from the Becs he married right out of high school. They had barely lived together before he went to Parris Island. His plan had been to move her to whatever base he ended up being assigned. That never came to fruition. Halfway through his time in training, he received the divorce papers. There'd been no letters or calls warning him. While he'd written to her, Rebecca had only mailed one or two brief notes in return.

In hindsight, he realized that should have clued him in. Instead of reaching out to her, he'd signed the paperwork without trying to reach out to his wife. Jay had just surrendered his marriage and focused on the Corps.

In the long run, he considered how that had changed him. He'd joined Recon and connected with people he would still die for. Had he stayed married, he might have taken a different course in the Corps. With a wife at home, he likely would have gotten out after a single tour instead of creating a career. In turn, that could have put him in another field that wasn't law enforcement.

"Chief, we should get lunch this week," Franklin suggested.

"Yes," Jay replied. "Good idea, Mr. Mayor."

"Oh, just call me Tom."

Jay didn't tell Franklin to refer to him as something other than "Chief," but he expected the man would do what he wanted, anyway.

"I'll text you," Rebecca said, squeezing his hand.

Jay smiled and nodded before heading inside to pick up his pizza. At least on the way out, he could hurry past with the excuse he needed to get the food home while it was still hot.

Luckily, on his exit, the pair were no longer sitting there. Jay got into his Jeep and drove to his father's house.

13

The Delp house sat at 212 Dewey Street beneath a massive live oak that shrouded the roofline from the Mississippi sun. Terry Delp bought the home in the late '70s when he married his new bride, Louise. At the time, Terry worked for the post office while Jay's mother taught art at the high school.

The cottage-style house sported its fifteenth or sixteenth layer of paint, at least by Jay's calculations. When Jay and Sam were boys, it was a biannual chore to scrape the old paint from the windows and soffits before applying a fresh coat. By the time Jay graduated high school, he'd slapped paint on that wood siding a minimum of eight times. He'd assumed Terry had maintained that schedule to some extent after he left, but he hadn't even considered his father's rigid maintenance routines. He hadn't missed them, either.

When Jay arrived last night, the storm preoccupied him. He hadn't noticed the new metal roof. That was a more recent addition that Sam, no doubt, had paid to have installed. As Jay pulled into the drive, he admired the gray tin color. It blended well with the beige paint on the siding.

"Why mess with something that works?" Louise asked Terry one day when Jay's father suggested a baby blue tint.

The Jeep's engine went silent, and Jay stared at his childhood house. The scent of greasy crust and melted cheese filled the interior of the Wrangler. He got out with the large Mississippi Meat Lover's pizza he'd gotten from Tom's.

"Hi, Caroline," Jay addressed the in-home nurse as he came through the door.

Caroline Snider rolled a long white stick of dough into aluminum foil. "Chief Delp," she greeted Jay. "I'm just prepping some sausage pinwheels for your dad. He likes those for breakfast."

Jay nodded. "Call me Jay, please," he urged her as he set the pizza on the table.

"Will do, Jay," the fifty-eight-year-old nurse responded.

"How is he today?" Jay asked, not quite sure what to say. Less than a day in town, and he felt life pummeling him like he was trying to drink from a fire hydrant.

"He's fine. Been watching that ESPN Classic. He is in the den, cheering for a game that aired in '87."

"At least he's happy," Jay remarked.

"He won't be when Georgia loses."

Jay frowned, and Caroline gave a coy smile. "He wanted to make a bet."

A laugh erupted from Jay's mouth. "You didn't."

"I did," the spritely nurse quipped. "Don't worry. We only made a one-dollar bet."

"No judgment here," he told her. "I'm jealous I hadn't thought of it."

She grinned. "It helps give him something to latch onto."

"Any problems?" Jay asked. "Besides his poor gambling skills."

"He got a little frustrated earlier looking for your mom," Caroline said softly, as if worried it might upset Jay.

"It's okay, Caroline. She's been gone a long time."

The nurse shrugged. "I understand. It can still be raw for some people." She folded the aluminum foil over the log and lifted it in her hands. "Of course, you see plenty of worse things, don't you?"

Jay considered the face staring down at him in his office. He nodded.

"Your dad calmed down," she added. "I think he realized he was having an episode."

"I haven't had to experience one of those yet," Jay admitted.

"They can be tough," Caroline explained. "The best thing to do is play along and let him figure it out. He could go on thinking your mother is at the store until he forgets. Or he might get clear all at once. Those are the most difficult moments."

Jay nodded, remembering what Sam told him about Terry realizing his wife or daughter wasn't there. It forced his father to relive the grief.

"Caroline, thanks so much for stepping in to help," Jay told her. "Sam's said great things about you."

"Well, your brother's known for exaggerating," she retorted.

Jay shook his head. "Nah, if you're taking the old man for a buck or two, he must have been right about you."

She smiled at him before sticking the foil-wrapped dough in the refrigerator. "I'll try to get here a little early so I can pop those in the oven before you leave in the morning."

"No need, Caroline," he assured her. "As long as I have some coffee."

His face dropped as soon as he said it. He'd forgotten to grab coffee before coming home. Now the only thing Jay would have until he got to work were the ancient grounds in his dad's freezer.

"I just want to help," she explained. "At least until you find your footing here. I'm sure this is all disconcerting."

"It's been a whirlwind day," he confessed.

"The poor girl is the talk of the town," she told him.

That reminded him again that he should have put out some kind of statement. He had no clue what the local newspaper was anymore. As a kid, he never read the paper, even when his name showed up in it. He recalled a weekly one in Ocean Springs, but with the internet, it might no longer exist.

"Tragic," he muttered. "Would you like some pizza before you go?"

"Oh, thank you, no. I'm making Quinn take me over to the casino for dinner."

"Sounds delicious," Jay lied. He'd never cared for that atmosphere. There was no way to know if the stench of desperation or cigarette smoke was the most powerful.

"Let me see if the old man wants something to eat," Jay commented, leaving the woman to finish up her work. "Dad, what's on?" he asked as he entered the living room.

Terry Delp reclined in his rocker with his feet raised up. On his stomach, he held a can of Diet Pepsi. His father lifted his eyes, taking his gaze off the television screen to view Jay.

"Oh, hey, Dale," he greeted him. Jay didn't know who Dale was, but he did like Caroline suggested and let his dad assume he was this person. "Georgia and LSU," Terry continued, answering Jay's question. "LSU is going down."

"Really?" Jay asked, plopping onto the sofa next to his father's recliner.

"Sure. You seen that Jackson kid throw?"

"Can't say I have," Jay replied. "Hey, I brought some pizza. You want a slice?"

Terry shifted his gaze back to Jay with a confused countenance. "Why'd you bring that? Louise went to the store to make her chicken and dumplings."

"Wasn't she going to her sister's?" Jay inquired, playing along with the delusion.

Terry's eyes brightened. "You're right," he declared.

"So, pizza?" he offered.

"Yeah, I'll take a slice."

"Stay there," Jay told him. "I can get it for you."

Jay left his father in 1987 and marched into the kitchen, where Caroline had already set out two plates for Jay.

"Thanks," he said.

"It's worse in the afternoons," she explained. "I think he gets tired. If I can force him to take a nap, he's a lot clearer."

"That's good info," Jay noted. "Although, if he thinks I'm this Dale guy, he might be easier to deal with."

"You never know," Caroline replied.

Jay plated up two big slices of pizza and grabbed one of the Bud Lights in the fridge. He carried the plates into the living room, handing one to his father. Terry took the plate and stared at the meaty pizza.

"Where'd you get this from?" he wondered.

"Tom's," he told his father.

"Where's that?" Terry demanded. "Is it new?"

Jay shrugged. "Guess so."

Terry opened his mouth and stuffed it with a bite of pizza. "That's good," he commented with a mouthful of cheese and sausage.

Jay smiled and started on his own piece.

"You positive Louise went to Sally's?" Terry asked.

"I think so," Jay said after swallowing his bite.

"Not sure," Terry remarked, gobbling more. "I wonder if she's with Jacob."

Jay's attention lifted from his slice of meat lover's pizza to his father. "Who?"

"You know, that SOB," Terry barked. "Jacob."

"What are you talking about?" Jay asked. "Who is Jacob?"

Terry stared at him for a long second. His face flooded with confusion. "You know," he muttered. His voice filled with desperation. "I can't. He's—I can't. What's going on?"

"You were telling me about Jacob," Jay pressed.

Terry's eyes cleared. "Jay, what are you doing here?" he demanded.

"I'm staying here," he told his father. "Remember?"

"Oh," Terry groaned. "Yeah, Sam told me you had to come back home. The job down in the Keys let you go?"

"I wasn't in the Keys, Dad. It was Palm County."

"How'm I gonna know where that is?" he growled.

"You could pay attention, I suppose," Jay snapped, immediately regretting it. "Sorry, Dad."

Terry blew out a breath of annoyance. "Where'd you say this pizza came from?"

"Tom's."

His father curled his lip in disgust. "That the place with the dogs?"

"I didn't see any dogs," Jay responded.

"Think it is," Terry mumbled. "Who lets dogs in a restaurant?"

"People who like dogs?" Jay suggested.

Terry ate some more pizza. "Why didn't you bring me a beer?" he demanded.

Jay stuck his partially drunk bottle of Bud Light out to his father. "Here, finish this," he offered.

"I don't want your beer."

"Would you like me to get you one?"

"No, I'll stick with my Diet Pepsi."

Jay took another bite. "Dad, who is Dale?"

"Dale who?"

"I don't know."

"How the heck should I know who Dale is? Dale Earnhardt? The chipmunk from that morning show? I don't know."

Jay rolled his eyes at his father's obstinance. "Who's Jacob?"

Terry's face puckered, and he cut his gaze to his son. "No idea," he replied.

"You were telling me about him."

"I did not," Terry insisted. "I never knew a Jacob."

"You kidding, Dad?" Jay asked. "You never met a single person named Jacob?"

"What did I say?" Terry snapped. "Do I need to repeat myself?"

Jay lifted his hands in mock surrender. "No, just pay attention to your game."

"This is an old game, anyway," he barked. "Why would you want to watch this?"

"I didn't, Dad. You were watching it."

Terry shook his head in denial. "How about just let me eat this crappy pizza in peace?"

"You got it," Jay declared, standing up and taking his beer and pizza back to the kitchen.

Caroline had left at some point. Jay hoped it was before

the father and son's disagreement. He needed to exercise more tolerance with his father. After all, he hadn't been around before his dad got sick, either. He shouldn't have expected anything new now.

Jay pulled out the stool at the kitchen counter and slid onto it. He ate the rest of his pizza, wondering who Dale and Jacob were. And how they were involved with his parents.

14

Another day, and Jay was still working on stomaching the generic, decades-old coffee. He thought if he added more grounds, it might offset the weak flavor. Instead, the freezer-burn taste he'd barely noticed yesterday popped out with more intensity.

His father hadn't spoken a word to him the rest of the night. When Terry fell asleep in his chair, Jay insisted on helping him to his bed. Terry Delp grumbled all the way to the bathroom, shooing Jay away from the doorway. The only words he spoke were after the door closed: "I can wipe my own butt."

Despite the lack of sleep the night before, Jay had struggled to drift off. Images of Jamie Rene trussed up as if she were a piñata for some killer's amusement pervaded his mind. More than that, there was an underlying worry that he wouldn't catch this guy before he killed again.

Jay had worked on a couple of serial murder cases. Most people did not know how many sadistic killers were in the world. Most flew under the radar because they were smart enough to change up their kills. Those were the cases that were far more difficult to solve. The sensational ones attracted attention. In a town as small as Ocean Springs, any homicide was sensational.

"Hey, boss," Jennifer Kelly greeted Jay as he came in. "There's a guy here to talk with you."

"Who is it?" Jay asked.

Her eyes cut to the right, and Jay turned to see a young African-American in his twenties seated in one of the metal seats along the reception area. "Reporter at the *Sun Herald*," Jennifer answered.

There it was. The news people had shown up.

"Thanks," he told her before turning to the man waiting. "Hi," Jay greeted the man. "Chief Delp."

"Marcus Taylor," the reporter said, rising to his feet. "With the *Sun Herald*. Do you have some time to talk?"

"Yeah, come along," he urged.

Taylor followed Jay as he jogged up the steps. Jay froze at the top landing, Taylor on his heels. He realized that he didn't want to take the reporter to his office. That would give the man full access to the murder board Towns was developing. Yet, Jay had no idea if there was a conference room anywhere that he could use. Now he wished he'd asked Jennifer about it before approaching Taylor.

He stepped through the door into the bullpen. Shannon Towns sat at her desk in her little cubicle.

"Officer Towns," Jay called.

"Morning, Chief," she responded, bounding to her feet.

"Do we have a conference room?"

"Yes, sir. Let me show you," she offered.

"Thank you," he replied as she led the two men down the hall.

Past the elevator, she opened a door to a space about the size of Jay's office. Instead of a desk, a laminate table sat in the middle with twelve chairs around it. At the far wall, a flat-screen television stared back at any occupants holding session there.

Jay motioned for Taylor to take a seat. Looking at his officer, he winced as he asked her, "Do you mind bringing us some coffee?"

She cocked her head.

He replied, "I know, please forgive me."

"No problem, Chief," she answered.

"Bring yourself a cup, too, please," he amended.

Towns furrowed her brow.

"I'd like you to sit with us," he explained.

She gave a nod before hurrying off.

"Sorry, Marcus, I didn't ask you how you liked your coffee," he said. "I'm kinda being baptized in fire."

"Yes, sir," Taylor noted. "Your first day was something."

"I assume that's why you're here?" he inquired.

"We hoped to do an interview with you at some point, but yes, this is about the body."

"If you don't mind, then, we'll wait until Officer Towns returns."

"Thanks for seeing me," Taylor said.

Towns returned with a pot of coffee and three paper cups. "Do you need cream or sugar?" she asked both men.

"Black is fine," both chimed in unison.

"Men," she muttered. "I happen to love myself, so I'll be having both."

Taylor smirked at Towns as she poured three cups of coffee before setting them in front of both men. She settled in next to Jay, proceeding to add cream and sugar to her cup.

"Let's get started," Jay suggested.

Taylor nodded as he pulled out a steno pad and pen.

"Do you want the quick basics?" Jay inquired.

"Please," Taylor said.

"Sunday night, we received a call to 911 that two fishermen hooked a body. Our team responded to find a deceased female."

Taylor stopped writing and looked up. "That's quick," he noted.

"And basic," Jay added.

"Do you have an ID on the victim?"

"Not a positive one yet."

"When do you expect to?"

"We hope today. We also want to make sure we inform the family before we release it."

"She was murdered?"

Jay nodded. "Yes, we believe so. At present, we are still awaiting the final autopsy results, but there were indications of multiple stab wounds."

"Was she raped?" Taylor queried while jotting down scribbles in his notepad.

"Inconclusive," Jay said.

"What have you learned?"

"Right now, very little that we are able to share," the chief responded.

"Do you have any idea of where she was put in the water?"

"We haven't confirmed that at this time."

"Is there anything you can tell me?"

"Again, nothing we can release just now."

Marcus Taylor's shoulders sagged.

"Sorry, Marcus," Jay said. "We're working it as best we can."

"Is there any indication that this was random or targeted?"

Jay shook his head. "Not yet," he replied as he took a sip of coffee.

"Is it okay if I ask about you?"

"I'm an open book," Jay said.

"You're originally from Ocean Springs, yes?"

Jay nodded. "Born and raised. Graduated from OSHS. My parents were married in the Lutheran church way back when. My brother, Sam, is on the town council."

"You came from Florida last, right?"

"My last position was Chief of Detectives for the Palm County Sheriff's Department. Prior to that, I was a detective in Panama City."

"Are you the local boy come home?" Taylor asked off-handedly.

Jay shrugged. "My father has gotten ill, and I came back to help my brother take care of him."

"That's nice."

"I'd prefer that not make it into print," Jay added.

"Just background," Taylor acknowledged. "Are you happy to be home?"

Jay considered that for a second. "Yes, I suppose I am. It could have been a better homecoming to not walk into a homicide, but it's been nice to reconnect with family."

Taylor turned to Towns. "How does the new chief compare to Chief Ward?"

Shannon smiled. "So far, he's been great. But if he asks me for coffee tomorrow, that might change."

"This is a one-off," Jay promised her.

"Before you became a police officer, you were special forces. Is that correct?"

"Marine Recon."

"Oh, sorry," the reporter mumbled, although Jay didn't think he understood why he was sorry.

"It's a common mistake," Jay said.

"What did you do in the Marines?"

"I was a sniper," Jay explained.

He felt Shannon's eyes tune into him.

"Nice!" Taylor jotted that bit down. "Kill anyone?"

Jay's face turned to stone, solidifying the half-smile he had on his lips. "Marcus, you're pretty young, right?"

"Not that young. I'm twenty-seven."

"Well, that's old enough to learn what questions not to ask."

"Chief, this is the news. Your military history is important to the people of Ocean Springs."

The half-smile remained on Jay's face. "You never ask a veteran if he killed someone. It's a highly personal thing."

"Chief, I'm sorry. It's what the townspeople deserve to know."

Jay shook his head. "No, it isn't. I was a sniper, which means in the name itself that most likely, I killed people. That's all you need. How many and who doesn't matter."

Marcus Taylor stared back at the chief for a beat before he let his chin jerk down once.

"We have work to do, and you have enough to write something down," Jay concluded.

"Yes, sir. I apologize if you feel I crossed a line."

"You did," Jay assured him. "Now, time to learn from it."

The reporter didn't acknowledge that.

Jay inclined his neck toward Towns. "Officer Towns, would you escort Mr. Taylor out? If you have any more questions, Mr. Taylor, you can direct them to Officer Towns here."

"Thank you, sir."

Jay picked up his coffee and carried it to his office. He stopped outside the door because a four-foot-tall package blocked the entry. Wrapped in clear plastic wrap, the object's identity remained obscured. However, the wheels at the base revealed to Jay what it was. He pushed it into the office and found a pair of scissors in his desk drawer. Careful not to cut past the layers of plastic, he removed the skins around it until it revealed an office chair.

Jay cocked his head with a smile. This chair wasn't as fancy as the one the mayor sent over, but it was still made of soft leather and brand new.

Three chairs! Yesterday at this time, he had a piece of junk. Now, he was sitting on a cornucopia of chairs.

Jay pushed the newest one to the side and settled into the one behind his desk that Shannon brought up. His attention turned to the murder board. Shannon had added a few notes about Clay Miller. His workplace: a Chrysler auto dealer near I-10. His parents: Jack and Shirley Miller from Saucier, Mississippi. His car: a 2014 Mitsubishi Mirage with Mississippi tags.

"Chief?" Towns interrupted his reading when she stuck her head in the door.

"Shannon, hey." Jay straightened up in his seat. "I'm sorry about the coffee thing. I was halfway up here when I thought I might not want to bring a reporter in here with this." He motioned at the murder board. "Which, by the way, is looking great."

"It's not an arts-and-crafts project," she reminded him.

"No, but it is getting very detailed."

Towns shook her head. "Not really. I still haven't located Miller."

"Interesting," Jay mused.

"Think he's our guy?"

"Boyfriend or husband often clicks the right box."

"Where is he?"

"Good question."

"No, Chief. I want to know if he killed Jamie and dumped her several days ago in the bay, why is he missing now? He'd be trying to look innocent, wouldn't he?"

"People are stupid. They can plan a perfect crime and forget to get rid of the bloody clothes. Who knows what he's thinking?"

"I guess that's true."

"Did we get the tape from Collins?" he asked.

"Yes, but it's not a tape."

"What do you mean?"

"Chief, you sound like a Luddite. It's digital. There is no tape."

Jay scowled. "I know that. It's just a term."

"We did get it last night. I haven't watched it yet."

"Let's see it," he declared.

"It's in your email," she told him.

"My email still isn't set up," he reminded her.

"Oh, wait," she said, hurrying out of his office.

It took her five minutes to return with a USB flash drive, which she handed to the chief. He inserted it into his computer and opened the file. The video started playing. Right away, the resolution was clearer, confirming Jay's suspicion that Collins's old PC was the problem.

"Hold on. Are those the guys hassling Jamie?" Towns asked over his shoulder.

"Yeah, those four."

"Pause it," she demanded.

When he did, she reached down and took his mouse, enlarging the image.

"What is it, Shannon?"

"That guy," she said, tapping her chewed but painted fingernail on one of the faces.

"He's the one that caused all the problems," Jay noted.

"Oh, you don't know the half of it."

"You know him?"

"That's Trip Franklin."

"Franklin?" Jay asked.

"Tom Franklin's son."

Jay cursed under his breath.

15

"This is bad, isn't it?" Towns stated.

"We have a logistical problem, to say the least," Jay admitted.

"What do we do?"

"I don't see a lot of options. How sure are you that's him?"

Towns tilted her head and stared at him. "He's the mayor's son. Do you have any idea how many times the kid has gotten into trouble and we've had to let him skate?"

"What kind of trouble?"

"You name it: speeding, DUI, public intox, vandalism, assault."

"Assault?" Jay echoed.

"If I recall, that was a fight at a juke joint on the edge of town. Trip hit on a guy's girl, the guy got upset, and Trip threw a punch. Course, when we get there, the stories are all over the place."

Jay nodded. "I imagine Mayor Franklin is aware of his son's legal issues?"

"Oh, yeah, he is," Towns confirmed. "I'm not sure how

much influence he put on Chief Ward, but Ward always made it go away."

"Hmm," Jay pondered. He wasn't fond of that, but it was part of the bureaucracy. In Panama City, the governor's son had gotten picked up in a drug bust. He, too, had conveniently avoided being included in the reports.

"Should we call the mayor?" Towns asked nervously.

Jay shook his head. "Did we call him when we questioned Crews?"

"Yeah, but isn't this different?"

"No," Jay told her, then added, "Actually, it is. We need to be far more careful with how we handle this."

"Chief, this kid's a troublemaker, but I never saw him as a murderer."

"Most people don't seem that way," he advised. "We have to assume everyone is a suspect until we prove otherwise."

"You are going to be kicking a can of you-know-what," she noted.

"Will you find where Trip Franklin lives? If he lives with his father, I'd rather not approach him at his home."

"You got it, Chief," she assured her boss.

"What about Miller? I see you've connected the dots on him."

"I have a phone number and the address we visited yesterday. There's been no answer so far when I've called."

Jay leaned back in his chair, enjoying the comfort it offered. He fought the curiosity to try the other two out right now. Instead, he remarked, "He might see our caller ID."

Towns nodded. "I considered that. So, I tried to call from my cell."

Jay cocked his head. "Smart, but be careful doing that," he cautioned. "We don't need the wrong person identifying you as part of the investigation team."

"I understand," she acknowledged. "We could drive by again and see if he's home."

"Who is in today?" Jay inquired.

"Marco, Tomlinson, and JD. Felton and Tomkins are on the roster for the afternoon shift."

Jay moaned. "We need more men."

Towns only offered a sympathetic shrug.

"Who do you want to go with you?" he asked.

"JD, I guess," she replied.

"Any reason?" Jay wondered.

"Nothing, really. Marco and Tomlinson are capable, but I've worked with JD a few times."

"Good. Grab JD after you find where Trip Franklin is. Send one of the other two to bring him in."

"Wanna guess how long it will take for Franklin to show up here?"

"Think he calls or just barges in?"

"He'll come running," Shannon stated.

"I'm betting twenty-five minutes," Jay wagered.

"Might be less than that," Towns countered. "I'd say fifteen."

Jay smirked. "Winner buys coffee?"

"We have free coffee," she pointed out.

"Good, that's a no-lose situation."

She nodded with a broad grin.

"I'll win, though," Jay informed her. "It's a ten-minute drive over from city hall. He'd have to make it from his office to his car in less than five minutes."

"Why couldn't he?"

"That will depend on what the mayor is doing. He won't cause a scene, so if he is in a meeting, he'll politely dismiss everyone before making his escape. That's presuming he answers his cell phone while he's busy."

Towns twisted her lips into a snarl. "Dang it."

He chuckled at his subordinate. "Go to it," he ordered in a light-hearted tone.

Shannon Towns bowed her head. "Yes, Chief," she replied before turning to leave the office. She stopped at the door and looked back. "Am I mistaken, or are there now three desk chairs in here?"

Jay shrugged. "My rickety chair plight escalated to an invasion."

She shook her head and left Jay alone.

He resumed staring up at the murder board. Rising from his seat, Jay marched over to what accounted for a puzzle with too many missing pieces. He picked up the Expo marker and added the name "Trip Franklin." His stomach tightened. This was going to be a challenge.

He returned to his desk and scrolled the video back to freeze the image of Trip Franklin with Jamie. Jay hit the "Print Screen" button. The printer in the bullpen hummed and buzzed as it spat out his picture. He retrieved it and stuck it to the board under Trip's name.

Jay lifted the receiver and called Sam's office at the bank.

"First Coast, how may I help you?"

"Can I speak with Sam Delp?" he asked the receptionist.

"One moment. Who may I tell him is calling?"

"Tell him the smarter, better-looking Delp," Jay joked.

"Uh... yes, sir?" she replied with some hesitation.

Jay smiled. He hadn't realized how much he'd missed his brother. The pair had still chatted when Jay was in Florida, but he liked how quickly the two had fallen back into their sibling routine. It had always been the Delp boys together growing up. They'd weathered the trauma of Sandra's death, followed too soon by their mother's. After that, it was riding out the storm that was Terry Delp.

"If you were the smarter Delp, you'd be making far more money than you are," Sam quipped when he picked up the phone.

"Watch your tone," Jay reminded him. "You might be the older brother, but I can kick your butt from here to Louisiana."

Sam chuckled. "Don't go all leatherneck on me. You're just a hick bayou boy."

"Sam, you got a minute?" Jay questioned, his demeanor sobering.

"What's going on?"

"It would be better in person."

"I have a meeting in half an hour," Sam said.

"It might not wait. I'll be right over if you have time."

"Come on over. I can push my appointment if needed."

"On my way," Jay acknowledged, hanging up and heading out the door. "Be back in thirty!" he shouted to no one in particular.

As expected, Shannon replied, "Roger, Chief."

The First Coast Bank was on Washington Street near downtown. It took Jay the ten minutes he'd calculated yesterday to get there. He left the Jeep parked on the curb and hurried into the bank.

First Coast had carried several names. It began over a century ago as the Biloxi Trust. Since then, it had changed hands countless times. However, the building was still the one built in 1926, and while it had undergone the requisite renovations over the years to bring it up to code, the lobby continued to display the glamor and allure of its Art Deco decor. Marble floors matched the countertops. While the teller booths had kept the classic brass bars, the bank had added plexiglass shields between the partitions and the tellers during the pandemic. That feature was the most modern and off-putting thing about the time-honored structure. To avoid permanently marring the institution's historic atmosphere, the bank had installed the clear panels by connecting the acrylic to the brass. Jay assumed, like so many companies, they'd expected the temporary fix to be just that—temporary.

The lobby had only one customer, an older lady at the second teller. The octogenarian had taken the time to dress, do her hair, and adorn her face with plenty of eyeshadow. Jay guessed the issue with most elderly women who put on too much makeup stemmed from their failing eyesight. However, there was no part of him that would ever verbalize that thought to anyone. He might have three failed marriages, but he knew enough to keep his mouth shut.

Sam Delp had been the vice president of First Coast for the last five years. As Jay understood it, Sam was one of several vice presidents in the company. However, in his role, he handled the branches in Ocean Springs, Biloxi, and a few smaller cities. Since First Coast portrayed themselves as a regional bank, they only had a handful of locations under that moniker. The larger corporation, though, was a national brand familiar to most people.

Jay knocked on the open door to his brother's office.

"What's up?" Sam asked.

"Mind if I close the door?"

Sam's eyes widened in surprise. "Go ahead," he said as Jay closed the door. "What's going on, Jay?"

"Since you pushed for me to get this job, I would otherwise leave you out of this."

Sam inclined his chin with a concerned expression. "What's the problem?"

"This is police business, and normally, I wouldn't bring

you in, even if you were my brother. But this has some extenuating circumstances."

Sam nodded. "Go on."

"This has to stay here," Jay emphasized.

"Of course," Sam agreed.

"We have a person of interest," he explained.

"Like a suspect?" Sam asked.

"Not even that yet," Jay informed him. "But a name came up."

Sam lifted his eyebrows. "Unless it's mine, don't hold back."

"Trip Franklin."

Sam stared at his brother. "You're kidding, right?"

Jay shook his head slowly.

"How so?" Sam questioned.

"That's more than I should share now," Jay told him. "However, I wanted to inform you. Shannon suggested there might be some blowback when we bring him in."

Sam released a dry chuckle. "Some blowback is an understatement."

"You know me, Sam."

His brother nodded. "And for that reason, I recommended you. Trip being the mayor's son won't stop you from doing your job."

"Will it affect you?"

Sam pursed his lips. "It could muddy my relationship with the mayor, especially if it turns out Trip was involved. Then again, if Trip is more than suspect, it might mean the mayor's authority wanes." Sam added, "Besides, I'm elected by the people, not appointed by Tom Franklin. The most he can do is stymie my influence in the council."

"Good, though it wasn't going to change what I did," Jay pointed out.

"Didn't figure it would," Sam replied with a proud grin.

Jay's shoulders sagged with relief. His only concern about bringing in Trip Franklin had been the effect it might have on Sam. While he'd suspected his brother would agree with him, he needed to talk to him first.

"How was Dad last night?" Sam asked, changing the subject.

"It was surreal," Jay recalled. "I came home to find him enthralled in a football game from 1987. He thought it actually was '87 and I was some guy named Dale. Do you remember a Dale?"

Sam pursed his lips as he seemed to search his memory. Finally, he shook his head. "No clue."

"Me either. He started talking about Mom being with a Jacob. It sounded... I'm not sure... risqué."

"You think Mom had a boyfriend?" Sam asked, his face contorting in confusion.

"I'd prefer not to," Jay admitted. "Dad's mind cleared right after that, and he insisted he didn't know who any of those people were. Not Dale nor Jacob."

"Weird," Sam declared.

"He got mad and refused to talk to me after that," Jay explained.

"That's a common occurrence," Sam stated. "What do you think of Caroline?"

"She's awesome," Jay said with a grin. "She bets with Dad about these game replays."

"What?"

"Yeah, she wagers a buck with him. Probably the same dollar, at that. She knows who won and bets against him."

Sam laughed. "I love it."

"At least she seems to handle him," Jay said. "Great job picking her out."

"That was all Danielle," Sam told him. "Speaking of, why don't you come over to supper tomorrow evening? Bring Dad."

"Sounds fun. Do you think one of you could sit with him tonight, though?"

"Need to work late?"

"I'm having dinner with Rebecca," Jay said. "We ran into each other last night."

Sam's left eyebrow shot up inquisitively.

"It's not like that," Jay insisted. "Just catching up."

"Yeah, but didn't you say when someone says, 'It's not like that,' it is, in fact, like that?" Sam reminded him. "You don't have the best track record there."

Jay groaned and waved him off. "I have to go interrogate the mayor's son."

"You realize Tom will be there fifteen minutes after you bring Trip in?"

"You and Shannon think alike," Jay replied, grinning again. "But it will be twenty-five minutes."

He rose and gave Sam a wink as he left the office.

16

Had Jay's door been closed, he assumed it would have flown open with a knock. Instead, Tom Franklin stormed through the ajar door into the chief's office.

"What is the meaning of bringing my son down to be questioned?" he demanded.

Jay checked his clock. Tomlinson had radioed when he picked up Trip Franklin at 10:11 a.m. His computer said it was 10:33. Twenty-two minutes.

"I'm guessing you weren't in a meeting this morning," Jay remarked.

"What does that mean?" Franklin spat.

"Nothing. Have a seat, Tom," Jay said, using his name with blunt intent. In this moment, Jay had to put aside the fact the man was his boss and the mayor of the city who had recently hired him. Instead, he needed to have Franklin understand that Jay viewed him as a suspect's parent, not a city official.

"Chief, you need to explain yourself," Franklin

announced. His face was reddened, and his cheeks were pinched tight.

"Sit down, Tom," Jay repeated in a calm, flat tone.

Mayor Tom Franklin stood on the opposite side of the desk, staring dumbfounded at his newest employee. He might be wondering how brazen the new chief was to arrest the mayor's son after only two days on the job, although Jay didn't care what went through Tom Franklin's mind. He only motioned with his palm up at the high-back chair across from Jay.

Franklin remained motionless for a second, his eyes darting from the outstretched hand to the leather chair. He relented after Jay didn't remove his outstretched hand. Franklin settled in the seat, both hands gripping the armrests as if the chair were about to race down a roller coaster track. He stared across the wooden desktop at the chief of police, sucking air through his teeth as he locked eyes with Jay. He steeled himself for the next words out of his mouth.

"Chief Delp, would you care to explain why you brought my son in for questioning?" he asked in a deep voice.

Jay gave him a subtle smile that could have been mistaken for him sucking on a mint. "Tom, I would not," he answered.

"What do you mean?" Franklin barked.

"I am saying this is an active investigation. Your son's name came up in it. We have to make sure he had nothing to do with this."

"Look here," Franklin interjected.

Jay raised a single index finger, and the mayor stopped talking before he finished his thought. "Mayor, can I ask you a question?"

Franklin glowered at Jay.

"Let me start with this. I doubt your son is involved. My officer stated the same thing. However, I'm new here. Since Trip's name came up as not only interacting with our victim but doing so in a..." Jay paused as he considered the correct word to use. "...Negative manner, I weighed how to handle the situation."

"Well, you handled it wrong," Franklin stated.

"Did I?" Jay asked. "I started yesterday. Today, somehow, your son's name appeared in our investigation. If I ignored it, then what would your constituents think?"

"I don't know," Franklin muttered. His tone was calmer now.

"Me either, but I considered a few outcomes. Just this morning, I had a reporter in here with the *Sun Herald*. Had he gotten wind that Trip was involved? How do you think he would handle it?"

Franklin remained silent.

"Exactly," Jay replied. "Again, I don't suspect your son at this point. He has only shown up as a person of interest. If it turned out he was involved and we suppressed it, it might effectively end your mayoral career."

"You should have called me," Franklin said in a pleading tone.

"Yes, but that might have the same result, don't you think?" Jay pointed out. "Like I was giving Trip a warning."

"Have you talked to him?" Franklin asked, his tone now shifting from demanding to demure.

"Not yet. He just got here."

"He's going to want a lawyer," Franklin stated in what he hoped came across as blustery but only sounded desperate to Jay.

"Of course," the chief acknowledged. "Trip is an adult

and has the same rights as everyone. If he wants to speak to us with his lawyer present, I don't blame him."

Franklin nodded curtly, as if he'd somehow gotten his way. "He is not that kind of boy," Franklin insisted, his voice returning to the pleading timbre of a worried father.

"Tom, may I be frank?"

The mayor gave a half-gesture of agreement.

"I'm a Marine. I have a solid career history as a police officer. That means I salute and respect my superiors. What I am not is a yes man. This city hired me to do a job, and I take that seriously. If I come across even my own brother breaking the law, I'd do my duty."

Franklin gave a reassuring nod.

"Of course, you could raise issues with the city council if I am not doing my job, as you should. But unless you want to be chief, you shouldn't be telling me how to run an investigation."

"Jay, I'm not doing that," he blubbered.

"Good."

"It's just as a parent," he said.

"I understand that, Tom," Jay assured him. "You're worried."

Franklin's face dropped a little.

"I haven't met your son, but he has a history in this department," Jay explained.

"He's only a kid," Franklin said defensively.

"Trip's twenty-five," Jay corrected him. "From his record, it appears the only reason he hasn't gotten into more trouble is your status."

"What are you implying?" Franklin demanded.

"Nothing. I'm saying that he has issues, Tom. I don't have kids, but I can see that. One day, you won't be mayor. Then this kid will step out of line with no safety net to catch him."

Franklin leaned back in his seat. Jay couldn't read his face. It reminded him of a story he remembered from junior high called "The Great Stone Face." He recalled little about the tale except that a young Native American found a cliff that resembled the countenance of a man. Jay guessed there was some symbolism or meaning that his seventh-grade teacher attempted to share to enlighten the class, but Jay had forgotten it. He only faintly recalled the premise.

"Trip's not a bad kid," Franklin repeated.

"His actions might have nothing to do with how you raised him," Jay pointed out. "My father was a disaster with Sam and me. Still, we are both fine."

"I'm sorry, Jay," Franklin apologized, and Jay sensed there was some sincerity there. "Does it look bad for him?"

"Listen, Tom, I'm not able to share that with you. It wouldn't be proper. You should get a lawyer in here, and then I'd suggest you scoot out."

"I can't cut him off," Franklin blurted out.

"Of course not. Return to your office and do your job, or go home and wait. But if you are hanging around here and word leaks, it might look bad for you."

"How will anyone know?" Franklin asked.

"The same way Rebecca heard about the body," he answered, silently accusing Franklin of leaking that information. "It's a small town. I could tell my guys to keep it to themselves, but I'd never be able to prove it if one of them told their spouse or significant other."

Franklin nodded without saying a word.

"Have you contacted his lawyer?" Jay asked.

"Yes, I called him on my way over here."

"Tom, I'd like to help more, but until I clear Trip, I just can't."

Franklin bowed his head and shook it. Frustration oozed from the mayor, and Jay assumed that while Franklin was directing some at him, a fair amount came from his son. It left him with a strange, empty feeling in his chest. There were no kids for Jay to worry about. He had his niece and nephew, but he hadn't watched them grow up. He hadn't been around.

It gave Jay something to consider. He'd just told Franklin what a terrible father he had growing up, and Terry Delp still wasn't winning any awards. But family was funny. There was an expected emotion tied to those related by blood. Yet, the men he'd served with and under in the Corps were closer to family than Jay's father had ever been. He thought of them the same as his brother.

"Will you let me know if anything changes?" Franklin asked as he pushed to his feet. "If you can, that is."

Jay marveled at his attitude change. Although he hadn't appreciated Tom's bluster when he'd barged in, he appreciated the parental concern he displayed. When he was sixteen, Jay got arrested for drinking and driving. While he'd only had one beer, the officer dragged him to jail, expecting his dad to come take him home. Only Terry Delp never showed. He allowed Jay to sit behind bars for twenty-four hours. Even after that, it wasn't his father who came to get him. The chief, then a man named Leonard, sat him down in his office and gave him a stern warning before letting him go. Sam ended up picking Jay up from the police station that morning because his father had decided he should learn his lesson.

Jay had learned it, too. That was the last time Jay reached out to Terry Delp when he needed something. It cemented his decision to join the military, although he thought he'd enlist in the army. It took a Marine recruiter who came to his high school to convince him the Corps was his path.

"Tom, I'll do what I can," he assured Franklin.

"Thank you," Franklin said. "I appreciate your understanding."

Jay stuck his hand out, and Franklin gripped it firmly. As his boss left the office, Jay wondered if they'd come to some new dynamic. Or had it just been as simple as Jay had snatched away any control the mayor thought he had? Jay wasn't searching for any power over Franklin. He only wanted the man to understand his position. Confident he'd made that clear, Jay stood up.

"Towns," he called across the bullpen.

"Yeah, Chief."

"You want to join me in the... where do we do the interrogations?"

Shannon came out of her cubicle with her little notepad in her hand. "Tomlinson took him to the conference room."

"Let's go," he announced.

The two walked down the hall to the same room where they chatted with Marcus Taylor earlier that morning. Shannon opened the door for Jay, who stepped inside. Tomlinson stood in his uniform on one side. At the other end of the table sat a young man with the same blue eyes as Tom Franklin and an older gentleman in a suit.

Jay blinked, staring at the other man. He looked familiar, but Jay couldn't place where he knew him. He assumed he was the lawyer that Tom called.

The supposed attorney rose to his feet. "You're Jay Delp?"

"Yes, I'm Chief Delp," he said, hoping to establish some authority with the lawyer. "This is Officer Towns."

The lawyer stepped around the table, extending his hand. "Calvin Calkins," he introduced.

Jay stopped in his tracks. "Calkins?"

Calkins grinned as if he'd just beat Jay in a round of Texas hold'em. "Yeah, that Calkins."

"The one with the billboards?" Shannon asked.

"He's also married to my ex-wife," Jay realized out loud.

17

———

"Dang!" Trip whistled. "He's with your wife?"

"Mr. Franklin," Calkins scolded his client, who dropped his head. Shannon Towns lifted her eyebrows in surprise before glancing at Jay.

"Calvin," Jay replied, "it's nice to finally meet you," releasing the man's grasp. "Do you mind if we all sit down and talk?"

"Is my client being charged with any crime?" Calkins asked.

"No, sir," Jay responded. "However, he has come up in our investigation. We'd like to speak to him about it."

"I didn't do anything," Trip griped.

Calkins held a hand up, signaling the young Franklin to hold his tongue. Jay understood why the mayor might want his son's lawyer present. Trip Franklin was an egotistical man who could not shut up when it was in his best interest. A skilled and unscrupulous detective could convince him to confess to something he hadn't done. While he refrained from playing those games with people, Jay had witnessed such things occur in the past. Detectives in urban areas often got inundated with crimes, and clearance records were important to the upper brass.

Trip closed his mouth again. Jay wagered it wouldn't be for long, though.

"Chief Delp, would you fill us in on what you are investigating?" Calkins suggested.

"Gladly," Jay agreed. "Let's sit."

Calkins sat next to his client while Towns and Jay took a seat opposite them.

"Before we begin, can I offer either of you anything to drink?" Jay asked.

Trip answered first, something that didn't surprise Jay. "Yeah, I'd like—"

"No, we are both fine," Calkins interrupted.

Jay nodded. "We should start. Mr. Franklin, do you know a Jamie Rene?"

Trip opened his mouth, and Calkins laid a hand on his client's forearm, stopping him from speaking. "Chief Delp, can you tell us who this Jamie Rene is?" Calkins asked.

"Mr. Calkins, Jamie Rene was murdered this past weekend."

Trip's head twisted from side to side in a rapid motion. Calkins squeezed his arm, signaling him to stop.

"Chief, may I speak with my client alone?"

Jay gave a nod. "Come on, guys, let's let Mr. Calkins have a moment to confer with Mr. Franklin."

Jay and Towns stood. As they walked out, Jay signaled Tomlinson to follow them into the hall. When he shut the door, Jay motioned for the two officers to step away from the conference room.

In a hushed voice, he asked, "Tomlinson, were there any issues when you picked him up?"

"Sir, he got belligerent, but he calmed down."

"Did you tell him what it was about?"

Tomlinson shook his head. "No, sir. I wasn't sure I should."

Jay looked over at Towns, who cringed a little. "It's okay. You both did fine."

"What's the lawyer doing?" Towns questioned.

"He's grilling his client about Jamie Rene."

"Think he knows her, sir?" Tomlinson inquired.

Jay shrugged. "He may or may not recognize her name. We have evidence that they met, though."

"What are you going to do?" Towns asked.

"We'll ask him some questions."

"But we don't even have the time of death yet," Shannon pointed out.

"True, which is why we won't be keeping him. Unless he confesses."

"Sir, Trip and I were in high school together," Tomlinson told Jay. "He was two years older than me, but we passed each other."

"Nothing to worry about, Tomlinson."

"I didn't want there to be an issue," the young officer remarked, and Jay appreciated his forethought.

"We're interrogating our mayor's son," Jay acknowledged. "We already have plenty of conflict to concern ourselves with. His lawyer is married to my ex-wife. That's going to be hard to get around in a small town."

Tomlinson nodded. Relief passed over his face.

"I think we can handle it without you, though," Jay told the young man. "Why don't you go about your duties?"

"Yes, sir," Tomlinson replied. "I'm slated to patrol this morning."

"That will be more fun than this," Jay assured him.

"Remember, let's not tell anyone about Trip or his connection to the case."

Tomlinson nodded before leaving Jay and Towns in the corridor.

"Should I have told him why we were picking up Trip?" Towns asked.

Jay considered it. "Yes, probably so. Someone killed Jamie, and he might try to do the same to any of us if he thinks it will save him."

"Sorry, Chief."

"It worked out," he assured her.

"Chief?" Calkins stuck his head out the door. "We're ready for you."

Jay motioned for Towns to go first. "You want to take the lead?"

Shannon's expression answered for her, but she said, "No, I'd rather let you show me how it's done."

He smiled. "Let's do it."

Calkins took his station next to Trip as Jay and Towns found their seats again.

"Chief, what reason do you have to ask my client anything?" Calkins asked.

"Mr. Franklin encountered our victim last week," Jay told them.

"He states he doesn't know a Jamie Rene."

Jay nodded. "Mr. Franklin, were you at the Biloxi Blues Crab Shack on Wednesday evening?"

Trip's face flashed with enlightenment. "Wait, is this that bi—"

"Mr. Franklin." Calkin's tone was sharp and short, cutting his client off. The lawyer turned his focus on Jay. "Would you elaborate?"

"Honestly, Mr. Calkins, I'm waiting for him to confirm whether he was at the restaurant."

Calkins's attention returned to Trip, and he gave an approving nod.

"Yeah, me and some buddies went there," Trip said. "But nothing happened."

"Did you make any advances on your server?" Jay asked.

"Chief Delp, is this about murder or a young man's dalliance?" Calkins asked.

Jay leaned back in his chair. "Counselor, it's about establishing a connection with your client and our victim."

"Can you?" Calkins pressed.

Jay gave Towns a quick glance, and she nodded. Shannon Towns produced a television remote and pointed it at the screen behind Calkins and Trip. Both men turned to see the display as it powered on, revealing the paused surveillance footage from the Biloxi Blues Crab Shack. The scene showed Trip reaching to touch Jamie as she walked away. This was the point in the video that seemed to be the last straw for Jamie. If Shannon pressed play, the group would proceed to see Jamie's volatile reaction, followed by Michael Collins approaching the men and throwing them out.

"Why don't we continue, Officer?" Jay suggested to Towns.

She complied, and the playback restarted. She let it run until the foursome of men left the table and Trip Franklin continued to argue with the manager. When they vanished from the scene, she paused the video.

"Was that you, Trip?" Jay asked, shifting to using the man's first name.

"Yes, but that bi—girl—blew it out of proportion," Trip argued.

"If we rewind that tape, we could count the number of times you groped her, if you'd like," Jay suggested. He focused on Calkins, adding, "It's five, just so you understand."

Calkins never flinched. Trip, on the other hand, did.

"I didn't kill her," he insisted. "Never saw her again after that. I just wanted to get to know her, and yeah, I probably had too much to drink that night."

"Is that what this was? Too much to drink?"

Trip nodded. "Yes, sir," he said, his tone becoming contrite. "That was it. I got out of line."

"Hmm," Jay mused. He turned to Towns. "Did the exterior camera show Mr. Franklin here driving away from the Biloxi Blues Crab Shack?"

"Yes, sir. It did," Towns confirmed.

"That won't matter," Calkins interjected. "You cannot prove the level of alcohol he had in his system now."

Jay stared at the lawyer. "Your client can't have it both ways," he admonished. "He can't say he had too much to drink so he sexually assaulted his server, but wasn't too drunk to drive."

"Did the waitress—what was her name? Jamie Rene. Did Jamie Rene press charges against my client?"

Jay shook his head. "No, she didn't."

"Then it isn't sexual assault, is it? As far as you can tell from this video, they were lovers who had a spat about something else."

"The manager will testify that she came to him feeling uncomfortable."

"Chief, that is nothing but hearsay," Calkins admonished.

Jay knew he was right. There wasn't much to go on, but he thought he'd push it, anyway.

"Listen, we just want to clear Trip's name for everyone's sake. How about he offers us a DNA swab of his own volition to prove his innocence?"

Calkins laughed. "That will not happen."

Jay shrugged. He realized the only way his ploy would work was if Calvin Calkins was the worst attorney known to man. But he gauged Trip's reaction. It appeared passive. The idea of a DNA test never registered with him. That was not solid proof of innocence, but given how obtuse Trip seemed to be, Jay didn't think he wasn't worried. Unless Trip Franklin was a full-blown sociopath. Jay didn't believe that was the case, though. Still, he had to follow the evidence.

"You never saw her before this evening?" Jay questioned.

Trip gave a sidelong look at Calkins before saying, "I doubt it. Maybe. I've been to Biloxi Blues before, but I don't remember her."

"And after that night?" Jay inquired.

Trip shook his head.

"Can you tell me where you were over the weekend?"

Calkins bent over and whispered something in Trip's ear. The younger man gave a little nod, leaning toward Calkins. When Calkins withdrew, Trip replied, "I drove over to Panama City with my friends Paul, Kyla, and Julia. We left Friday night and came back Sunday."

Jay nodded. "We will need to corroborate that with them. If you would provide their information."

"I can get that for you, Chief," Calkins stated, casting a glance at Trip.

"For the moment, we don't have any more questions for you, Trip," Jay said.

"Is he clear?" Calkins questioned.

"Once we establish his whereabouts, probably," Jay assured him.

"Good. Mr. Franklin, we can go."

"Wait," Jay said, stopping the two before they exited. Both men eased back down in their seats, their eyes fixed on Jay. "Trip, I reviewed your record. You've skated by with some luck when Chief Ward was here. I'm about to be blunt and off the record here. This won't be a department that allows DUIs, assaults, and vandalism. A few of these are charges you seem to have avoided in the past. It doesn't matter to me who your father is. I've already had the same discussion with him."

"Look, Delp," Trip began.

"Trip, you're twenty-five," Jay cut him off. "If you don't want the next possession or DUI to stick to your record, you need to straighten up. I will not sweep things under the rug because someone tries to pressure me."

"Whatever," the younger Franklin moaned. "May I go?"

"By all means," Jay told him.

Trip Franklin stood up and marched out. Jay stayed in his chair along with Towns and Calkins.

"I'll send you those contacts as soon as I return to the office."

Jay nodded. "Thank you, Mr. Calkins."

"We're done being official. Call me Cal."

Towns squirmed next to Jay, and Jay leaned toward her. "Thanks, Officer. You can get back to whatever you need."

"Okay, Chief," she responded.

When she left, Calkins said, "Off the record?"

"Go ahead," he told the attorney.

"Trip Franklin needs a good scare," Calkins told Jay. "He didn't do anything like murder. I'd bet my life on that, but he thinks he's untouchable."

"You will end up chatting with the mayor today, if not in

the next fifteen minutes. It might benefit both Franklin and his son if they understand that."

"I'll do what I can to share that," Calkins agreed. "I apologize for springing my appearance on you."

Jay shrugged. "Nothing to be sorry for."

"It felt like I was waylaying you."

"Nah, I've dealt with far worse. How is Katie?" Jay asked.

"She's fine," Calkins told him. "I bet she'll have something to say tonight when I tell her I met with you."

Jay smiled. "I'm sure she will," he replied. "Katie never kept her opinions to herself."

Calkins laughed. "No, that she does not. You know, she heard you were coming back to become chief and said it was what the department needed."

"What does that mean?" Jay questioned.

"There were some things happening with Ward that, while never proved, might have bordered on shady."

Jay lifted an eyebrow. "Such as ignoring the transgressions of the mayor's wayward son?"

"If only," Calkins replied. "More like some under-the-table dealings, falsified reports, planted evidence. That kind of shady."

The chief couldn't resist rolling his eyes. Why was this job getting more and more complicated? "That won't happen under my department," Jay insisted.

"That's what Katie said. She called you 'honest to a fault.'"

Jay cracked a smile. "That might have been half our problem."

"Look, Chief—"

"Call me Jay," he interjected.

"Jay, I'm sorry about what went down back then."

"Cal, it was the past. That water has long since flowed downstream. The bridge isn't even in sight."

"I realize that, but it never sat quite right with me," Cal commented.

Jay stared at him. "Didn't stop you from sleeping with her," he pointed out.

"I know."

"Cal, it's fine. If Katie's happy, that's good."

The lawyer nodded. "I need to go speak with my client and send those contacts to you."

"Thanks, Counselor," Jay said, standing and extending his hand.

Calvin Calkins left Jay seated in the conference room. For a few seconds, he reveled in the silence. Katie came to mind. She'd been his second wife, and in hindsight, the one he wished had worked out. Part of the reason he didn't fault Cal, or really even Katie, was that he hoisted the blame on his shoulders. He'd been in Afghanistan, and when he came back, he just wasn't as present as he should have been. Jay blamed himself for putting that distance between him and Katie.

With a sigh, Jay pushed to his feet and walked toward the bullpen.

"Chief," Towns called from her cubicle. "I think we found Clay Miller."

Jay stopped and stepped over to her desk. "What? Where is he?"

"He's dead."

18

The whiteboard serving as their murder board had a circle drawn around Clay Miller's name. Jay stared at the flat surface, feeling somewhat dumbfounded.

Towns appeared in the doorway with a small cup of coffee. "Here, you won the bet," she told him, setting the black coffee in front of the chief.

"I missed by three minutes," he pointed out.

"Yeah, well, your logic was sound."

Jay raised the cup to his lips and sipped. When he pulled the rim from his mouth, he motioned toward the murder board. "What about Clay Miller?"

"He was found in a rundown house on the edge of Slidell, Louisiana," she explained. "Stabbed multiple times."

"Slidell," Jay mused. "What is that, like, an hour from here?"

"Yes, close to that."

"Do they have a suspect? If this is our guy, we might wrap this all up."

She shook her head. "I talked with a Detective Warren

over there. He thought this was a drug deal gone wrong. They found residue of crystal meth on Miller's body. He didn't have a wallet, either."

Jay pursed his lips. "How did they ID him?"

"He's in the system. They printed him."

"When was he killed?" Jay asked.

"I'm waiting on Warren to call me back. He wasn't in the office, and he told me to give him five to ten minutes to get back."

Jay reclined in his chair, and Towns asked, "Did you swap chairs?"

"Yeah, I needed to try them all out."

She smirked. "You're just living the life, ain't ya?"

"Sure thing," he retorted. "While we're waiting, we need to hire some new officers. Any idea how that's done?"

"I wouldn't know," she admitted. "You should reach out to Alicia at city hall."

Jay searched his brain. "Alicia's the woman in HR? Forties?"

"Yeah, the blond one," Shannon told him. "She's married to a manager over at the Golden Nugget."

Jay nodded.

"Don't let her suck you into her personal life, though," she warned.

"Why?"

"Her and her husband are swingers. Not that I'm judging, but she often feels out people's reactions before inviting them in."

"Is that true?" Jay asked.

"Talk to Rick about it tomorrow when he's back," she suggested.

Jay curled his lip. "That's a surefire way to end up in HR."

The phone rang. Towns motioned toward it, asking if she could answer it. Jay threw up his hands, giving her room to grab the receiver.

"Ocean Springs Police Department, Officer Towns here." She paused and listened before punching a button and replacing the receiver. "Detective Warren, I have you on speakerphone with Chief Delp."

"Detective," Jay greeted the man on the line.

"Hey, Chief, your officer said you've been searching for Clayton Miller?" a loud voice on the other end asked.

"Yes, sir. Miller is—or, rather, was—dating a woman we pulled out of Biloxi Bay Sunday night."

"Gee, sounds like we have a matching pair," Warren said.

"That's what we thought," Jay said. "We were looking for Miller in conjunction with this murder."

"I found him," Warren said wryly.

Jay lifted his gaze across the desk to his subordinate, who never flinched at the man's dark humor. Most cops didn't. They often saw the worst of humanity, and such light-heartedness in the face of death helped them cope.

"What can you tell us?" Jay inquired.

"We got a 911 call earlier today from a landlord who discovered Miller in his empty house," Warren told them. "He's been dead since we think Saturday morning sometime."

Towns eyed Jay with the unspoken conclusion that the two murders were too close to be coincidences. "You just found him today?" Jay asked. "Was that the ME's time of death?"

"Still waiting on that," Warren admitted. "Bureaucracy, right? No, the house was empty Friday. The landlord had a plumber there doing some repairs. Obviously, he didn't notice a corpse."

"One would hope he would mention that," Jay noted.

"Have you confirmed the plumber wasn't the killer?" Towns asked. Jay gave her a nod of approval. He'd been thinking the same thing.

"We don't think so," Warren stated. "Once we confirm the time of death, we can iron out his alibi. The guy's a local fireman and a pastor. It's not outside the realm of possibility, but seems unlikely. We'll cross our T's and dot our I's, though, just in case."

Jay gazed at Jamie Rene's two faces. "Detective Warren, what we have is a twenty-three-year-old student stabbed, likely raped, and dumped in the bay. We're also waiting on a confirmation of the time of death. Our ME's pre-autopsy guess was that she'd been in the water since Saturday morning."

"Sounds too close for comfort," Warren remarked.

"My thoughts, too," Jay agreed.

"You thinking my guy did yours, then came here and someone else killed him, or what?"

"My gut says it's more likely the same unsub got both our vics," Jay suggested.

"Makes the most sense to me," Warren agreed. "I'll be honest—until Officer Towns called, this one was at the bottom of the stack. Miller fits the profile. We found some crystal on him."

"Be interesting to read what the tox screen shows," Jay pondered.

"Would be," Warren said, adding, "I'd like to see if he died in there, too."

Jay lifted his eyes to the murder board. "What about his car?"

"Know what it was?" Warren asked.

Jay shot Towns a look. She pulled out a notepad and

read, "A 2004 Mitsubishi Mirage. Mississippi plates RDP 412."

"I'll check, but there weren't any vehicles at the house," Warren said.

Jay glanced at Towns. "What about a white Honda CRV?"

"Nothing there," Warren stated. "That your vic's?"

"Yes, but we haven't located it, either."

"Maybe they parked together," Warren quipped.

"It seems unlikely," Jay commented dryly.

"Odd that neither car has been found," Warren pointed out.

Towns gave Jay a knowing glance, and Jay suppressed a grin.

"How about we keep each other updated?" Jay suggested.

"Yeah, sure thing," Warren agreed. "After all, you made my case a bit more complicated."

"We strive to serve," Jay remarked before hanging up the phone.

"I don't understand," Towns said. "Why would he take Miller that far?"

"He hoped no one would come across Miller," Jay speculated. "At least for a few days. The boyfriend is usually a suspect, and if he's missing, we'd be chasing around for him instead of looking for the actual killer. Of course, he probably didn't expect Jamie Rene would wash up so quickly."

"Why not get rid of that body, too?" Towns wondered. "Could've dumped him in the bay with her."

"Just a guess, but we might find that Clay was dead before Jamie," Jay suggested. It occurred to him that he'd switched to using Clay's first name once he was no longer a suspect.

"What if they'd been together?" Towns contemplated.

"Still doesn't explain the cars," Jay considered. "The killer could have taken them both, but the cars have to be someplace. If he wanted to make it look like Clay killed her, he should have left her car at Clay's place."

Towns shrugged. "That might be too obvious."

Jay pondered that for a second. He turned to study the board. "We need to track Clay Miller's whereabouts, too," he said. "Why don't you head over to this Chrysler dealership and start asking there?"

"Okay, Chief."

"Shannon, take JD with you," Jay ordered.

She offered him a nod as his computer dinged. Jay gave it a quizzical glance.

"Oh, IT got you all set up," she explained to him. "Your email, server access, the whole shebang."

"Do I need a password?"

She smiled. "It's 'password,' but I suggest you change it."

"I'll try to manage that," he told her as she left him.

Jay scrolled to the email icon, which now showed the number "32" in red. The phone let out a shrill screech, and Jay snatched it up before it repeated the sound.

"Delp," he muttered into the speaker.

"Chief Delp, this is Dr. Harley," the other voice responded. "Did you get the autopsy results?"

"Not yet," Jay answered.

"It should be in your email," the coroner replied with a sigh of frustration.

"Sorry, Doctor. IT just got my email working. Let me check."

He scrolled through the new messages to find one from the Jackson County Medical Examiner. Jay clicked the attachment to read a detailed report.

"Wanna give me the synopsis so I understand?" Jay asked.

"I assumed you might want something like that," Harley remarked with sullen superiority.

"Please," Jay said with a hint of concession.

"The victim's time of death was, in all likelihood, Saturday morning. But the water temperature affected my determination. The ligature marks were made at least eight hours prior to her death. I found some residue in her vaginal cavity that likely came from a condom."

"She had sex?"

"Not consensual," Harley amended. "The bruising on her body suggested she was bound during the rape."

"Like she'd been hanging from straps?" he asked, recalling the way Harley had described the marks in the morgue.

"Yes. The angle of the knife wounds suggests the killer made them while he was, er, inside her," the doctor explained.

Jay groaned. "How long did it take her to die?"

Harley cleared his throat. "At least five to ten minutes."

"What about the killer's DNA?"

"Unfortunately, I found nothing. The condom would have prevented any seminal discharge, and the time she was in the water washed away anything else."

"Tox screen?"

"There was some gamma-hydroxybutyrate—GHB—in her system."

"Any chance she was out of it while this was happening?" Jay hoped.

"Not likely," Harley explained. "The amount was minimal, suggesting the effects were diminishing at the point of death."

"Geez," Jay muttered. "What else can you tell me?"

"There was some bruising that might have come from a hand. Hard to determine, but I'd suggest a medium-build male. Not a female, unless she was a bit bigger and stronger than the average woman."

"That's something," Jay considered, though he doubted this new information helped. He'd already suspected it was a male. That he could be an average-sized one didn't help at all.

"Her stomach was virtually empty. It seemed to contain some protein, possibly chicken, though not a significant amount."

"It had been a while between her last meal and her death?"

"Appears so," Harley confirmed. "I believe her killer shaved her."

"Really?"

"Her pubic area had very little hair, but not none. It was a meticulous job, but not perfect. I found some irritation and two minor cuts. The angle of those cuts didn't seem like something the victim could do herself."

"Interesting," Jay remarked. "Is it possible to identify the razor used?"

"Not likely," Harley admitted. "Any small blade could have inflicted these injuries. If you had the actual razor, we might be able to match it to the slice. That would be a stretch, though."

Jay sighed. It wasn't a lot to go on, but it lent to the killer's profile. Not that it helped him much. An average-sized man who liked shaved vaginas did not make up a niche population.

"Thanks, Doctor," he told the medical examiner.

"Reach out if you need me to explain anything further in

the report," Harley added with more than a bit of conde-scension.

"Of course," Jay conceded. "You're the expert, right?"

Harley let out a slight, satisfied chuckle. "I suppose I am."

19

Jay slid his Jeep Wrangler into a space on the curb in front of the taco bar he and Sam ate at yesterday for lunch. The thoroughfare was busy with pedestrians walking dogs or strollers or significant others. He stared east down Government Street. The speakers in his car played that Rascal Flatts cover of the old Tom Cochrane hit. He paid no attention as they sang, "Knock me down. I'm back up again. You're in my blood. I'm not a lonely man." Instead, Jay pondered poor Jamie Rene. In fact, that had been almost the only thing he'd done since hanging up with Dr. Harley.

After he spoke with the medical examiner, the chief scoured the report Harley emailed to him over the next hour. Each time he reread it, he hoped that some insignificant detail might spring off the screen and signal to him what he should be looking for. Despite how many times the *SVU* or *Criminal Minds* teams did it on network television, it never worked that way in reality. No, instead of some breakthrough, Jay felt an overwhelming gloom descend on him. Each pass through the details painted a grimmer picture of

Jamie Rene's last hours, adding to the image that formed in Jay's mind.

Someone took Jamie Rene and probably Clay Miller, too. This monster bound Jamie in straps that, for some reason, Jay continued to imagine as leather, although nothing in the report indicated that. While she was helpless, tied up like a rabid animal, he raped her. Somehow, though, that wasn't enough. He wanted to violate her while she died.

What kind of demon could hurt someone that way?

It was a question he'd confronted more times than he liked to count on this job. Often, he considered police work far more traumatizing than anything he did in the Corps. At least in Afghanistan, the Taliban, albeit evil, did so from an indoctrinated belief. It was utter crap, but they thought the West were the vile ones—the infidels.

Whoever tortured Jamie Rene did so because they wanted to. They sought some perverse pleasure from it.

Again, the question rose in his brain: Was this his first murder?

The only answer he knew was that if Jay and his team didn't find him, it wouldn't be his last.

Tap. Tap. Tap.

Jay's mental exertion ceased, and he turned to his window to see Rebecca standing on the other side of the glass. Her smile shone with perfectly white teeth, the red lipstick contrasting with the bright enamel.

He glanced at the clock: 6:05. His thoughts had consumed him for too long. Consequently, he was late.

"Sorry," he muttered as he opened the door.

"You looked confused or something," she said, her expression softening but still present.

"Or something," he admitted. "This case."

"You wanna forget about it?"

"You have no clue."

Rebecca's head tilted to the left, and her expression melted into empathy. "Jay, if you aren't up for doing this, it's okay."

"No, Becs. I need to get out of my head."

"They make a martini here that might help you do just that," she said wryly.

"Will they give me six of them?" he asked.

"Oh, sure. But you might want to have a connection in the police department who won't ticket your car when you walk home."

"I'm not sure if I have that much clout yet," Jay confessed. "I just got access to my email there this afternoon."

"Please," she muttered, taking him by the hand. "Let's eat, drink, and be merry."

Jay returned her smile. Her palm felt cool and soft, and as soon as she squeezed his fingers, he was eighteen again. He followed her across the street to the two-story brick edifice surrounded by a short wrought-iron fence. The architect designed the structure after the Creole townhouses of New Orleans, with a full-width balcony stretching along the front of the building.

As the pair entered the restaurant, a young woman in a white blouse and black pants standing behind a podium with a crane-necked lamp greeted them. The girl, who Jay guessed to be close to Jamie Rene's age, offered a gracious grin.

"Welcome to Evergreen," she said. "Do you have a reservation?"

Rebecca returned the hostess's welcoming smile. "It's under Thomas."

The girl's blue eyes scanned down a list in front of her. "Rebecca Thomas?"

"That's me."

"Oh, you're with the mayor's office," the woman realized as she read a note next to Rebecca's name on the list.

"Yes, I am."

Jay thought about pointing out he was the chief of police, but he also realized that was an ego issue on his part. With his mouth shut, he followed Rebecca, who trailed behind the hostess to the back of the restaurant.

Gold lamps with reddish-orange shades adorned the tables, each of them covered with an ocean-blue cloth. When the hostess stopped at a table in the corner, she pulled out the seat for Rebecca while Jay took care of seating himself. Two menus appeared from thin air. Jay hadn't seen her take menus from the front. In fact, her hands, he was certain, had been empty when she pulled the chair out.

"Gamiel will be your server," the hostess explained.

"Thank you," Jay told her as Rebecca nodded.

He was about to turn his attention to his ex-wife when Gamiel appeared from thin air. "My name is Gamiel," he announced. "Can I offer you a cocktail?"

Jay's eyes shot to the menu in front of him like a fifth grader trying to cram one last bit of knowledge into his brain before a pop quiz.

While he panicked in silence, Rebecca said, "I'll have the Blueberry Smash."

Jay scanned the page for that cocktail, finding it under the specialty menu. Blueberry syrup, gin, St-Germain, and mint. It sounded too complicated for a guy who normally stuck to Bud Light, yet drinking a Bud Light in a place this nice seemed like a faux pas. Lucky for him, next to the Blueberry Smash was an old-fashioned, and it appeared to be a fancy one with bourbon. That was right up his alley.

"How are your folks?" Jay asked after Gamiel left to get their cocktails.

"They are good. Moved down to Tampa," Rebecca explained. "Said it got too cold here."

Jay shrugged. "After being in West Palm, I might think the same thing."

Rebecca shook her head. "I have to admit, I always thought you'd end up on some mountain in Canada."

Jay furrowed his brow. "Why?"

"I don't know. Just figured after you went to the Marines, you would come out not wanting to be around anyone."

"Nah, I like people," he countered.

"My father messaged me a few weeks ago when he heard you were the new chief," she told him.

"I always liked your dad," Jay said with a smile.

"Dad loved you," Rebecca recalled. "He was ecstatic that you were moving back. Both of my parents reminded me a hundred times a year how I screwed up leaving you."

"I'm not sure that's true."

"Oh, Dad mentioned it to Chris more than a few times."

"I bet your husband got a kick out of that," Jay said, stifling a grin.

"Go ahead and smile. He hated it," Rebecca replied. "It wasn't why the marriage broke up, but it didn't help that my parents pined for my first husband."

"At least you turned out okay," Jay stated, not sure how to traverse the verbal minefield.

"Eh, I got Robbie. So, if nothing else with Chris worked, there's that," she declared. "But otherwise, no, my folks were right. Don't you ever tell them I said that."

Jay shook his head and mimed zipping his lips closed.

"It really was my biggest mistake," she admitted. "I never told you that."

"Becs, we were kids."

"I don't think that's an excuse," she responded. "And you were never a kid."

"Sure I was."

Her head shook more. "No, you had a plan. I didn't comprehend it until much later, but you knew what you wanted."

Jay bit the inside of his bottom lip. She wasn't wrong. When they graduated high school, it took no time to realize his father couldn't afford to send him to college. Jay remembered talking to Rebecca about it. If he stayed in South Mississippi and attended community college, which was the most he could manage then and even that was questionable, he would end up in some nine-to-five job that would take him nowhere.

Instead, he joined the Corps. He could get the government to pay for a degree. At the time, he considered becoming a lawyer or at least something that would have long-term success. Rebecca could work when the Corps sent him overseas, and they'd bank plenty of cash to live off while he attended school.

Of course, none of that happened. When Rebecca divorced him, he never looked back. Or at least, he told himself he never looked back.

"It doesn't matter anymore," he emphasized.

Rebecca grinned again. "It's good to see you, Jay," she told him. "I never realized how much I missed that face."

"It is quite adorable," Jay quipped with a wry smirk.

"Are you seeing anyone?" she asked.

"I just got to town," he reminded her. "I mean, I'm fast, but dang."

"What about back in Florida?"

"Seeing is a stretch, I guess. My last—well, anything—was a fling with a Homeland agent."

"Indeed?" she remarked. "How did that end up?"

"She ended up getting shot and returned to D.C."

"At least you didn't marry her," she joked.

"Oh, you sound like my buddy Chase. Just because I'm adorable, I get blamed."

Gamiel reappeared from the mist somewhere with a tray and two cocktails. Rebecca's blueberry drink came in a short champagne coupe. The blue from the syrup swirled in the liquid, resembling some beautiful science experiment. Jay's old-fashioned looked identical to most old-fashioned, with one giant cube of ice and a sprig of rosemary.

"Can I get you anything to start with?" Gamiel asked.

"Want to slurp some oysters?" Rebecca questioned Jay with a wry grin. It had been a joke with them during their early dating years. She referred to the way people ate the oysters with an exaggerated slurping sound.

"Let's do it," he replied, returning her smile.

"A dozen, then," she told Gamiel, who only nodded before vanishing the same way he came. "Where were we?"

"You were giving me grief about not being married."

"Oh, right," she said with a broadening smile.

"You know, that's probably all your fault," he said, only half-joking.

She bowed her head slightly, her expression souring a touch. "I'm aware. If I hadn't derailed us, I figure we'd be living in Atlanta or Chicago somewhere, and you'd be a partner in some law firm."

He shrugged. "Guess it's just as well."

Rebecca's eyes glistened slightly, and he started backpedaling on his last statement when Gamiel saved him with a platter of raw oysters. Rebecca reached out quickly to scoop up the closest one. With the shell in her fingers, she tossed the meat down her throat, swallowing it in a gulp. Jay followed suit.

"Slurp," she said with another exaggerated sound effect.

Jay mimicked her in response.

Dinner arrived—the duck for Rebecca and the blackened snapper for Jay. They ate and chatted for the next hour. At some point, Jay thought the evening reminded him of a hot shower. It was one of those things he often put off, but once immersed in the steam and coursing water, he found it to be the most enjoyable thing ever.

"No, this is my treat," Rebecca demanded when the check came.

Jay's arm had reached across the empty snifter glass that a few minutes earlier housed some warmed Grand Marnier. "Becs, let me," he argued.

Her head tilted, allowing a lock of hair to fall in front of her face. He stared at the brown curl and the green eyes staring back at him. He retracted his hand, leaving the check on the table.

"You could buy me dinner next time," she suggested.

Jay's stomach tightened, but he nodded. "That would be nice, yes."

20

Jay considered walking home, but he'd only had three drinks over the several hours he was at dinner with Rebecca. Still, he almost felt like the fresh air would do him good. Jay remained in the street after she pulled away from the curb. Her taillights stayed in his sight until she turned two blocks down.

Had she been watching him in the rearview mirror?

Stop it. You aren't seventeen anymore.

On the other hand, she wasn't, either. Tonight wasn't like their dinners in the past. Back then, a fancy dinner involved pizza from Pizza Hut, followed by a movie over in Biloxi.

But he still remembered the day those papers showed up. It hadn't even been the regular mail call; they arrived from a process server. It took less than two hours for the entire barracks to find out, and while the guys were supportive, Jay sulked for weeks, keeping the pain to himself.

That was a lifetime ago.

It was, but the nerves often seemed raw. Logic reminded him that those feelings were lying. Sure, it still hurt. His wrist panged during the rain, too, from when he broke it in eighth grade. That didn't make the injury nearly as bad as it had been when it initially happened.

Was he being stupid?

He walked down the sidewalk toward his Jeep. The drive home took him only two minutes. He parked next to a silver Lexus. Despite the lingering anxiety, he bounded out of the vehicle, his boots thudding against the concrete driveway. The night air carried a breeze. The beach was several blocks away, but the northern edge of Weeks Bayou was a lot closer. Jay rejoiced that the wind was strong enough to cut down on the swarms of mosquitoes normally coming off the wetland.

He pushed through the kitchen door to hear the television in the den. Jay crossed the linoleum floor that had the same design he recalled as a child. The square designs made perfect roads for his Hot Wheels, and he and Sam often reenacted car chases from the latest movie or TV show they'd seen.

Jay opened the refrigerator, pulling a cold Bud Light from the shelf. As he cracked the cap, he walked into the den. Danielle, his sister-in-law, sat curled up on the sofa watching Jimmy Fallon on the television. She looked up, noticing Jay in the doorway.

"Jay," she said in what might have been an exclamation for her. Danielle stood up and crossed the room, wrapping him in a big hug. "I'm so glad you are here."

He returned the embrace. "Good to see you, too."

"Sam mentioned you were out with Rebecca," she noted, stepping away from him.

"Yeah, we ate at Evergreen."

"It's great, isn't it?"

"It was."

She settled back on the couch, muting Jimmy, who was talking to Nathan Fillion. "So," she pressed. "Rebecca, huh?"

"We were just catching up," Jay explained.

"Oh, 'catching up,' eh? That was a long time."

"It's been a long time," he pointed out.

"She's divorced," Danielle told him.

"Danielle, we were together all night. I'm well-aware that she's divorced."

"Just saying," Danielle continued. "Like you said, it's been a long time."

Jay shook his head and took a drink of the beer. "Where's Dad?"

"Asleep," she answered.

"What about Sam?" Jay asked. "I figured he'd be here."

"Someone needs to put the kids to bed," she reminded him.

"Sorry," he apologized.

"Don't be," Danielle explained. "Your dad's easy. Half the time, he thinks I'm your mom. That makes him super docile. The rest of the time, he tells me I'm too good for your brother."

Jay smiled. "Aren't you?"

"Oh, I don't think so," she demurred. Jay believed her. Or at least, he believed she thought that.

"How are the kids?" he asked.

"Jenson's playing football this fall, with the JV."

"Isn't he in eighth grade?"

Danielle nodded.

"Wow, that's great for him."

She nodded but said, "Makes a mama nervous. One of those bigger boys is going to clobber him."

Jay smirked. "That happens."

"I don't like it."

"Sam's probably ecstatic."

"Over the moon," Danielle confirmed. "He told me you're coming to dinner tomorrow night?"

"Yeah, I'm looking forward to seeing the kids. It's been too long."

"You never came home," she accused, but her face shifted as soon as the words spilled out. "I'm sorry, Jay. That was uncalled for."

"No, you're right. I dropped the ball," he admitted. "It never had anything to do with you or Sam."

She nodded. "Sam's told me enough stories over the years."

Jay's eyes drifted to the hallway leading to his father's bedroom. "Never expected him to get sick like this," he commented.

"Remember when I lost my mom?"

Jay nodded.

"She and I had a rough relationship. I was so ready to run away. Then one Monday afternoon, she has an aneurysm at the church. The preacher found her two hours later. She'd been putting together school supplies for the poor kids in Panola County."

Jay kept listening.

"I had so much guilt."

"Danielle, that's not your fault."

"Of course not. Aneurysms happen, especially to people her age. But it was my fault I didn't go back. Don't get me wrong, Jay. She was horrible. Nothing I ever did was good enough for her, including marrying Sam."

"Staying wouldn't have been healthy, either," Jay reasoned.

"No, and I've dealt with it. However, you have at least a shot at something with your dad. You might be lucky and have some time with the Terry Delp you knew before your mother died. Or your sister," she added after a beat.

Jay dipped his chin. "Let me ask you something."

"Go ahead."

"Did Dad ever mistake you for Mom and discuss a man called Jacob?"

She cocked her head. "Once, he yelled at me about him."

"What did he say?"

"He started complaining about dinner and said Sandra saw Jacob over at the bridge. After that, he got agitated and shouted, 'Where'd Jacob go?' Jay, he jumped up like he was a kid and barged into the other room, looking for Sandra. I tried to calm him down, and he was suddenly back to now."

"Did you tell Sam about it?"

Danielle considered it. "We talked about Dad getting worked up about Sandra. That happens a lot. I figured Jacob was Sandra's friend."

"Did he say that?"

Danielle shook her head. "No, I just assumed it. I never push it, though. Sometimes that only makes it worse for him when he's dissociating."

Jay nodded. "What about Dale? Ever hear him mention a Dale?"

"That doesn't sound familiar," she replied. "Honestly, Jay, I sometimes don't correct him and play along without paying attention."

"It's okay, Danielle. I didn't mean anything by it."

"Are you bringing Rebecca tomorrow night?" she implored.

"No," Jay said. "That would be a bit presumptuous."

Danielle shrugged. "Were you dating anyone in Florida?"

"Geez, everyone wants to know, don't they?"

"We just want you happy."

"How about I get settled first?"

"Okay, okay." Danielle waved him off. "I'll let it be for now."

Jay gave his sister-in-law a comforting smile. He realized how much he'd always liked Danielle. When Sam married her, Jay was the best man. Rebecca was a bridesmaid because in the South, one didn't leave out the brother-in-law's fiancée from the wedding party. That was a major no-no. During that period, Jay found Danielle to be a witty addition to the family.

"How's the murder case going?" she asked.

Jay frowned. "A little sickening, if I'm being honest."

"Really? What about it?"

He shook his head. "I probably shouldn't get into it."

"I can keep a secret," she said. "If you need to talk."

"It's just complicated. The poor girl had a rough end, and the person responsible is... well, sick."

Danielle nodded. "Don't let it devour you," she warned.

Jay affirmed, "I won't."

She stared at him for a second.

"I promise," he added.

"I'm going to head home before Sam falls asleep."

Jay checked the time. It was after eleven. "Is he still up?"

"If he isn't, I can sit up and stream something in peace," she explained. "Your brother can't make it through a show without talking."

Jay chuckled. "He never could. Used to ruin *X-Files* for me."

"He hasn't changed," she remarked as she stood. "Night, Jay."

"Text me when you get home," Jay told her.

"You aren't my father," she joked.

"No, I'm a cop, and there is a guy out there who killed a girl."

"Thanks for the concern, but I'm far from a girl." She hugged him and kissed his cheek before leaving him alone in the den.

Jay settled on the couch and scanned the den. Since he'd been in town, he hadn't had time to look over this room. Very little had changed about it since he left for the Corps. There was a new carpet, and his dad had painted the walls. All the furniture remained in the same position. Even the replacement carpet was just a shade off what the original one looked like. Terry Delp didn't care for change. At least, not since Jay's mother passed.

Or maybe he fears it, Jay thought. This was the place where he and Louise Delp watched the ten o'clock news every night.

Jay gulped some beer and crossed the space to the bookshelf that came directly from 1978. Rows of photo albums lined the shelf. Jay's mother, Louise, had been diligent in documenting their life with her Polaroid or the thirty-five-millimeter Canon her husband bought her one Christmas. The spines of each book noted the year in bold, black, hand-printed letters. Jay traced his finger along until he found 1994.

That was the year Sandra died. August 20, 1994.

The album was significantly lighter than in the previous years. While Louise Delp meticulously maintained the catalog of photos, after Sandra's death, she hadn't taken any pictures. Jay remembered the following Christmas, a subdued holiday for the Delps. His mother had been lifeless. Later, Jay concluded she'd received tranquilizers, though the family never broached the subject.

Jay flipped to the front of the album, scanning the image

of Jay, Sam, and Sandra under a banner reading "Welcome 1994." Sam stood in the center of the trio with his arms around both of his siblings. All three grinned those toothy smiles kids that age did when the camera pointed at them.

Jay smiled at the photo. His sister was eleven in the picture, her blond hair pulled into dog ears that flopped down, covering her lobes. The two front teeth looked too big for her mouth, and Jay regretted the number of times he called her "chipmunk."

Sandra Delp had fair features, and Jay recognized that if she had grown up, his sister would have been pretty. Looking at her now, he saw his own mother in her face. In the picture, Sam loomed the way an older brother does. Even how he held Jay and his sister showed how he'd been the mentor for both of them.

Jay flipped the page. The rest of the January pictures showed the various Delp kids on the beach or at the park. A few photos showed Sam playing basketball. A couple from a warm Saturday on the bay. Sandra held up a small snapper she'd reeled in on her own. Her bucktooth grin glowed from the past as Jay examined it.

He flipped through February, where pictures captured Sam dressed for his first dance, holding a Valentine's Day card. Another showed Jay with his mother, holding a picture he'd drawn for her. The next photo had been taken by one of the kids, probably Sandra. Terry and Louise Delp were dancing in this very den with wide smiles on their faces.

Jay froze on that photo, the little snippet of time captured on this page. An instant when his parents both seemed happy. Terry Delp was a good father who took his children fishing when he could. Louise was a devoted mother who brought joy into the house. It was a moment that never repeated itself after that year.

Jay wiped a tear that had formed in the corner of his left eye. He flipped through March's pictures that immortalized the kids playing in the park. One Polaroid showed Sam and another boy from the neighborhood. In the white pouch under the image, "Sam" and "Jeremy Counce" were scrawled in Louise Delp's handwriting.

More photos started documenting May and June as the Delp siblings were out of school and off on various adventures. Photos from all three kids' end-of-the-year parties and get-togethers filled the pages. His mom had diligently noted the people in the Polaroid pictures. He assumed the names would be on the backs of the ones developed at the Fox Photo Booth over by the grocery store.

His fingers stopped on a Polaroid, showing his father and another man. Both men were cramming burgers into their mouths. Jay glanced at the past few photographs where his mother had documented a Memorial Day Picnic down at the beach. The same penciled handwriting adorned this picture. Beneath the image, Jay read, "Terry and Dale."

21

———

When Jay walked into his office, he found an actual mug of coffee on his desk. It wasn't a small cup, either, to his relief. He picked it up by the handle, bringing it up to inhale the aroma of roasted beans. The smell didn't impress him, and he decided that whenever they ran out of the coffee stocked in the office, he'd find a better brand. Coffee cost little, and it was the lifeblood of a police force. It had been that for every military base he'd ever set foot on, too. Cut off the coffee, and the troops might rise against their leaders.

The murder board hadn't changed since Jay left last night. If only he'd come in to find an answer jotted down with an Expo marker that gave the killer's name.

"Morning, Chief," Towns called from the door.

"Shannon, are you to thank for this?" he asked, lifting the mug that read "Ocean Springs High School Orchestra."

She grinned at him. "I have this immense collection of coffee cups at my house. I like to dump them off on folks whenever I can."

"People might ask me to play the cello," Jay commented as he regarded the mug.

"You are tall enough," she remarked.

"Well, thank you," he told her, though he didn't understand that statement. "What have you got today?"

"I read over the autopsy after you emailed it to me."

"Light reading for you at night?" he asked.

"I like dark fiction, but this was a bit much. The poor girl," she empathized.

"Yeah, it wasn't pretty. Have you heard from Warren yet?" She shook her head.

"Morning, boss," Rick Lawson announced. "Shannon, how are you?"

"Great, Rick. How was your day off?"

"Wife had me cutting grass and weed-eating the front yard."

Shannon frowned. "Figured you'd go fishing."

"No luck," he confessed. "She hooked me. What have we got today?"

Jay reclined in his chair and lifted his orchestral mug to his lips.

"Hey, boss, you have a cup?" Lawson noted.

"Officer Towns has been taking care of me," Jay revealed.

Lawson cast a playful side-eye toward Towns.

"Shut it, Rick," she told him.

Lawson eyed the whiteboard. "You ID'd her?"

Towns answered, "Yeah. It's a lot more complicated, too."

As Lawson scanned the information on the murder board, he nodded. "Looks like it. The boyfriend is dead, too?"

"Yes," Towns replied. She paused and looked to Jay, who motioned for her to continue. "We think the same guy killed him in Slidell."

"Why?" Lawson asked.

"That's the question," Jay said.

"Dang, I missed a lot yesterday."

"You deserved a day off," Jay reminded him.

Lawson nodded. "What's the plan today?"

Both officers turned to their chief for the answer. Jay took another sip of coffee before answering. "Shannon, we should go to the college and talk to her instructors. Focus on the ones she saw on Friday."

"Could it be one of them?" Lawson asked.

Jay shook his head. "Anyone, at this point, is a suspect. But if we can establish her whereabouts, we could develop a pattern. If this was an acquaintance, it means we need to put a name to anyone who interacted with her."

"Do you think that?" Towns asked.

"What?"

"That it's someone she knows?"

Jay let out a sigh. "I don't have a clue. My gut suggests something, but I've learned to never trust it. All we are certain of is at some point, Jamie and Clay came into contact with the man who killed them. He tortured Jamie for hours before raping and killing her. We have no idea how long it took him to kill Clay."

"What does your gut say?" Lawson pressed.

Jay lifted an eyebrow. "I think it was someone she crossed paths with. Maybe on a regular basis or a one-time thing. But there's no evidence of that, so we investigate what we can. That's running down everyone she had contact with. It could have been a jealous lover or a potential one, which might explain why he killed Clay. Or, Shannon, it's like you said yesterday, that Clay and Jamie could have been together when they encountered the killer."

"Geez," Lawson whistled.

"Rick, can you get with Detective Warren over in Slidell?" Jay asked. "He's going to send us crime scene photos and the autopsy results once he gets them. Forward what we have. There's always the possibility that both of them were killed in the Slidell house."

"Really?" Towns asked.

"I find it unlikely," Jay conceded. "They both lived twenty minutes from here. If they were in Slidell when they were murdered, why would the killer bring her an hour back to dump her? He already had an empty house there."

"Good point, I guess," Towns replied.

"I could be wrong," Jay allowed. "It's happened once before."

"Only once?" Lawson retorted.

Jay lifted the corner of his mouth in a half-smile. "Yep, as far as you are aware."

Lawson grinned, flashing a broad white grin. "I'll call the guy. You don't need me to drive over there, do ya?"

"No point. At least not yet. Let's run down what we can here," Jay answered. "Who else is in?"

"Tomlinson and Baker," Towns told him.

"Rick, you man the office and research from here. Shannon, reach out to the public safety officer or whoever is in charge over at the college and tell them we are coming."

"Yes, Chief," she agreed. "When do you want to go?"

"About an hour."

She gave him a thumbs-up and started for the door.

"Towns," he called, and she turned back. "Thanks for the cup," he told her again.

"You bet, sir," she declared.

"Dang, you really got things going around here," Lawson admitted. His gaze shifted to the extra chairs behind his desk. "What's up with all those?"

"I have an embarrassment of chairs," Jay informed him.

Lawson only shrugged in response.

"Rick, sit down real quick," Jay said, and Lawson settled in the high back across from him. "I've heard some rumors about the department," Jay began.

Lawson nodded. "I bet you have."

"What do you think they might be?"

"Sir, I don't like to tell tales."

"I understand," Jay responded. "But if what I'm hearing is true, this could be more than just tales."

Lawson tilted his head forward. "Chief, I wasn't a part of anything like that."

"But?"

He shrugged. "I heard things."

"Such as?"

"Nothing concrete. Captain Lee bought a Corvette. He claimed it was a pre-retirement thing, but it was brand new. How many police captains you met can afford to buy one of those?"

"They make nice financing options," Jay suggested.

"Might be so, but word was he purchased with cash. Of course, that's all hearsay."

Jay nodded. "What kind of things were going on?"

"This is a decent area, but there's still an underbelly. We have a couple of families that are part of the Dixie Mafia. Word was they were untouchable around here."

"Just in Ocean Springs?"

"Dixie Mafia was based in Biloxi. At least to some extent. I expect Biloxi doesn't press those cases, either. Of course, they aren't about to tell me that, are they?"

Jay bit his lip. "I suppose not."

"They pretty much think us colored boys shouldn't be

hanging around them, 'less we're hanging from a live oak," he replied in an exaggerated dialect.

"Yeah, that's not going to fly around here, Rick."

"You won't make too many friends, then," Lawson cautioned.

Jay shrugged. "I've faced smarter, more dangerous foes."

"No doubt," Lawson remarked.

"Anyone ever give you any trouble here?" Jay asked.

The African-American officer shook his head. "It's never been like that here."

Jay raised his eyebrows, displaying an obvious amount of skepticism.

Lawson added, "No, don't get me wrong. We had plenty of good ole boys on the force, but no one said anything. That didn't mean they'd step between me and a bullet from a racist Dixie Mafia gunman."

"It's not going to happen here," Jay promised. "Not under my watch."

Lawson nodded, but Jay suspected the officer had his doubts.

"I get it. I'm new," Jay told him. "But you ever have a problem in here or on the streets, come directly to me."

"Yes, sir," Lawson replied.

"Rick, I'm not pushing any of the rumors. Like you say, most of it is hearsay. For now, we're going to rebuild this department, and I hope you'll help me keep it clean."

"Thanks, boss."

"Also, I appreciate the heads-up on Towns. She has really taken to the investigation."

"She's smart," Lawson told him. "Too smart to run errands."

"We had a big head start yesterday, but I need you on this, too."

"Of course."

"I want the two of you to work it for the next couple of days. I'm still trying to get my feet wet," Jay paused. "Or is it, I'm trying to get my feet under me?"

"Both make sense," Lawson said, breaking into a smile.

"Good. I'll go with Towns to the school."

"You don't think she knew the killer?" Lawson asked.

"No, I don't," Jay admitted. "He took too much pleasure in it. In fact, my concern is that it's going to happen again."

"You ever work a serial killer, boss?"

Jay gave a nod. "A couple. Most metropolitan areas have one. The media doesn't always know it. Some guys kill once a year. Some are smart enough to change up their MO. Most target demographics that don't report missing people."

Lawson nodded in understanding. "Is this guy one, in your opinion?"

"I'm the farthest thing from a psychologist, but yeah, what he did to her suggests to me he's a psychopath."

"We must find him," Lawson agreed. "Other than this Warren in Slidell, you want me working on anything else?"

Jay pointed at the board. "Right now, whatever we don't know, we must know. I'm especially curious about where Jamie and Clay's vehicles are."

"See what I can do," Lawson answered. "Anything else?"

Jay shook his head, and the officer got to his feet. As he walked out to the bullpen, Lawson paused at the door. "Glad you're on board, boss. I hope you can do what you say."

Jay dipped his chin slightly in response and watched the black officer walk away. Lawson wasn't throwing down a gauntlet or even casting shade at Jay. At least, Jay didn't interpret the comment that way. No, it was skeptical, but not about Jay's intent.

Jay was growing concerned by the extent of corruption

in the city, which surpassed his estimations. One thing that bothered Jay after his conversation with Lawson was how connected the Dixie Mafia might be. It seemed unlikely that the criminals with their fingers in the department would risk losing all their dirty cops. In fact, it was odd they had let any leave.

Jay knew all about the Dixie Mafia, but he had never crossed paths with them. There was a case in Panama City involving an alleged hitman for the mob, but the DA never pressed charges, stating there wasn't enough evidence. It hadn't been Jay's case, so he was sketchy on the details. However, now he wondered if that was the only reason it didn't go to trial.

He had crossed paths with the cartels in South Florida. They operated on a different level than the Dixie Mob, although he suspected that was for similar reasons. The cartel's operation, depending on which one it was, remained in the hands of the Cubans or Mexicans or whatever other country they might originate. He'd dealt with the Cubans mostly, and even that had mostly been on the outskirts, like an occasional stiff connected to a cartel who the police believed ran drugs or money and then crossed the powers-that-be.

The Dixie Mafia worked differently. They dug their fingers into the society around them. Cops and district attorneys had been bribed or blackmailed. If that didn't work, they'd be threatened or killed. However, they were thorough. If they had a handhold on the department under Ward, they wouldn't give it up easily.

Jay suspected they still had some eyes in his bullpen. The problem was, who? He felt sure that Lawson was clean. The Dixie Mafia tended to be, on the whole, a bigoted bunch. None of them would trust an African-American cop.

Towns seemed unlikely, too. She was a woman, and while it wasn't unheard of, it didn't fit the pattern. Feminism hadn't made it to organized crime yet. While there were plenty of women who had become leaders of criminal organizations, most females worked the bottom rung as prostitutes or drug runners. Otherwise, they were just some guy's "old lady." If the corporate world struggled with gender equality, a group of thugs wasn't making any progressive strides, either.

Although it didn't preclude the station from being threatened. A man or woman might do anything if their family's lives were at stake. He'd remember that as they moved forward.

Trust was something Jay normally dealt out until someone proved they were unworthy of it. He didn't want to approach everyone with distrust, but he planned to be careful for the moment.

22

"Most of Jamie's classes were at the Harrison campus," Towns explained to Jay as they drove over the causeway again.

Jay listened as he stared out across the bay at the IP Casino. It marked his fourth day on the job—his third, technically, but he counted going to the body Sunday night—and he had a serial killer and a possible infiltration by the Dixie Mafia. He'd figured this might be an easy role for him, to transition into the head of a department, but he'd already bumped up against roadblocks. Well, potential roadblocks. No evidence yet suggested that Jamie Rene's murderer was a serial killer, only his gut feeling. The same held true for the mafia. Only hearsay from Lawson and whispers that corruption ran rampant in the department under Ward.

"You aren't listening to me," Towns stated.

"What?" Jay sat up straight. "Sorry, Shannon. What did you say?"

"Nothing important," she told him. "Just that Jamie stayed at the Harrison campus."

"How many campuses are there?"

"Like ten or eleven, but they are scattered everywhere. Her advisors were at this one, though," she added.

Jay nodded. "Good."

"You seem preoccupied," she noted.

"This has been a busy week," Jay explained.

"Yeah, just imagine your second week," she joked.

"Let's hope it's a lot calmer."

"Hope springs eternal," Towns replied.

"Dickinson?"

"Alexander Pope," Towns corrected him.

"Huh, thought I knew something."

"Do you like poetry?" she asked.

"As well as the next guy."

"Around here, that would be not at all."

Jay shrugged. "It's one of those things I appreciate but don't study. Like art. I've been to my fair share of galleries and museums, and I admire the skill and talent to paint masterpieces. However, I rarely understand them."

"You and me both."

"Sam was a little more into it than me," Jay said.

"No, Sam hates poetry," she said knowingly.

Jay shifted in his seat. "I meant artwork."

"Oh, right. That's true, isn't it? He paints, doesn't he?"

"You like both?" Jay asked, biting back the other question in his head.

"I don't paint, but I've dabbled in poetry. Mostly I read it now. But in another life, I'd write some down. Always wanted to publish a book of poems."

"You should."

"No. Are you aware of how little poets make?"

"Less than cops?" Jay guessed.

"Way less."

"That's pretty crappy," he said. "How did you know Sam painted?"

"Oh, we talked one day. At the station. I forget how it came up. He told me he enjoyed painting."

"He's good," Jay noted.

"Yeah, at least as far as I can tell," she agreed.

"What did the school say?" he asked, changing the subject.

"Carl Stone, the head of campus safety, is going to meet and escort us around. He promised to have her schedule, too."

"Are her teachers expecting us?"

Towns grinned. "No. I figured we wouldn't want them to think about it too hard."

"Good," Jay told her. She had a point. If they wanted to catch someone off-guard, giving them time to cement a story in their mind was bad. On the other hand, they needed details about Jamie's last day. That might require some consideration and recollection. These professors saw hundreds of students daily. If Jay had to guess, he'd say they paid very little attention to them individually. It would depend on how outgoing Jamie Rene was.

"Did you talk to Clay's work?" he asked her.

"Yes, they didn't give me much. Clay worked in the service department. It seems he was nothing more than the bottom rung of the grease monkey ladder."

"Oh?"

"His supervisor stated he wasn't bad with cars, but he hadn't gotten his certification in whatever they certify mechanics. So, he did the grunt work—cleanup and such."

"How long had he been there?"

"A few months. Four, if I recall. Those notes are on my desk," she explained. "He seemed well-liked. However, they do drug test, and his boss told me the dealership wouldn't hire him if anything dinged on his test."

"But that was months ago, right? He could have gotten into it since then."

"His supervisor said he showed up on time and worked hard," Towns countered. "He mentioned he'd dealt with junkies before, and Clay wasn't that. Pot, maybe. He said he swore that Miller didn't do anything harder. I got the impression he might enjoy a bit of weed now and then."

"You talked to him on the phone?"

Towns nodded.

"Might be good to chat with Clay's coworkers, too," Jay added.

"I can get out there," Towns assured the chief.

"First, we should follow up with Crews and her boyfriend—what was his name?"

"Kyle Rose," she answered.

"Yes, give them a call later. Don't ask straight out, though. Try and go at it from an angle."

"Of course," she said as if he'd suggested something obvious. "People get sketchy about that."

He nodded in agreement.

"What if this was a drug deal?" Towns asked.

"I doubt it," Jay said. "Her tox screen showed GHB, not meth."

"No, I understand that. But suppose Jamie finished up this big exam, and she was looking for a way to let loose. What if she just wanted to try it, so they decide to do it together?"

"I see," Jay considered. "They aren't regular users, so they find someone who is selling crystal and arrange to meet him?"

"Exactly. Two naïve kids. Warren said Clay didn't have a

wallet or money. What if the deal turned into a robbery and kidnapping?"

Towns presented as viable a theory as Jay had. They found no evidence that either Jamie or Clay used drugs regularly, but he'd seen plenty of purely recreational one-off users who just wanted to experience a substance once.

"Plus," Towns added, "a dealer could have connections up and down the coast."

"Meaning it would be simple for them to find a place to dispose of a body? For example, in Slidell?"

"Possibly."

"It's possible," Jay acquiesced. "That will be hard to trace, but let's see. Someone at the restaurant or Clay's work might have known a guy. If they sent Jamie to them, they won't be quick to divulge that voluntarily."

"Yep, people are sketchy about that," Towns agreed as she pulled into the drive, passing a beige sign reading "Gulf Coast Community College Harrison Campus."

After parking in front of the administration building, they entered to find a rotund black man in his fifties standing next to a water cooler with a younger woman. The gentleman lifted his eyes to see the pair and excused himself from the conversation.

"Are you Officer Towns?" he asked as they approached.

Shannon extended her hand. "Shannon Towns. This is Chief Delp."

"I'm Carl Stone. Head of Campus Safety."

"Mr. Stone," Jay greeted. "Thanks for taking the time to assist us."

"The news is terrible," Stone said, shaking his head. "I saw the paper this morning."

Jay nodded. He'd read the same article. It had been front-page stuff, but the attribution to Jay was minimal.

Marcus Taylor had found a criminologist from the University of Southern Mississippi to weigh in on the murder. Even without having the actual details, Taylor's piece suggested a crime as vile as what had really happened. Jay expected a backlash from citizens after the television stations picked it up.

"I've reached out to all of Ms. Rene's professors," Stone said. "Only two are on campus here, but they were the ones she had on Friday."

"Good," Jay told the university employee.

"Dr. Browne had her in psychology. Dr. Hardy taught her Secondary Education Theories class."

"That's a mouthful," Towns remarked.

Stone shrugged. "You know academics."

Jay nodded, though he didn't quite understand what he was agreeing with.

Stone escorted them outside. They crossed the courtyard, and Jay scanned the quad where students occupied benches with open books.

"We'll hit the psych department first," Stone explained.

"Have you had any incidents on campus recently?" Towns asked.

"Officer, that's like asking if y'all gave out any traffic tickets," Stone stated. "We have a couple of thousand students on any one of our campuses. Luckily, that's not as big as some schools, but it's enough to have some rotten apples in the bunch."

Jay understood that. The larger the community grew, the greater the chance of people problems. He recalled a captain in Panama City referring to it like that: "All cop problems are people problems. Remove the people, and the problems disappear."

It was a cynical viewpoint, but it also made sense. Large gatherings garnered more issues.

The cops followed Stone up two flights of stairs. They exited into a corridor lined with offices on either side. Very little traffic passed through here. It was the professors' office space, and few students ventured up there without a purpose.

Stone rapped his knuckles on the door.

"Enter," an aged voice called from inside the office.

Stone pushed the door open, revealing a man in his sixties. He fought against the years with copious amounts of hair dye. The mop on his head was unnaturally black. He shaved his goatee into a point, reminding Jay of a villain in a James Bond movie. Add in his rail-thin build, and the professor looked like he had a master plan.

He rose to greet the three, and Jay realized he was only about 5'2".

"Dr. Browne, Carl Stone," Jay said, "I called you earlier."

"Yes, of course," Browne acknowledged. He gestured for the visitors to step inside.

Jay stepped forward. "Dr. Browne, I'm Chief Delp from the Ocean Springs Police Department. This is Officer Towns."

Browne's eyes widened a bit. "Chief, how can I help you?"

"We want to ask you about a student," he explained.

"Is this Ms. Rene?" he inquired.

Jay nodded.

"I saw the news report. Tragic."

"It is, sir. We suspect your Friday class was among her last actions."

"Oh," the professor said. "I heard she'd been abducted after work?"

"We aren't sure," Jay admitted. "Sometime after she left her work, she was."

"How can I help you?" Dr. Browne asked. "She was an outstanding student, but we weren't close."

Jay glanced at Towns. He hadn't intended on taking the lead, but now that he had, it felt awkward to throw it back to Towns.

"Did she ever talk to you?" Jay asked.

"Yes, but only casual conversation. She asked me after class last week about her paper. Our discussion was inconsequential."

"What did she ask?" Jay pressed.

"It had to do with a source she wanted to quote. She wondered about the legitimacy of the publication. It was an article in a pop science journal."

"Pop science?"

"The internet has brought about a plethora of information, but it's also generated countless quote-unquote online journals. Most are—what is it?—clickbait. Not run by reputable scientists or researchers. You've no doubt seen a number of these articles. Lately, they drop hot topic words like 'narcissists' or 'sociopaths' to target people. The one she found was dubious at best, but I guided her to research the article's author. I'm not sure what she decided about using it, though. I left that up to her."

"Did she turn in the paper?"

He shook his head. "It was due today."

"Do you know if she had any problems with anyone in class? Or someone in the building?"

Dr. Browne scowled. "No, I can't say. I am not close to my pupils in that way."

"Dr. Browne, speaking of sociopaths, as a psychologist, did any of your students stand out as anti-social?"

"Chief, I don't practice psychology in my classes. Determining whether an individual is a sociopath requires a lengthy course of therapy."

"I understand, Doctor. I'm more curious about your gut. Did it tell you if you had someone in your class like that?"

"Most of my students aren't twenty-one yet. By most metrics, I'd consider almost all of them sociopaths."

"I see," Jay acknowledged. The doctor wasn't about to diagnose a student at random, but Jay hoped if one came to him, he might mention it.

He didn't, though.

"Thank you, sir," Jay said.

Browne gave an approving nod. "Anytime, Chief."

"I think that's all," Jay said. He signaled for Towns to give the professor a contact card. "If anything comes to mind, can you call Officer Towns?"

"Of course," Browne replied as if that was a given.

Stone escorted them out of the office and to another building, where they found Susan Hardy grading papers.

"It's horrible," Hardy stated after they introduced themselves. "Jamie was such an outstanding student. So kind. How can I assist?"

"We're trying to find the connection to Jamie's killer," Towns said, having taken the lead again.

"I'm not sure how I can help," Hardy replied.

"It might be one of those things you don't realize is important."

"Then I'll do what I can," the education professor said.

"Did Jamie have any problems in your class?" Towns asked.

"Not that I was aware. She was at the top of the class."

"What about conflicts with other students?"

Hardy shook her head. "Nothing that I knew about."

"No conflicts?"

"Again, not that I'm aware of," Hardy repeated. "We do have a lot of group projects in this class, so it can be ripe with issues. Jamie never came to me with any, and no other student did about her, either."

"Could we get the names in her group?" Towns asked.

"You don't believe one of them could do this?" Hardy questioned. "These are almost all young women. The news made it sound more—uh, I don't know—sinister."

"No, we don't think that," Towns replied. "However, we have to acknowledge that anything could have happened. It's possible that Jamie confided in one of her classmates if something was going wrong."

Hardy just shook her head in disbelief. "I can't believe it. She just started her student teaching last week. She was doing great despite everything."

"Despite what?" Jay interjected.

"Oh, it was nothing. Finding student teaching spots has gotten difficult. Not enough openings."

"But Jamie found one?" Towns asked.

"Yes, though it's quite a drive. She didn't care, though," Hardy explained. "Luckily, she only had to drive to Slidell twice a week."

"Wait," Towns said. "Her student teaching was in Slidell?"

"Yeah, the professor answered. "We had to finagle to get her approved to do her teaching in Louisiana, but once we did, she started there. Shame, all that work for nothing."

Towns turned to look at Jay with an obvious question in her eyes.

23

———

"Is it a coincidence?" Towns wondered in Jay's office. "She gets a teaching job in Slidell where someone killed her boyfriend?"

"I'm not a big fan of coincidences," Jay confessed. He leaned forward in his new chair, the one the mayor sent over. "They happen, though."

"What's the play?" she asked.

Jay considered the options. They had the name of the elementary school where Jamie had been working. He considered calling Warren, but that left it up to the Slidell detective to get the information Jay needed. He didn't want to disparage the man, having never met him, but he preferred he and Towns go visit the school. Preferably without warning the teachers. If that was the connection, he wanted surprise to be on their side. Their arrival might generate enough fear, causing someone to split. It happened on TV. Why not in real life?

"Fancy a drive to Louisiana?" he asked Towns.

"Now?"

"We'd be back by five," he promised.

"Yeah, let's go," she replied, enthusiasm filling her eyes. Jay appreciated the vigor with which she had tackled this investigation. He considered how she might do as a full-time detective. But did the department need that right now? He filed the question away for the moment. After they got through Jamie Rene's case, he would focus on rebuilding the department.

His phone rang, and Jay picked it up. "Delp."

"Chief, this is Jennifer. I have a lady on the line who would like to speak to you."

"What is it about?"

"Her daughter didn't come home this morning. She's worried that something happened to her."

Jay sighed. "Okay, why don't you put her through?"

"Yes, sir."

Jay lifted his eyes to Towns and raised a finger, signaling her to wait. The speaker clicked as the line transferred to Jay's office.

"Chief Delp," he announced himself.

"Chief, this is Amanda Haywood," the woman on the other end of the line said, sounding distraught. "My daughter hasn't come home yet. She's not answering her phone, either. I'm scared this monster got her."

"Ms. Haywood, let's take a breath," he advised. The mother held her silence for a second, but Jay heard the minute gasps as she attempted to control her crying.

"What's your daughter's name?" he asked in a flat tone.

"Angel Haywood."

"Okay," Jay acknowledged. "When did you last see Angel?"

"She left for a run this morning. I thought she'd be home when I came back from church."

"Is Angel a jogger?"

"Yes, sir. She got a track scholarship to Southern Miss."

"Good for her," Jay said. He'd taken similar calls during his career. Most of the time, the panicked parent overreacted, and the kids turned up later. Especially the ones who were adults. However, Jay never assumed that was the case. He handled each call like something was truly wrong, though his job grew more difficult if the person on the phone remained too worked up to communicate the details. Keeping a loved one calm required a great deal of skill. Fortunately, Jay had been blessed with his mother's mild-mannered temperament.

"Ms. Haywood, this is probably nothing," he assured her. "It's only been a few hours. You said you were at church?"

"Yes, today is our Wednesday morning Bible study. We are reading through Esther."

"Is it possible she came back from her jog and left?"

"Her car is still here," Ms. Haywood explained.

"What about with a friend?"

"Her running shoes aren't here."

"Could she be wearing them?" Jay asked, though he already knew the answer.

"Of course not," Ms. Haywood declared. "She only wears them to run in. And her clothes aren't here, either. They would be in the laundry."

Jay glanced at Towns. He scrawled the name "Angel Haywood" on a notepad before turning it to show Towns.

"What can you tell me about Angel?" he asked.

"She's twenty-six, 5'5", and 104 pounds."

Jay jotted down that data. "What is your address, Ms. Haywood?"

She gave it, and Jay wrote that down.

"Ms. Haywood, if you will give me a few minutes, I will come by with an officer to take a statement. However, let me put this information out there in case anyone comes across her."

"Thank you, Chief," Ms. Haywood replied before Jay disconnected.

"Shannon, why don't you get Rick and go to Slidell? Start with the staff and students, but don't rule out parents, either. We want to find out if anyone has ties to the house where they found Clay."

"What about this new girl?" Towns asked.

Jay shrugged. "Right now, it might only be a distraction. She may turn up and just wanted an afternoon away from her mother."

"You could send someone else," Towns suggested. "One of the black-and-whites?"

Jay shook his head. "We're short-staffed. Besides, she called me. I should take the opportunity to make brownie points with the citizens."

Towns nodded. "I'll call you if we get something worthwhile."

When Towns left, Jay headed for the stairs. The drive from the police station to the Haywood residence only took ten minutes. Ms. Haywood lived in a modest residence built in the early '70s. Hundreds of flowers sprouted along her front walk and sidewalk. Verdant shrubs with a few withering azalea blooms enshrined the red-bricked house.

Ms. Haywood spent a lot of time or money on maintaining this yard. Jay assumed it was the former. Most people in this neighborhood weren't spending a fortune on a landscape company. Ms. Haywood, or someone in the home, had a green thumb and a passion for using it.

He rang the bell. The classic Westminster chime echoed from inside the home. A second later, the deadbolt clicked, and the door swung open. An African-American female in her forties stared at him. She was dark-skinned with short hair. Her red-rimmed cat's-eye glasses matched her bright lipstick.

"Ms. Haywood?" he inquired.

"Are you the new chief?" she asked.

"Yes, ma'am," he replied. "Can I come in?"

The woman nodded. Jay considered her quite attractive, and the little white cotton dress she wore gave a simple but pretty look. She had been to church, though. Jay's mother hadn't done much with the congregation, but if she had, hell would have frozen over before she showed up in anything less than what Ms. Haywood wore today. This was the South, and proper was proper, after all. As those words flowed through his head, he recalled his mother using that exact phrase about something Sandra wore one day. He couldn't remember his sister's infraction, but he could still see his mom standing at the kitchen door, spouting off, "Proper is proper" to Sandra.

Inside, the Haywood residence was well-maintained if not modernly decorated. Wood paneling in the den matched the time period when the house was built. Neither the Haywoods nor any other residents had remodeled the dated decor. However, Ms. Haywood kept a clean, simply furnished home. Family pictures adorned the walls, shelves, and any available space. Jay circled the room, taking in every image he could.

The Haywoods seemed to comprise a Mr. Haywood, a man a few years older than Ms. Haywood; Ms. Haywood, put together like a proper Southern woman in each picture; a younger girl, presumably Angel; and two identical twin boys in their teens. More pictures showed Angel sprinting down a track and another of her holding a trophy. Images of the twins playing basketball for Ocean Springs

High School filled an entire shelf, book-ending several trophies.

"Can I get you something to drink?" Ms. Haywood asked.

"No, ma'am," Jay answered. "Have you heard anything from Angel yet?"

She shook her head. "Not at all."

"Okay, I'm going to be blunt first. Understand?"

Ms. Haywood nodded.

"Normally, Angel hasn't been missing long enough to worry about filing a police report. Most of the time, it isn't something serious. She might have dropped her phone and broken it. Or a friend picked her up."

Ms. Haywood shook her head. "Angel would have called," she insisted.

"I understand," Jay continued. "I'm taking it very seriously. When did you last see Angel?"

"She left about eight. I had to be at the church by half-past nine."

"What church do you go to?"

"Second Baptist," she said, but Jay did not know where that might be. He didn't think asking would render the confidence he hoped to exude for the mother.

"And what time did you get home?"

"One o'clock."

Jay nodded as he listened. "How long does she normally run?"

"An hour. Sometimes two," Ms. Haywood clarified. "She's never been gone this long, though."

"Have you called any of her friends?"

Ms. Haywood looked down. "I don't know many of her friends now. Tried Kira, but she said she hadn't talked with Angel in a few months."

"Kira who?"

"Walls. She and Angel grew up together. Ran track in high school. Kira's living over in Biloxi and works at the hospital. She's a nurse, you know?"

"I did not," Jay admitted.

Ms. Haywood motioned at Jay with a wave of her hand. If she'd said, "Pshaw," the gesture would have made sense.

"Can you get me her number?" he suggested. "What about your husband or sons?"

"My husband divorced me and is living in Pascagoula with his new skank wife. The boys are with him this week."

"Have you called him, though?"

She shook her head.

Jay pursed his lips. "Why don't we do that first?" he advised. "It could be as easy as she paid him a visit."

"She hates him," Ms. Haywood pointed out.

"I understand, but let's check." He motioned for the cell phone lying on the coffee table.

Ms. Haywood picked up the device and dialed a number. "Al, it's Amanda. Have you talked to Angel?"

There was a pause.

"No, I understand that. But she went out running this morning and hasn't come back."

Pause.

"I know, Al. What about the boys? Have they talked to her?"

Pause.

"Well, ask them once they're back from school."

A longer pause.

"I will, Al. I will."

She hung up, shaking her head. "He hasn't spoken to her in months, but he said he'd ask the boys when they get home."

"Do you have a picture of her?"

Ms. Haywood nodded, rose to her feet, and disappeared into the other room. She came back with a framed image of the same young woman Jay saw in the family photo. Angel was pretty, black, and close to Jamie's age. It didn't mean this was another abduction, but something in Jay triggered as he inspected the photo.

"What route did she jog?" he asked.

"She had several. Usually, she'd run toward downtown and past the beach before crossing the bridge and coming back. I just don't know for sure."

"Did she use a Fitbit or Apple Watch to track her running?"

Ms. Haywood gave a nod. "She has the Apple Watch. I think she uses an app on her phone to map the route."

"If you can get me the carrier information, I can try to search for her phone. Is she on your plan?"

She nodded.

"I'll likely need your information to get the carrier to cooperate," he explained.

"Of course," she agreed.

"I don't have a card yet, but if you call the switchboard again, I'll tell them to send you right to me."

"Chief, I'm scared." Tears welled up in her eyes.

"Stay calm," he assured her. "We have nothing suggesting anything bad happened yet. Angel might show up for dinner unscathed. In which case, call me, and we can celebrate together."

Ms. Haywood smiled slightly, but she looked anything but soothed.

24

———

"I thought we were going to watch Perry Mason," Terry Delp complained as Jay drove down the street.

His father had been griping since he heard they were heading to Sam and Danielle's for dinner. It disrupted his routine, something Caroline suggested would be both frustrating and stimulating for his father. So far, Jay only found it frustrating.

"Sam invited us over, remember?" Jay reminded his father.

"Why didn't he just come over to our house?" Terry asked. "Your mom said she was making meatloaf."

"No, Dad. That was Danielle last night. She promised you she would use Mom's recipe and cook the meatloaf."

"I don't want her to make it," Terry whined. "Your mother makes it best."

In the few days Jay had spent with his ailing father, he was already learning about the different moods. Like Sam and Danielle had explained, sometimes he appeared coherent, cranky, and in the present. Other times, he was just as lucid but living thirty years in the past. But then there were more perplexing occasions when Jay decided his father was stuck between two eras. He seemed aware that his wife wasn't with them, but he didn't acknowledge it.

"Danielle is making it tonight, Dad. So be nice about it."

"I like Danielle," he announced, his tone shifting and sounding almost childlike. "She doesn't boss me around."

Jay assumed there was an unspoken "unlike you boys."

"Good," Jay said. "I like Danielle, too. She has to put up with Sam and you, so we need to be extra polite to her. Otherwise, she won't want to take care of you."

Terry grumbled under his breath.

Jay pulled the Jeep into the driveway at Sam's two-story turquoise beach house overlooking the sand. The path to Sam's house was behind the house and only accessible from the side streets. While he had a spectacular view from his veranda of the sound and Front Beach Drive, there was no way to get to the house from the busy avenue.

"Come on, Dad," Jay urged as he turned off the Jeep.

Terry ran his hand over his graying mop. "Why'd you have to leave the top down? I gotta comb my hair now."

"No, you don't," Jay corrected him. "Besides, it's a perfect afternoon for letting the wind blow your hair."

That afternoon had also been a distraction for Jay after leaving the Haywood house. He drove across the highway, following the sidewalk where he imagined Angel Haywood had jogged earlier. Once he was on the opposite side of the main road, there were far too many side streets throughout the historic section to be sure which way Angel ran. He cruised along the streets, nonetheless, feeling a glimmer of hope that he'd pass a young woman jogging back from the seaside. It had, after all, been a beautiful afternoon, just like he told his father. It would have been nice if Angel had stopped at the beach to get some sun and let the day slip away from her.

While that was his desire, he had a different urging in the pit of his belly. Whether Angel had fallen victim to Jamie's murderer, he had no proof. Despite that, he sensed something had run afoul.

Shannon and Rick called him as they were heading back from Slidell. From the initial report, they hadn't come up with anything workable, but he told them he would sit with them first thing in the morning to dissect what they had discovered.

Worried that Angel was going to show up as another victim, Jay wanted to at least find a lead. So far, Jamie's whereabouts after work on Friday remained a mystery. Tomorrow, he could send Towns to scour the neighborhood where Clay lived. Possibly a doorbell camera had caught Jamie arriving at his house late Friday or early Saturday.

Doorbell cameras?

As Jay walked up the steps to Sam's front door, he noticed his brother had one on his porch. Jay turned and looked at the other houses on the street. How many of them had them, too? Perhaps a door-to-door search would turn up a couple of cameras with footage of Angel running past.

Who are you going to send on that wild goose chase? He was understaffed, and if he pulled Towns or Lawson to do it, he'd hurt Jamie's investigation. Of course, they could be the same case. Or, he reminded himself, they could be unrelated.

"Uncle Jay! Grandpa!" Julia Delp, Sam and Danielle's eleven-year-old daughter, answered the door.

"Julia, you've grown," Jay admired.

"Of course she's grown," Terry said happily. "Come give Grandpa a hug, sweetie."

Jay eyed his dad, who seemed at the moment to be in the moment. Julia wrapped her arms around her grandfather, and Jay noticed the old man's face softening. When she let go of Terry, he kissed her forehead. For a split second, Jay recalled his father doing something similar with a young Sandra Delp. He also saw how Terry's confusion toward Julia led him to think she was Sandra. Her facial features were close to his sister's. Had he not been looking at the photo album last night, he doubted he would have made that connection. For his father, who regularly time-traveled in his world, the resemblance was probably uncanny and unsettling.

Julia embraced Jay, who squeezed her once and ruffled her head as she pulled away. He wasn't sure what caused him to do it, but it struck him as something an uncle would do.

"Come in," Julia offered. "Daddy's in the den."

"Let's go, Dad," Jay urged his father, who stepped into the bright entry hall.

Danielle had decorated the home with the same style that matched the exterior. Even without considering the setting sun over the Mississippi Sound, it was obvious from the décor they were in a coastal house. Even the family photo, framed in a giant four-by-six-foot frame over the fireplace, showed Sam, Danielle, Julia, and Jenson all in white with their feet in the ankle-deep surf. Jay cocked his head as he studied the image. The beach wasn't in Ocean Springs. In fact, he bet it was down in Panama City or Pensacola. The sand was too white and the sea too clear to be here. Or anywhere on the Mississippi coast.

Jenson came through the room with AirPods in his ears. "'Sup, Grandpa!" he called to Terry, who grinned at his grandson. "Uncle Jay."

Jay reached out and grabbed the fourteen-year-old's hand. The boy shook it, but it lacked the confidence of an adult. He was in that in-between age when he wanted to embrace manhood but hadn't quite figured out how.

"Your mom says you're playing JV?" Jay asked.

"Yes. Not starting yet, but it's something," Jenson explained.

"Give it a few months. Even next year," Jay stated. "When things change, they change fast."

Jenson nodded, but only to be polite. At fourteen, Jay remembered, time already seemed to run like molasses. The boy had gotten that same crappy advice from every adult. Jay berated himself for being so trite with him. That wasn't the way to connect, and he knew that.

"Come on in here," Sam called from the den.

Jay followed Terry into the expansive sitting room. Vaulted ceilings and a wall of windows overlooking the sea made the space feel larger.

Sam rose from a leather recliner and came toward the other two Delps. He grabbed Jay and hugged him before turning to Terry and wrapping an arm around his father.

"Don't be mushy," Terry warned as he marched across the room to a matching recliner. "Can someone get your grandpa a drink?"

Jenson replied, "Whatcha want?"

"Jack and Coke," he answered.

"Only one," Sam cautioned, to which Terry growled something under his breath.

Jay responded by rolling his eyes so only Sam could see the expression. Jenson walked over to a nook in the corner where Sam had set up a bar with a handful of liquor bottles, a countertop ice maker, and a mini-refrigerator.

"You want anything, Uncle Jay?" Jenson inquired.

"I'll take the same," Jay answered.

"Might as well make it three," Sam added.

"How about four?" Jenson asked with some futile hope in his voice.

"In about seven years," Sam shot back.

"You know, by then, I may miss the chance to drink with my grandfather," the boy pined.

"That will suck, then," Sam responded with a smile. "Just prepare Grandpa's special now."

Jenson gave a knowing nod, and Jay gathered that some secret message had just passed between father and son. After a few minutes, Jenson brought over three drinks. Jay noticed him hand one to Terry with extra care.

"Cheers," Sam toasted, raising his glass in the air. Jay leaned forward and clinked glasses with his brother before tapping the bottom of the tumbler on the table and taking a drink.

"Why'd you do that?" Jenson asked.

"It's a tradition, although I think it transcends just the Corps. That's the toast to those who aren't with you anymore."

"Like guys that died in battle?" Jenson wondered.

"Or died in general," Jay corrected. "It's to anyone who went before us."

"That's nice," Julia remarked from the door.

Jay shrugged.

"Mama said it's time to eat, though," the girl added.

Jay pushed to his feet and stopped as his father chugged the cocktail in his hand. He didn't remark but motioned for his father to follow the kids into the dining room.

Dinner was meatloaf, and while it had been decades since Jay had eaten his mother's version, his recollection was that it had never been as good as this. He would share that with Danielle in private so as not to upset his father, who might consider that a disparagement of Louise Delp's cooking.

"Everyone's talking about the girl you found in the bay," Jenson said. "Is it a serial killer?"

"We only have one victim, so we aren't saying that at all," Jay clarified.

"Oh, I hope not. How scary would that be?" Danielle remarked.

"Are you going to catch the guy?" Jenson asked.

"We usually do," Jay told him. "Everyone messes up."

"I mean, a serial killer would be cool. Nothing interesting happens around here," Julia remarked.

Jay didn't respond. Instead, Danielle stepped in. "No, that would be scary. People shouldn't kill others, anyway. We don't want someone skulking about looking to kill girls. This poor thing was tortured, wasn't she?"

Jay's gaze shifted to Sam, but it was Terry who intervened. "They killed my Sandra," he muttered.

Jay and Sam locked eyes for a split second.

"Murdered her," Terry continued.

"Dad, Sandra drowned on accident," Sam explained.

"Wasn't no accident," Terry blurted, his excitement exaggerating his Mississippi twang. His face twisted, and clarity filled his pupils. "It was just tragic," he added.

"Maybe no more talk of murder," Danielle suggested. "Would anyone like some dessert? I made a blackberry cobbler."

Both kids responded with a resounding "yes."

"Jay? Dad?" she asked the other two.

"I'd love some," Jay replied, and Terry nodded. His father's countenance was wrinkled with some internal struggle. Was he still thinking about Sandra?

"What about me?" Sam demanded in a jovial tone.

"I know your answer," Danielle quipped. "You've never turned down dessert of any kind."

"I don't care for bread pudding," Sam pointed out.

"There's nothing wrong with being wrong sometimes," Danielle told him. "Julia, can you come help me? Everyone want ice cream?"

Again, a collective "yes" echoed in the dining room.

Terry pulled into himself, leaving Jay to wonder if this was a shift in his personal timeline or ordinary confusion. Or was his declaration that someone murdered his daughter weighing on the man?

After dessert, Jenson and Julia cleared the table while the adults moved into the den again. Sam prepared another round of cocktails, and this time, Jay eyed Sam as he fixed the drinks. He only splashed a bit of Jack Daniels into his father's tumbler. Enough for the man to taste the whiskey without causing too much intoxication.

Despite the smaller portion of alcohol, the late hour caught up with Terry. His eyes closed, and soon a soft purr of snoring came from their father.

"What was that about at dinner?" Jay asked Sam.

"He's never said that before. Talking about Sandra being murdered? I've never heard that."

Danielle shook her head. "Me either. He has talked about her a lot, but not like that."

Jay straightened in his seat. "Remember when I asked you both about someone named Dale?"

His brother and sister-in-law nodded. Jay produced the picture he'd found the night before with the caption "Dale." He handed the Polaroid to Sam.

"I found that in a photo album after Danielle left," he explained.

Sam studied the image. "I don't recognize him," he confessed before passing the picture to his wife, who just shook her head.

"They look friendly," Jay suggested. "That's how Dad treated me when he thought I was this Dale."

"When was this taken?" Sam wondered.

"I think it was the Memorial Day picnic before Sandra died."

"Someone should know him," Danielle remarked. "Have you asked Dad?"

Jay shook his head. "Not yet. I was worried it might trigger something."

"That could be exactly what you want, though," Danielle replied as she handed the Polaroid to Jay.

Taking it back, Jay tapped the edges of the picture against his palm as he stared at the face of the unknown Dale.

25

"We interviewed all the teachers and the custodial staff," Towns explained as she nibbled a donut, careful not to let the jelly filling drip out of it.

Rick Lawson had no such concern for the jelly or its final destination as he opened his mouth wide and shoved in half a raspberry-filled donut. He chomped down, sending an ooze of red goo out the side of the pastry. His index finger shot out, catching the excess jelly and scooping it into his stuffed mouth.

"We're cross-referencing names with Warren, but so far we've drawn a big goose egg," Lawson mumbled with a donut-filled mouth.

"Rick, chew your food," Towns admonished. "Were you raised in a barn?"

"Nope, in a shack out on the Biloxi River," he clarified as he swallowed his bite.

"Any news on Angel Haywood?" Jay asked.

Both Lawson and Towns shook their heads. Towns added, "I reached out this morning to Amanda Haywood. They still have no word."

"What about tracking her run?"

"I've got a call through to a tech at the phone company. He's working on it. Right now, he's been able to ping her off the same tower. It doesn't do us a bit of good because it covers the downtown area."

"We already knew she was there," Lawson moaned as he shoved the rest of the jelly donut past his lips.

"Disgusting," Towns commented.

"I've asked Jennifer to call people in the neighborhood," Jay said. "I'm hoping someone can review their doorbell footage or security cameras to find Angel as she ran by. Maybe we can piece her run together."

"You think it's connected?" Lawson inquired.

"Two women, roughly close in age, go missing within a week of each other. I don't care for the coincidence."

"Could be a copycat," Lawson advised. "Someone waiting until something like this happens. Gives them a good excuse to act on their impulses."

Jay had considered that. "Right now, in this room, we investigate this like it's the same case. However, until we have any confirmation that it is, we don't let it out. Panic about a serial killer is the last thing we need."

"What's the play?" Lawson wondered.

"We split up," Jay answered. "You two, go back to Danni Crews and Kyle Rose. Let's see if we can fill in any blanks. Look at drug usage but also any friends that we might have overlooked."

"Roger," Lawson said.

"What about you, Chief?" Towns asked.

"I'm going to talk with Clay's coworkers," Jay said when a knock at the door interrupted them.

All three turned to see Tim Lamb standing in the doorframe. "Hey, guys, just checking in."

Jay nodded. "Join us, Lamb," he replied. "How was your time off?"

Lamb shrugged. "Same old. Went fishing yesterday. Got some snapper if anyone wants some."

"Totally," Lawson interjected.

"I threw it in the freezer in the break room," he told Lawson. "Where you want me today, Chief?"

"Why don't you come with me?" Jay suggested. "I need to go to D'Iberville, and I don't care to drive."

"Sure thing," Lamb agreed. "You getting anywhere on the stiff from the other night?"

"That's what we're working on," Jay explained.

"Good."

"Get moving," Jay told Lawson and Towns. "Lamb, give me five minutes, and I'll be ready."

As Lawson and Towns exited, Rick snatched a chocolate donut from the box on Jay's desk. Lamb eyed the remaining donuts.

"Grab one," Jay told the man. "In fact, carry the rest out to the coffee pot for everyone."

"You got it, Chief."

Lamb disappeared, and Jay pulled the Polaroid of his father and the mysterious Dale. He had already tried checking the police records for anyone named Dale who matched that description. Unfortunately, this was Southern Mississippi, and Dales were a dime a dozen. Too many parents named their kids after Dale Earnhardt.

He could run the picture through a reverse image search, but those weren't great for current pictures. Even the FBI's facial recognition software would struggle against a face three decades old. And if Dale never had a record, that made it more difficult.

Instead, he typed Sandra Delp's name into the Ocean

Springs Police Department's database. A file popped up with an orange banner: "Located off site."

What the hell did that mean? He didn't have time to dig around. After they all came back, he'd get Towns to help him decipher what that meant.

Jay rose from behind the desk. Now he was using the one Sam sent over. So far, Jay had decided that Sam's chair was the most comfortable, but the mayor's had the most gadgets. The latter's electric seat warmer had potential this winter when the temperatures dipped below tolerable.

"Lamb, you ready?" he called as he crossed the bullpen.

"Aye, sir," Lamb announced in a pirate voice. He appeared near the elevators, pressing the button.

"Stairs," Jay advised as he approached. "It's only one flight."

"Whatever you say."

"How long you been with the department, Tim?" Jay asked as Lamb cruised out of the parking lot and west on Highway 90.

"Ten years next May," he answered.

"What did you do before this?"

"Spent a decade in the Air Force."

"Stationed here?"

Tim nodded. "Yeah. Met my ex-wife here. Had kids, so when I got out, I stayed."

"Where you from originally?"

"Virginia."

"Ex-wife, huh?"

"Pain in the wife," he joked.

"I have three myself," Jay commiserated.

"Yikes. The one's bad enough."

"All my marriages ended before we had any kids," Jay told him. "I'm not sure if that makes it easier or not."

"Definitely easier," Tim assured him. "No swapping weekends. No juggling schedules. No being bitched out because she thinks she knows how to raise your children better."

"But you get your family," Jay remarked.

Tim nodded. "There is that. Mine are the best, too."

"What do you have?"

"Two girls and a boy. Twelve, ten, and seven."

"Fun."

"Yeah, and the oldest currently hates her mother. So, guess what? That makes me the favorite."

Jay smiled. He often wondered what could have been if he'd had a family with one of his wives. It had always been something on the horizon until he realized he had missed the destination. Now all his exes had kids and somehow he was still alone.

The Chrysler dealership was right off I-10 in D'Iberville, and it opened at eight. It was nine now, and there were only a few customers milling around the lot. The service bay, though, had several cars lined up outside. Tim parked next to a maroon Sebring, and they entered the service entrance.

"Can I help you gentlemen?" asked an employee in a blueish-gray shirt with the Chrysler logo on one side and his name, "Gary," stitched into the other.

"Hi, Gary," Jay said. "Who is in charge here?"

Gary turned to point at a man behind the counter. "Lawrence is your guy."

"Thanks," Jay told him as he moved to the man Gary

singled out. "Lawrence?" Jay asked, despite the man's name being embroidered on his lapel.

"Can I help you?" Lawrence responded.

"Jay Delp. I'm the chief of police over in Ocean Springs. You might have spoken to one of my officers yesterday."

His face melted into a somber expression. "About Clay?"

Jay nodded. Tim stayed a foot behind the chief, allowing his boss to lead the interrogation. "Do you have time to chat?"

"Not sure what I can tell you more than I already did with Officer Towns."

"I'm hoping we can talk with a few of Clay's coworkers," Jay explained. "We're trying to figure out his last few hours."

"I mean, he worked Friday, but he wasn't on the schedule until Monday."

"Yeah, we understand," Jay acknowledged. "Is there anyone here he was close with?"

Lawrence considered it. "Clay worked a lot with Jimmy out back. Not sure how close they were, but I saw 'em having lunch a few times."

"Could I speak with him?"

Lawrence nodded slowly before saying, "Let me get him. Do you mind using my office, though?"

Jay pursed his lips.

"It's just that the topic isn't something we want spread around the waiting room with our customers," Lawrence elaborated.

"Of course," Jay agreed.

Lawrence pointed toward a small office no larger than the cubicles in the bullpen. The room had glass walls on all sides, offering only audible privacy. Jay and Lamb moved to the office behind Lawrence, who said, "You can sit there, and I'll send Jimmy in."

"Thank you for your help," Jay replied.

"I hope you catch whoever did this," Lawrence stated. "Clay was a good kid."

He left the two men alone in the room. Tim stood in the corner as Jay settled into the chair at the desk stacked with paperwork that ranged from invoices for parts to estimates for customers.

"What do you want me to do?" Lamb asked.

"Feel free to interject if you have a question," Jay told him. "Otherwise, just take notes for me."

"Okay," Lamb replied with a hint of trepidation in his throat. He removed a notepad from his pocket.

Lawrence returned with a black man in his twenties. Like the rest of the service crew, Jimmy's name displayed itself on his uniform.

"If you need anything, call me," Lawrence offered before leaving.

"He said you wanted to talk about Clay?" Jimmy asked.

"Please, have a seat," Jay told Jimmy. "What's your name?"

"James Turhill," he answered. "People call me Jimmy."

"Can I?" Jay questioned.

Jimmy gave a single nod.

"Jimmy, did you hear what happened to Clay Miller?"

"Yeah, sir. I can't believe it."

"What part?"

"Ain't none of it believable," Jimmy clarified. "Clay didn't do drugs. Why would he be over in Slidell, anyhow?"

"Do you know where he was supposed to be?" Jay questioned.

"He told me he and his girl were going to stay around the house. He planned on working on her car."

"What was wrong with it?"

"The car? He said it was the alternator. She'd broken a belt last week, and he fixed it. But he complained it was too small. Clay worried he'd torn up the alternator."

"Sounds annoying," Jay acknowledged, although he had so little mechanical ability, even an oil change sounded painful to him.

"Yeah, he griped about how much they cost for that Honda."

"What does an alternator run nowadays?" Jay asked, as if he had some measure of the costs of alternators over the years.

"Think he said it was $500."

Jay nodded. "That's just for the part?"

"Yep. He asked Lawrence about ordering one through here. Not sure if he did or not."

"Did you ever spend time with Clay outside of work?"

Jimmy shrugged. "Some. Mostly we'd hit the bar."

"Which one did you go to?"

"We didn't go all the time. But when we did, we went to Jackson's near the river."

"Where's that?"

Lamb interjected, "It's a fishing camp down by the bayou. Most of the clientele are locals and river rats."

"Yeah, it's cheap," Jimmy admitted. "They got two-dollar Busch."

"Listen, Jimmy," Jay began, "I want to ask you some things, but right now, our concern is finding who killed Clay and his girlfriend. We aren't looking to come after you."

Jimmy bit the corner of his lip. "Whatcha wanna know?"

"Did you ever see Clay use drugs?"

His head shook. "No, he didn't do any of that. Think he smoked some pot sometimes, but that was it."

"No crystal meth?"

Jimmy continued to shake his head. "No, sir. Clay never touched none of that. Certainly, his girl wasn't into it. He said she only smoked pot one time back in high school."

"You don't know anyone who wanted to hurt Clay or Jamie?"

"I didn't know Jamie all that well, but Clay was a great guy. Funny. Ever'body liked him."

Jay scrawled his office number on a scratch piece of paper and handed it to Jimmy. "If you hear anything that might help us find Clay's killer, call me."

"Will do, sir," Jimmy agreed. "Is there anything else?"

"Was Clay close to anyone else here?"

Jimmy shook his head. "He liked everyone, but the mechanics tend to stick to themselves."

"Did Clay want to become a mechanic?"

"Yes, sir. He was studying to get certified ASE," Jimmy explained. "He kept trying to talk me into taking the test with him."

"You weren't going to?"

Jimmy scrunched up his face. "I don't test so good."

"Thank you," Jay told Jimmy, who stood and left the office.

Lawrence slid past the door before it closed. "Did Jimmy help you?" he asked.

"He answered some questions we had," Jay commented.

"Is there anything else we can do to assist?" the supervisor asked, eagerly anticipating the police's departure.

"Jimmy mentioned Clay tried to order a part through you?"

"Yeah, he asked me last Thursday. An alternator, if I recall. But it was too much for him."

"No discount?" Jay wondered.

Lawrence answered, "The discount isn't bad, but even

with it, the part was over $400. Clay told me he had to wait until he got paid."

Jay nodded. "Thanks, Lawrence."

"Good luck, Chief Delp. We hate this happened to someone as nice as Clay."

"It sucks for anyone," Jay corrected the man.

26

____

"Crews and Rose are both adamant that Jamie and Clay didn't use drugs," Towns explained to Jay.

Lawson occupied the other high-back chair beside Towns while Lamb reclined in the desk chair Towns brought up.

"Not even in a celebratory manner?" Jay asked.

"Danni says no. She admitted to doing some coke and crystal herself—recreationally, of course—but she said Jamie wouldn't touch it."

"Did lend credence to her statement," Lawson said.

"Yeah," Jay agreed. "We heard the same thing from Clay's friend."

"Leaves us at square one," Towns conceded.

"At least we can rule out a bad drug deal," Jay reminded them.

"But we don't have anything else," Lawson retorted.

"There's that."

"What about this Haywood girl?" Lamb asked from the side of Jay's desk. "Have we confirmed someone grabbed her?"

"Jennifer located three people who discovered footage of her running past their houses yesterday morning," Jay said. "With any luck, we will find a few more and iron out the route she took."

"The tech guy said he could ping her watch's last location at the beach. Not far from your brother's house," Towns explained.

"We already know she ran that way," Jay noted. "Let's get a map up on the board. As we pinpoint sightings, we can draw out her path."

"You got it, Chief," Towns said.

"Do we have a police golf cart?" Jay asked.

"Yeah," Towns and Lawson replied in unison, but with a questioning look on their faces.

"Tim, would you take the cart through the neighborhood? Hit the three houses Jennifer found where Angel passed and the last location of the Apple Watch. Look for other cameras. Try to find out if anyone else filmed Angel."

"Isn't Jennifer calling around?" Tim asked.

"Yeah, but I've found that people are far more willing to help in person than over the phone."

"At least it's not raining," Towns said.

"No, just ninety-five degrees," Lamb complained.

"Wear some sunscreen," Lawson suggested.

Lamb rolled his eyes. He looked to Towns. "I'll call when I get there."

"Tim, if you spot anything suspicious, call me ASAP," Jay said.

"Roger," he said before leaving the office.

"What else?" Towns asked.

"You help put together the route. Rick, grab JD or Tomlinson—wait, I don't know his first name."

"Will," Lawson supplied.

"Thanks," Jay told him. "Go to Clay Miller's house. Check if the landlord will let us in. If not, search around as best you can."

"You got it, Chief," Lawson replied as he rose from the high-back leather chair.

"I'll get started on the route," Towns offered.

"Before you do, I need some help," Jay admitted. "I tried to access the records from my sister's death, and I keep getting this notification." He turned the monitor for her to see the banner that said: "Located off site."

"That means it was an older file that never got digitized," she explained to him. "Is that the right word, 'digitized?'"

"Where would the physical file be?"

"The old precinct in city hall," she told him. "The file room is on the second floor. Be warned—it's a mess."

"Great," Jay replied without enthusiasm.

"Plan to spend half a day finding what you want," she warned. "That's assuming the files are even there."

"Then it will wait," he decided.

"What are you looking for?"

"Last night, my dad blurted out that Sandra was murdered."

"Your sister?"

Jay nodded. "We'd always been told she drowned."

"You and Sam were young, though?"

"Teenagers," he said.

"It might not be uncommon for a parent to shade the truth about something like that to their kids," she considered. "I'm sure it was easier than the truth."

Jay shrugged. "Makes sense, but why keep up the pretense?"

"Your dad is in bad shape," she reminded him. "He may

be struggling with what was real and what was a fabrication."

"I'm trying to temper my curiosity with that, but it's still strange. Why carry the lie like this?"

"Didn't his world pretty much fall apart?" Shannon pointed out. "He lost his daughter. Then his wife. Maybe he struggled to face the truth, whatever it was."

Jay shrugged. "I'd be remiss if I didn't look into it, though."

"I understand," she agreed. "We can go over to city hall whenever you want."

His head shook. "No, I can do it on my own time. No point pulling my top investigator to dig into a thirty-year-old death."

"Your top investigator?" Towns repeated.

Jay smiled. "Don't let it go to your head."

"Just nice to be appreciated," she responded.

"Can I interrupt?" a familiar voice called from the open door.

Jay looked up to see Rebecca standing in his doorway. She leaned against the door jamb with a plastic bag looped over her right wrist. She wore a dress that declared she was a professional while still highlighting her legs and hips in a way that reminded everyone that she was an attractive woman.

"Becs?" Jay asked.

"Thought I'd bring you some lunch," she explained. "Hey there, Shannon."

"Hi, Becs," Towns greeted. "You look great."

"Oh, thank you."

"I'll get out of the way," Towns announced. "Great to see you, Becs."

Rebecca gave Towns a nod as the officer left Jay's office.

"Have a seat," Jay offered, and Rebecca rounded the leather high-back chair before settling into it. Her right leg crossed her left leg, offering Jay an ample view of her thigh.

"Hope you don't mind," she told him. "I was getting a po' boy from Fayard's and thought you might like one, too."

"What kind did you get?" Jay asked, eying the plastic bag.

"Roast beef," she answered. "Even got them to throw in some au jus."

"You trying to seduce me?"

"If I was doing that, you'd know," she promised.

"I'm not so sure," he countered. "I've always been aloof."

Rebecca laughed. "Tell me about it." She pulled out a long sandwich wrapped tightly in white butcher paper and handed one across the desk to Jay. Rebecca fished out a sealed plastic container of brown liquid, which she gave to Jay.

"Thank you," he said. "This is two meals you've bought me."

"I told you that you could return the favor."

Jay nodded as his ex-wife unrolled her own sandwich. Steam drifted up from the piles of sliced beef between the flaky white loaf of bread.

"How's the head cop doing?" she asked before dipping her bread into the au jus.

"I suppose he is good. I'm getting baptized with a fire hose, but at least I'm up against the worst of it right now."

"Meaning it can only get better from here?"

"That's the hope."

Rebecca put her sandwich down. "Is this weird?"

Jay lifted his eyes to her as he chewed a bite. "What do you mean?"

"Me just dropping in like this?" she explained. "Am I getting ahead of myself?"

"Wow, Becs, you don't beat around the bush."

She shrugged. "I'm not going to lie. When I saw you the other day at Tom's, I realized how much I regretted what happened with us."

Jay leaned closer.

"I'm not the same woman who divorced you," Rebecca told him. "Somehow, you don't seem the same while still seeming exactly the same. How does that work?"

He gestured vaguely with his hand since he had no words to answer with.

"I really enjoyed dinner the other night, and I didn't want to wait on you to ask me out again," she said.

"Was that a date?" he asked.

She smiled. "Very aloof."

"I warned you."

"It could have been," she said.

"Becs, I'm not sure what to say," he admitted. "It's been a crazy first week here."

"I know," she replied. "I'm not trying to pressure you. But I'm also not going anywhere anytime soon."

"That sounds like a threat," he joked.

"Not at all. But who else do you know in town?"

Jay considered that for a second. Outside of Sam and his family, Jay hadn't reconnected with anyone from high school. Over the last couple of decades, Jay lost track of all the people he considered friends from school. That was par for the course, he thought. At least for people in a bigger world.

"I'm not saying that I'm not interested," he replied. "In fact, the opposite. But Becs, it's been a long time for us, and I'm not sure."

"But that's not a no?"

"Uh," Jay stammered. "I guess not."

With a satisfied grin, Rebecca replied, "Good," and took a bite of her po' boy.

"This is an interesting turn of events," another voice said from the open office door.

Jay froze with his sandwich almost to his lips. His eyes met those of the woman's in the doorway.

"Two ex-wives in the room at the same time?" Katie Calkins noted. "What are the odds of that happening to a guy like you?"

"Katie? Wow," Jay muttered.

Rebecca turned to stare at Katie Calkins. "Katie," she said dryly.

"Cal said he had a nice chat with you," Katie said to Jay. "I thought I might swing by and see you as well. Guess it wasn't a unique thought. Wonder if we wait long enough, will number three show? What was her name?"

"Rachel," Jay offered.

"Oh, I didn't really care," Katie declared. "Did you, Rebecca?"

Rebecca didn't respond.

"What can I do for you, Katie?"

"Nothing, Jay. I truly did only come by to welcome you back. I was dropping something by Cal's office here and figured I'd say hi."

"It's nice to see you," Jay told her.

Katie's expression softened. "Look, I didn't mean to interrupt anything. You guys go on with your lunch."

"Thanks," Jay said. "Why don't you come by another time? We can catch up."

"That would be nice."

Rebecca's mouth turned up slightly. "You know, Katie,

we could all get together for dinner one night. You and your lawyer husband and me and Jay." The way she lumped her and Jay together prompted him to cast a glance her way.

"That would be lovely," Katie said. "I'll get Cal to schedule something."

"Perfect," Rebecca replied. "That would be nice."

Katie saluted with two fingers. "Great seeing you both," she announced before she turned to leave them alone.

"Bet you weren't ready for that," Rebecca remarked.

"Not in the least," he admitted.

"Jay Delp, the only man I know still loved by all his exes. I mean, I guess the other one still likes you, too."

Rachel? I haven't talked to her in years."

"She's married to that minister, isn't she?"

"Last I heard," Jay answered. "If all these women loved me so much, why'd they all leave me?"

"I can't speak for all of them, but I was stupid," she confessed.

Jay shook his head and took another bite of his po' boy. He found himself at a loss for words at the moment, and rather than dwell on the awkwardness, he stuffed his mouth with shaved roast beef and bread. That made it a lot easier to avoid talking.

Rebecca watched him closely as he did, and she smiled. Jay had to admit that he liked that smile. But then again, he always had.

27

"Two women at once?" Lawson asked, eyebrows raised.

"Two wives," Lamb corrected.

"Geez. The one I have is enough," Lawson said.

"You should have seen Rebecca," Towns quipped. "That girl wants to hump the chief so badly, you can smell it."

Jay, Lamb, and Lawson turned to gaze at Towns, who only shrugged. "A woman knows these things."

"She's a keeper," Lamb remarked.

"The chief knows that," Towns said. "They were married, remember?"

"Oh, I do," Lamb stated. "I wonder why my ex-wife isn't a smoke show and bringing me lunch."

"No wonder there, bud," Lawson answered. "Your ex can't stand you."

"Doesn't explain the smoke show biz," Lamb retorted.

"You don't know how to pick 'em," Lawson replied.

"As if you get to pick," Towns joked.

"If we can move past my private life, have you guys found anything worthwhile?" Jay asked wryly.

Lamb raised his hand. "I spoke with five homeowners whose cameras spotted Angel Haywood."

He rose to his feet and walked to the murder board, where Towns had hung an enlarged map of the downtown and historic area from Highway 90 to the sea. Lamb marked the additional houses he'd discovered.

"Jennifer also got one more," Towns added, joining Lamb at the board. She took the marker from him and applied a black dot to the new house on Angel's potential route. "With that, we have most of where she ran."

Shannon Towns traced a line between all the dots, following the streets. She stopped where Angel Haywood's Apple Watch last registered its location.

"Tim, you find anyone along Front Beach Drive who had a camera?" Jay asked.

The officer shook his head. "Negative, sir. I'll keep trying."

"What about the yacht club?" Jay pointed at the building at the north end of Front Beach Drive.

"Not yet, but I can check."

"If we presume that someone kidnapped Angel, the last known location of the watch is where he grabbed her or where her abductor tossed it. Either way, she was in the vicinity."

"Probably her phone, too," Towns amended.

"Yes, that, too," Jay agreed.

"Could we search the area?" Lamb asked.

"Not sure how effective it would be," Jay admitted. "If he threw the watch into the sea, we'll never find it."

"Someone will eventually," Towns told him. "Beachcombers hit at low tide, searching for lost stuff."

"By then, it might be too late," Jay said. "It's a lot of manpower for little effort. Better if we focus on what information we have. We should treat it like that's the point of abduction and search for evidence from there."

"Such as?" Lamb asked.

"If we narrow the window down, we can look for all cars in the area. Pull any traffic cams, visit all the businesses, and track down some footage of this guy leaving the historic district."

"If that isn't a needle in a haystack," Lamb moaned.

"I get it, Tim," Jay sympathized. "This is a long shot. However, there's a girl out there now. If we don't find her before it's too late, we'll end up fishing her out of the bay, too."

Lamb nodded, looking contrite. "Sorry, boss."

"No need to apologize," Jay scolded. "We're a team, and our goal is to bring Angel Haywood home."

"Yes, sir," Lamb acknowledged. "I'm on it."

"Rick, can you help Tim with this?" Jay suggested. "At the moment, we seem to be hitting a wall with Jamie's case. Unless we uncover something new, we don't have a lot to work with."

"You got it, Chief," Lawson responded with a cheery voice.

The two men left Towns and Jay alone.

"What do we do?" Towns asked the chief. "I'm at a loss."

"I'm going over to city hall," he told her. "We still need to find Jamie and Clay's cars."

"If Clay was working on Jamie's, could it be in a garage somewhere?"

Jay leaned forward in his chair. "That might make sense. Like one of those self-storage places?"

Towns nodded. "My ex used to work on his motorcycles in that storage unit heading out of town. Why not?"

The phone on the desk rang, and Jay lifted the receiver. "Delp."

"Chief Delp, this is Marcus Taylor again."

"Marcus, how can I help you?"

"Chief, we're doing a follow-up on the Jamie Rene story," Taylor declared.

While Jay hadn't released Jamie's name, it hadn't taken the media long to find it.

"We have nothing to say," Jay stated.

"Could you corroborate that your department is now looking into another missing woman?" Taylor inquired.

Jay's head popped up. "What missing woman?"

"Come on, Chief. Do we have to play games? Angel Haywood has been missing since yesterday morning."

"Marcus, you also realize that it's difficult to declare someone missing for only twenty-four hours. She's an adult who might just as easily have jumped on a bus."

"Her mother thinks otherwise," Taylor countered. "What do you say?"

"No comment," Jay replied before hanging up.

"How did it get out?" Towns wondered when Jay replaced the receiver.

"My guess is Ms. Haywood pulled out all the stops to find her daughter."

"But does she think our killer took Angel?"

"It's not an enormous leap," Jay pointed out. "After all, we came to the same conclusion."

"That's going to add some pressure."

Jay nodded. He expected the mayor to be back in his office before too long. He figured that because he'd questioned Trip, Franklin would avoid confronting him for a while. However, if the tables turned again with another victim, it would give the mayor plenty of ammo to come skulking by.

"Let's think about your idea," he proposed, shifting gears to their earlier discussion.

"What do you mean?"

"The storage unit. Start calling around. We need to see if Clay Miller rented one. Or Jamie. In lieu of that, ask if they have a Honda CRV or—what was Clay's car?"

Towns pointed at the whiteboard. "A Mitsubishi Mirage."

Jay pursed his lips. "Right. I wasn't paying attention."

"Did the women throw you off?" Towns asked bluntly.

Jay reclined in his seat and folded his arms.

"Too personal?" Towns asked.

The chief shook his head. "No, just confounding."

"Do you like Rebecca?" she pried.

"I've always loved her," he answered. "But I'm just not sure."

"What's the worst that could happen?"

"I fall in love, marry her, and we get divorced again."

"That's a bit pessimistic."

"I have been married three times," he reminded her. "It seems realistic to me."

"Sign a prenup, then."

"I have nothing."

"Then think about what's the best thing that could happen, Chief."

Before he could respond, she rose to her feet and headed out the door.

"Towns," he called after her.

"Yeah, Chief," she answered, stopping in the doorway.

"I'm going over to city hall," he said.

"Good luck," she replied, rolling her eyes.

Jay watched her leave. She wasn't much better than the rest of the women in his life. There was a mystery that lingered under the surface with Shannon, and Jay suspected it was connected to his brother.

Tomlinson appeared at his door. "Chief, you got a second?"

"Will, yeah, come in," he told the officer.

"I wanted to talk to you about something."

"Grab a seat," Jay offered.

"Mind if I close the door?" Tomlinson queried, his voice vibrating with nerves.

"Sure," Jay agreed, eying his officer as the man shut the office door. "What can I help you with?" he asked when Tomlinson took his seat.

"I heard a disturbing thing last night," he said. His neck swiveled from side to side as he verified they weren't being watched.

"What is it?"

"I was down at County Line," he told him.

Jay shook his head. "Forgive me, I'm still getting my bearings. Where were you?"

"County Line Saloon. It's over near Biloxi on Race Track Road. Just a little roadhouse bar."

Jay nodded.

"Couple of guys came up to me," Tomlinson explained. "They were asking a lot of questions about the new chief."

"Go on," Jay urged.

"They didn't say anything unusual," Tomlinson clarified. "At least, not at first. And I figured they were curious about the girl's murder. Of course, everyone is talking about it."

Jay nodded but let Tomlinson talk.

"I wouldn't share any details, of course," he stated. "But they were more interested in you. One of them asked the other something—they didn't realize I could overhear them. He said, 'Will this one play ball?'"

"What did the other guy say?" Jay asked.

"He said it was his job to make sure you did."

"Who were these guys?"

"I only recognized one, boss. Tommy Calhoun."

"Is he the one who's supposed to make me 'play ball?'"

Tomlinson shook his head. "No, that one I didn't know."

"What can you tell me about Calhoun?"

"He's a good ole boy. But he's been in trouble for some stuff. He runs meth—supposedly—but we've never arrested him. I know he's dealing some, though. Someone said he's running a few girls, too."

"In our city?"

"Not that I know of," Tomlinson answered. "I'm sure there's some, but mostly he's over in Biloxi."

"Thanks, Will," Jay acknowledged. "I'll keep an eye out."

"I just didn't want anything to happen," he said.

"How long you been with the department, Will?"

"Two years," Tomlinson replied.

"You enjoy it?"

He shrugged. "Most of the time, yeah."

"You ever see anyone else like Calhoun and his buddy hanging around here?"

"You mean lately?" Tomlinson questioned.

"When Ward was chief, but yes, anyone since Ward quit?"

He shook his head. A grimace crossed his face at the idea he might be disloyal to his previous boss.

"If you do, tell me about it," Jay said.

"Yes, sir."

"Do you need anything else?"

"No, sir."

"Okay, thanks for bringing it to me," he told his officer again.

Tomlinson got up and left, leaving the door open and Jay behind his desk. The new chief considered Tommy Calhoun and his mysterious friend. If he searched Calhoun in the database, would he find connections to the Dixie Mob? It struck Jay as an even money bet.

28

"Afternoon, Chief," a woman greeted as Jay entered the city's human resources office.

"Alicia, right?" he asked.

The human resource manager flashed a coy smile. "That's me."

"I hear you're the woman to speak to about hiring more officers."

Her sultry grin lingered. "I'm the girl you talk to about anything you need."

Jay smiled back. "I need bodies."

"Don't we all?" she remarked. "I assume officers?"

"Yes, but a detective or two might not be bad."

"Have you checked your budget?"

He hadn't. In the days he had been in the office, he'd only been running around after a serial killer. Budgets, forecasts, and profit-and-loss statements seemed trivial compared to Jamie Rene's life.

"Not yet," he admitted. "I still need officers, though."

"Shame you lost so many before you got here."

"Yep, but I heard most of them were trouble."

"Oh, really?" she asked, a pitch of surprise in her tone. "No one brought any complaints to my office."

Jay didn't mention that was likely because either the Dixie Mob or Chief Ward handled any grievances. One didn't sell services to organized crime and advertise that fact to human resources. At least, not generally.

He shrugged. "Look, that was before my time."

She nodded as if she understood. "What would you like, then?"

"Let's start with ten officers. We'll see what kind of applicants we get."

"Should be a lot," Alicia remarked.

"Good, but I want the right ones," Jay explained. "I'd rather be short-staffed than have hot-headed cops causing problems."

"Understandable," Alicia agreed. "I'll post the job based on what we did last. Is that okay?"

"Perfect," he said, because he wasn't sure what other criteria to use.

"Glad to help," she told him as he left the office.

While he was in city hall, he searched for the file room. The space wasn't much more than twice the size of Jay's office, but it had dim fluorescent lighting. He stepped inside and sucked in a dusty breath of air. Towns had been correct. A tornado could have hit that storage space and left it less disorganized. Containers piled on the floor with numbers and letters on each one.

He flipped through a box marked "Da-De" in black handwritten print. He pulled the cardboard lid off and scanned through the yellow folders. The tabs started with "Inez" and ended with "James." Even those weren't in a specific order. He spent ten minutes sorting all the files alphabetically. When he was done, he marched out of the file room and found the nearest desk where he stole a Sharpie. After he returned, he scratched through the "Da-De" and wrote "In-Ja." It wasn't exact, but at least he considered the update an improvement. Now that left only a few hundred more boxes to wade through.

No chance of finding his sister's file in here today. This was going to be a multi-day exercise, and already he realized his time would be more productively spent doing anything else. In fact, all this visit did was show Jay where to go to stash a file. It would take forever for someone to search through this collection of manila folders.

Jay stopped, still holding a folder marked "Delaney" that he'd pulled from the last box. The idea dawned on him that this was the perfect place to hide a manila folder. Similar to hiding a couple of cars on a car lot.

He dropped the folder onto the top of the cardboard lid and charged out of the room. He was outside and in his Jeep before he realized it. An idea now wriggled in his brain. A long shot. But it was something.

The drive to the Chrysler dealership took twenty-five minutes. It should have taken less than twenty, but Jay missed a turn.

"You're back?" Lawrence asked when Jay came into the service area.

"Yes, sorry to barge back in. I have a question."

"Go ahead."

"If someone parked a car on this lot, how long before anyone would notice it?"

Lawrence cocked his head as he considered the query. "I don't know. Not long."

"Why?"

"We move vehicles around here daily. Weekly at the minimum. Sales guys are adjusting the lot, not to mention test drives and sales. Those cars rotate out regularly. Besides, if it's not a new Chrysler, it would stand out."

"Even in the service area?"

"Not as much," Lawrence conceded. "But we still shift the cars constantly. Nothing stays in the bays overnight, so even a big job gets moved out. If someone just left a car in the service lot, one of my guys would complain when it blocked them in."

"Would it have to block them in?" Jay wondered.

Lawrence nodded. "Yeah, pretty much."

"Do you care if I walk the lot?" he asked. "Just to satisfy my mind."

The service manager shrugged. "Be my guest. We want to help however we can. Are you looking for Clay's car?"

"And Jamie's."

Lawrence shook his head in dismay. "Still heart-wrenching."

Jay nodded as he stepped into the August heat. Over the next hour, Jay walked up and down every aisle in the lot. He turned away three salespeople. Despite the sweat pouring from his forehead and drenching his shirt, he ended his walk empty-handed.

It was a shot in the dark. Perhaps Shannon was on the right track with the storage units. But how many of those were along the coast of Mississippi? It was still a daunting task.

As he walked back to the Jeep, he saw Jimmy watching him from beside the dumpster. The kid sat on a stack of six pallets. Jimmy took a drag from a cigarette as Jay detoured toward the young man.

"Jimmy, how ya doing?"

"What are you looking for?" he inquired.

"Clay's car," he explained. "Or Jamie's. A Honda CRV."

"Why would they be here?" he asked. The question itself didn't mean much, but his tone had a note of condescension.

"They have to be somewhere," Jay remarked.

Jimmy shook his head. "You think they might go unnoticed here with all these cars?"

Jay nodded. "It occurred to me."

"Like hiding a tree in a forest?"

"Exactly," Jay declared.

"Too many folks here," Jimmy pointed out. "Someone would notice. You'd need a lot where no one comes through."

"Like customers?"

Jimmy curled his lips. "No, man. Customers don't know nothing. It's the employees. The guys around here talk when the newest minivan arrives. Car salesmen are the most bored people in the world."

"Oh?"

"Yeah, most of the time, they got nothing to do. When a customer shows up, they work and usually make a nice commission. The rest of the day, they're watching Netflix on their phones."

"You're probably correct," Jay conceded, kicking himself for wasting his afternoon.

"You need a repo lot or something," Jimmy recommended.

Jay nodded. "You might be right."

"Sometimes," was all Jimmy said as Jay left him to suck down the second half of his cigarette.

When he got in his Jeep, Jay called the precinct and asked Jennifer to connect him to Towns.

"What if the cars were in a parking lot?" Jay proposed. "Maybe airport parking."

"Too many cameras," Towns countered.

"You know how CCTV works, though," Jay considered. "Most people don't bother with manned security watching the monitors. Too expensive. They only go review the footage if there's a problem."

"Right," Towns agreed. "If there's no issue, no one reviews the video. Too much of it."

"It would be easy to drive it up, pay the fee, and leave it."

"He would have two cars, though," Towns reminded him.

Jay leaned his head back against the seat. With the top down on the Jeep, the inside hadn't gotten hot like most cars on an August afternoon down south, but it still heated the fabric until it was sizzling to the touch. Jay ignored the heat as his scalp pressed against the headrest.

Two cars. But one wasn't running. Or, at least, it wasn't running well. Jamie's boss said Clay had jumped off Jamie's battery earlier in the week. Jimmy told them it needed an alternator. What if Jamie and Clay had taken it somewhere to be worked on?

Jay straightened in his seat. Of course, if a person took a car to the shop, they always required a ride home. That could be why there were two cars missing.

"Chief, you with me?" Towns asked through the phone.

"Yes, hang on," he said. "I'm thinking." He paused for a moment. "A garage or service station?"

"What about them?"

"If Jamie took her CRV to a mechanic, she'd need a ride home."

"Yeah," Towns replied with uncertainty.

"Stay with me, Shannon. She would likely get her boyfriend to pick her up, right?"

"But wasn't he going to fix it for her?" Towns wondered. "Why pay someone else to do it?"

"I'm not sure yet," Jay admitted.

"You know I could throw a rock outside the city and hit a hometown mechanic with a hundred-parts vehicles littered around his property."

"That's still a needle in a haystack," Jay stated. "How do we even go about searching for that?"

"Got me," Towns confessed. "If it were me, I'd strip those cars down until they were unrecognizable."

Jay considered that. "It would take too long. A crew could do it in a day, but we have to assume this is a lone individual."

"So, the cars are still wherever they were abandoned. We presume they are mostly intact."

"Fair assumption," Jay agreed.

"Doesn't help us at all," Towns groaned.

"Nope. Let me think on it," Jay said. "I'll be back in a bit."

"Okay, I'll hold down the fort for you," she replied. "But hurry, you have a message to call the mayor."

"Dang, guess my reprieve is up," Jay commented as he hung up.

He got out of the Wrangler and walked into the service area. Jimmy was cleaning the partition around Lawrence's office.

"Jimmy, one more quick question," Jay called.

The young man stopped wiping down the glass and turned.

"If Jamie's car had to be fixed, where might Clay take it?"

Jimmy furrowed his brow. "To his house. Can't imagine Clay'd spend the money to take it anywhere else."

"And he couldn't afford the part, right?"

"That's what he said," Jimmy confirmed.

"There's nowhere to get some cheap work?"

"Sure, but Clay would do it himself. He was good at that."

"What would you have done in his position?"

"Me? I'd've hit up the scrapyard for a used alternator. Prolly cost me fifty bucks."

Jay cocked his head to the side. "Scrapyard? Which one?"

Jimmy shrugged. "Used to go to one up near Latimer, but I think they closed up. There are a bunch around here."

"Clay ever talk about going to one in particular?"

"Not that I recall."

Gary, the mechanic Jay met when he came in yesterday, passed by. Jimmy flagged him down. "Gary, you know a good scrapyard to get an alternator?"

Gary nodded. "Try Kimmell's over near D'Iberville. There's a few."

"Any near Ocean Springs?" Jay asked.

"Best one out there was Carl's, but he died last year."

"Where is it?"

Gary narrowed his eyes as he tried to recall. "It's out on Ocean Springs Road, heading into the county. I don't remember exactly where. Used to go out there for old Chevy parts when we rebuilt that Silverado a few years back. Guy had so many cars lined up in those woods."

Jay nodded. "Thanks, guys."

Jimmy smiled. "Good luck, man. Hope you catch 'em."

"Me too, Jimmy."

29

Jay's phone buzzed, and he saw Sam's number. "Delp," he announced out of habit.

"You hear that Franklin's on a tear?" Sam asked.

"No, I didn't," Jay said. "Is this about the other girl?"

"That's part of it," Sam explained. "He's hot under the collar about you now. Jason Regal and Lanie Dinn told me he is trying to drum up council support to oust you."

"Guess he took offense when I pulled his son in to question," Jay remarked.

"No kidding. I wouldn't worry, Jay. He has fewer friends than I do on the board."

"Sam, don't go sticking your neck out," Jay warned. "I can handle myself."

"Oh, I have no doubt," he responded. "Any luck with the murder?"

"No. It's nothing but long shots at this point."

"I just wanted you to not fret if word got to you about Franklin."

"Sam, I rarely worry," Jay assured him. "However, once I

put this to bed, Tom Franklin and I should have a nice discussion."

"Geez, Jay. You sound like someone from *The Sopranos*."

"It's not that dramatic," he promised his brother. "We just need to understand each other."

"You must know some dirt on him," Sam stated.

"Brother, I'm the most ignorant fool in this town right now," Jay said.

"Give it time, Jay," Sam encouraged. "You'll be on top pretty soon."

"Honestly, bro, I just want to find this guy."

"I won't keep you then."

"No worries, Sam," Jay told his brother. He hung up as he pulled into the Ocean Springs Police Department's parking lot.

"Chief!" Towns called to him across the bullpen. "We might have something."

Jay crossed the room to where Towns hovered over Lawson's cubicle space. Tim Lamb leaned against the cloth-covered partition where he stared at Lawson's monitor.

"Whatcha got?" Jay inquired.

"A minivan," Lawson announced, tapping the screen with his right index finger.

The man's computer showed a grainy surveillance photo from one of the traffic cameras set up along Front Beach Drive. A silver and red Ford Windstar cruised past the camera's angle. Nearly black tint covered the windows.

"Can you zoom in on the driver?" Jay asked.

"Already ahead of you," Lawson informed his boss as he tapped the keyboard.

Another image appeared. The single frame showed the windshield of the Ford zoomed in closer to reveal a figure wearing a red balaclava over his face and a tan Carhartt cap pulled down over a hooded sweatshirt. Neither the shirt nor the hat had any logos or writing other than the small orange Carhartt emblem embroidered just above the bill.

"Seems a bit warm to dress like that," Jay remarked.

"Our thinking, too, boss," Lawson agreed.

"Can we follow him?" Jay asked.

Lawson nodded but added, "For a short way. We lose sight of him as he heads east on 90."

"Don't we have cameras along the highway?"

"Yep, but he must have turned off between them. We're scouring the side streets, but so far we found no sign of him."

"Where do you lose him?" Jay asked.

"Between the hospital and here," Towns answered.

"Show me a map," Jay said.

Lawson opened his browser to reveal Google Maps already loaded and zoomed in on that stretch of highway.

Jay chuckled. "You guys are on it," he praised.

"There are a few streets he could have taken," Lawson said. "Also, plenty of parking lots."

Towns interjected, "I asked Tomlinson to cruise through the businesses in case he dumped the van there and swapped vehicles."

"Good call," Jay remarked. That had been the next thing he considered doing. "How soon can he do that?"

"He should be on site now," she stated. "It'll take him a few minutes to circle through all the lots."

"If he took some side streets, where could he have gone?" Jay asked.

"I'd bet he went north," Lamb speculated. "Going south pens him between the National Park and the coast. He has a lot more room to get away if he heads north."

"Makes sense," Jay agreed. "We can't rule out that he has

waterfront access, though. Jamie Rene ended up in the bay from somewhere."

"I spent part of the morning looking at the weather conditions last weekend," Towns said. "That storm sent some strong winds into the harbor. That created a lot of chop. The currents could have carried her from anywhere in the back bay, but it would have been tough for her to float in from the sound, even with the wind and rain."

"He could have a boat," Jay pointed out. "Doesn't everyone around here?"

Towns nodded. "Maybe we check the marina," she suggested.

"Good idea," Jay said before leaning over Lawson and touching the screen. "That road there?" His index finger tapped on a line called "Ocean Springs Road."

"What about it?" Lawson asked.

"The mechanic at Miller's work mentioned a scrapyard out on Ocean Springs Road."

Lawson nodded. "Carl's Scrap. Used to be out there. I heard it closed when old Carl had a heart attack."

"When did that happen, Rick?"

Lawson glanced up between Tim and Shannon, hoping either had an answer. Both shook their heads.

"Not sure," Lawson finally answered. "A year or two. I was on the call with Letterman—he's one of the guys that quit last month. We found Carl in the yard. It wasn't a pretty sight."

"Right. He'd been there awhile, hadn't he?" Lamb asked.

"Yeah, scavengers picked him apart. Think he'd laid out there over a week."

"Do you remember the COD?" Jay asked.

"ME said heart attack. Nothing foul about it," Lawson clarified.

"He have any family?" Jay wondered.

"Not that I recall," Lawson replied. "We busted him for taking in stolen vehicles, though. He got probation, claiming he had no way to know. Most of them had come from out of state, so it wasn't quite a slam dunk."

Jay straightened up.

"What are ya thinking, Chief?" Towns asked.

"A scrapyard is as good a place to hide a couple of cars as anywhere else," Jay commented.

"Want me to send Tomlinson to check it out?" Towns asked.

"No, how about Tim and Rick go investigate the marina? Towns, you and I can drive out to Carl's."

"You don't need us?" Lawson questioned.

"We are only working on a hunch," Jay reminded them. "Can't get a search warrant based on that. We might do better to just visit."

"Should we check property records?" Towns asked. "If it changed hands, we'd know who has it now."

"Ask Jennifer to do that," Jay directed. "She can call us on our way out there if she gets anything."

Towns nodded.

"Let's do it," Jay said.

The four of them split up into pairs.

"Oh, Towns?" Jay said. "You're driving again."

"Do you ever drive?" she asked.

Jay shrugged. "It's good to be chief."

As they headed across town, Jay commented, "Sam called to tell me Franklin is after my job."

"He didn't let you finish out the week yet?"

"I'm skilled at pissing folks off."

"Might be a talent this city needs," Towns noted. "Franklin has had a little too much power over the last ten years."

"You think?" Jay pressed.

"He wasn't happy that Ward resigned," Towns told him.

"No?"

"I was in the office when he came to talk Ward out of it."

"That's not strange," Jay pointed out. "It's a pain to hire anyone new."

"True, but he sounded more angry than frustated."

Jay considered that. "Lawson implied there were some alleged dealings with the Dixie Mob. You know about any of that?"

"I never saw any of it, but I was told that several of the council members wanted to find someone from outside the area to fill the chief role because of that."

Jay narrowed his eyes at her. "Who told you that?"

"Just gossip," she answered. "Probably Jennifer spilled something."

"Sam didn't mention it to me," Jay remarked. In fact, when he spoke to Sam regarding corruption, his brother claimed to have no knowledge of it. How likely was that if the council shared the same concerns? "Was it Sam?"

"Was what Sam?" Towns asked.

"Did Sam tell you that?"

She shook her head, but it lacked conviction. "I don't think so."

"Shannon, do you and my brother have something going on?"

"No!" she blurted out. She didn't sound angry, just surprised.

"Have you ever?" he pushed.

"Chief, no. We're friends. That's all."

Jay nodded.

"Seriously, Chief."

"It's fine, Shannon," Jay assured her. "I'm not judging. But the two of you act a little weird about the other."

"What does that mean?"

"Well, Sam doesn't tell anyone he paints. Never has. That isn't something he shares much with me. Perhaps not even Danielle, but I can't say."

"It's just a thing," she blathered.

"Yeah, but in our house, it was a thing our father thought girls did. He was sure football players shouldn't be painting."

"Since your dad is, shall we say, less present, it might not matter to Sam as much."

Jay shrugged. "Could be."

"Ugh, fine. We were close," she admitted. "Nothing happened, though. Ever."

"I told you I wasn't judging."

"Whatever. You can't tell him this. After my divorce, we ran into each other one night. It was after a council meeting, and Danielle stayed home with the kids. We had drinks and chatted. He was a good listener."

Jay kept quiet, encouraging her to talk.

"I started going to the council meetings for Ward. After they ended, Sam and I would grab a bite to eat and talk. But that was all it ever was."

"But it stopped?" Jay asked.

Towns nodded. "Yeah," she replied. Her tone came out laced with regret.

"It happens, doesn't it?" Jay commented.

"Suppose so," was all Towns said back.

Jay focused his attention out the window. The municipal streets gradually became more rural as they drove away from the city center. Neighborhoods devolved into larger lots with bigger houses, which transformed into even larger plots with older, smaller homes.

Towns gripped the steering wheel at ten and two, her knuckles whitening from the grip. Jay regretted triggering her emotions. He'd been prying for sure, and that bothered him. Sam and Shannon were adults, and what they did together was none of his business. He knew he should have stayed out of it, or at least confronted Sam instead of Shannon.

Towns pumped the brakes as they passed a weathered plywood sign that read "Carl's Scrap Next Right." She turned on a red gravel road that hadn't been graded in years. Stagnant puddles of water collected in potholes and ruts. The brush at the roadside carried a thin crimson layer of dust on all the leaves and branches less than a few feet from the ground.

When they approached another hand-painted placard that read "Carl's Scrap," Towns stopped the car at the end of a drive. A galvanized cattle gate hung from a post at an angle. Chain looped around a railroad tie standing vertically on the ground.

The two cops sat in the cruiser, staring at the dilapidated entrance and the "No Trespassing" sign hanging from it.

"Guess we're here," Jay remarked.

30

Live oaks loomed over the galvanized gate. Jay exited the car and held up a palm, signaling Towns to wait. He approached the gate and stared over the fence. Rows of ancient rusting hulks lined the field. Grass grew up over many of the fenders, obscuring a lot of the different makes and models. Beyond the first few rows, someone appeared to have mowed the paths between the vehicles more recently. It might have been closer to a few months' growth in some places.

There was no intercom or bell to ring, and from his vantage point, Jay thought the junkyard looked to be permanently closed. He pulled at the chain wrapped around the pole. A newly placed padlock secured the gate.

The new lock wasn't confirmation someone was home, though. Whoever inherited the land from the now-dead Carl had justification in securing the property. That current owner might even be the bank or state that had taken over the real estate.

Jay turned back to the car, his eyes drifting down to the gravel drive. Tire tracks marked up the loose pebbles. They were fresh. At least, fresh like the grass had been recently cut. Of course, the storm the other night would have washed away some ruts, meaning they were a few days old at most.

Towns observed him as he walked back and forth before the gate. She was unable to witness the debate in his head, though. He had no cause to enter the property, and he had no warrant.

He scanned the trees, stopping when he spotted a trail camera strapped to a limb. Whoever was on the other end of the camera may be watching him now. He shifted his eyes toward Towns before returning to the car and getting in.

"Drive down the street some," he suggested.

"No one's home?" she asked.

"Not sure yet. There's a camera, though."

Towns pulled onto the dirt road and drove away. "What are we going to do?"

Jay took out his phone and dialed the station.

"Ocean Springs Police," Jennifer answered.

"Jennifer, Chief Delp here," he announced into the speaker. "Have you gotten any records on that property?"

"The land is still in Carl Cooper's name," she informed.

"Anything in probate?"

"Everything he owned went to a Paul Cooper."

"Son?"

"No idea. No info on him, either."

"Thanks," Jay replied before hanging up. He looked over at Towns. "Land is likely held by a Paul Cooper. Same last name as old Carl."

"Son?" Towns repeated Jennifer's question.

"Don't know. Good guess. Jennifer says there's nothing on him, though."

"He could be in there," she pointed out.

"Yep, but we can't just walk in," Jay advised. "At least not on camera."

"What do you mean?"

"I want you to drop me off up here," he explained. "And what happens next, it's best if you don't know."

"Are you going in?"

"What did I say?"

"Do not start with me," Towns scolded in what sounded like her mom voice. "I'm coming, too."

"Shannon, did you forget who is the boss? No, you aren't."

"Wait," she blurted as she slammed on the brakes. "Did you hear that?"

Jay looked at her.

"Someone just screamed for help."

Jay's eyes rolled, but he smiled. "I thought I saw something, too."

Towns threw the cruiser into park and got out. "We going over the fence?"

Jay came around the car and grabbed her arm. "Shannon, you stay close to me, understand?"

Towns cocked her head. "Would you be telling Rick to do the same thing?"

He nodded. "When we are breaking all sorts of rules to investigate, yes, I would."

"Fine," she said, scowling.

Jay climbed over the cattle barrier, using his hand to push the barbed wire strung across the top of the fence down. While he held the barbs back, Towns jumped over as well.

"You sure there aren't more cameras?" she asked.

"I kinda expect there are," he answered. "I'm hoping mostly on the gate, though."

"Hope springs eternal."

"Still quoting poetry?" Jay mumbled.

She shrugged and followed as the chief started for the tree line. The edge of the woods bore giant live oaks, pushing back any other growth. Once past the line of oaks, stands of pines filled in the gaps between more Spanish moss-covered specimens.

He raised a hand, signaling Towns to stop. With two fingers, he pointed at a deer stand about fifty yards north of them. The blind sat about twenty feet off the ground and was aimed to the west. Jay scanned the trees for more game cameras. He spotted a couple on the far side of the deer blind.

"This way," he rasped before heading in a large arc to avoid the stand. Motion often activated trail cams, and since living, moving things inhabited the forest, these cams didn't usually trigger until something came much closer.

"Keep your eyes peeled for more," he warned.

"Roger, Chief," Towns whispered.

As they approached what must be the center of the property, they came across the first line of cars. Hoodless, windowless, and doorless, these sentries sat like they had for decades. The newest car Jay identified was a mid-'90s sedan. Or what remained of a sedan. He thought it had once been a Buick, but it wasn't recognizable now without a much closer inspection. Unless it was a Honda CRV or a Mitsubishi, he had no time to investigate it.

"Stay low," he urged as they hurried beside the rusting automobiles.

Past the next line of pines, he stopped, dropping into a crouch. In front of him, an open area lined with vehicles spread out. He counted twenty rows of them, with over a hundred per row. They ranged from totaled trucks to slightly dented Volkswagens to several boats with a layer of pine sap covering the hulls.

Beyond the automotive field was a single-wide trailer with orange siding and a wooden porch that leaned to the left. The two officers sat still, gazing intently at the mobile home for any movement.

"What do we do?" Towns asked.

"We wait for a minute," he suggested.

"If nothing happens?"

He shrugged.

Five minutes passed in silence. Towns shifted from one leg to the other.

Jay reached over and grabbed her arm, pulling her down closer to the ground. Towns spun her attention in his direction, and the chief gestured across the field. She shook her head when she couldn't understand what he was pointing toward.

"Follow me, stay down," he ordered under his breath.

Jay crawled away from Towns along the dirt on all fours. His eyes were up, and his neck was swiveled 180 degrees. Towns tried to copy his movements, but Jay moved faster than she imagined possible. He didn't wait for her, instead scampering like a squirrel across the grass.

Jay had years of practice infiltrating places he wasn't supposed to be. As a sniper, he'd have to get into position, often under the noses of the enemy. Now, he was employing the same tactics to stay out of sight. When he traversed the field, he looked back to locate Towns on the other side of the overgrown scrapyard. She motioned for him to continue, and he debated waiting for her.

Instead, he rounded the corner and crawled ahead. He stopped next to a white Honda CRV. Jay raised his head over the hood, searching the junkyard for any movement. Towns scuffled along, and he registered her shuffling through the grass even though she was still fifty feet away.

Other than that, the yard seemed quiet. He tried the handle, and the door opened. Jay slipped into the front seat and stretched toward the glove compartment.

Empty.

He ran his fingers between the seats, searching for anything. There was nothing. He flipped open the ashtray. Also empty.

Jay slid out of the car and moved around to the rear. No license plate, either.

"Is it Jamie's?" Towns asked when she reached him.

"No idea," he admitted. "Right year, though. And it doesn't look like it's been sitting here for a decade."

"Let me get the VIN," she suggested.

He motioned for her to do it, and Towns stood up, pulling out her phone to take a picture of the vehicle identification number on the dash. She slid back down to the ground.

"Send it to Lawson," he advised. "He can run the number."

She nodded and typed out a message before sending it.

"Stay put," he ordered. "I'm going to look at the trailer. If Lawson responds, text me."

Jay didn't wait for her to respond. He scurried down the row of cars, leaving Towns cowering beside the Honda CRV.

When he reached the front line of junk cars, he crouched behind a Chevrolet Caprice Classic that was missing the entire trunk. The trailer looked lifeless. Past the trailer, he noted more vehicles lined up like soldiers. Toward the tree line, he saw three large cabin cruisers propped up on giant Styrofoam logs similar to what was used for docks before someone realized how much crap they were putting into the water.

None of the boats would ever float. He spotted no breaches in the hull; however, the ship's state made him question the soundness of the core.

Something flashed in the window of the middle cruiser, and he squinted as he tried to make out more movement. Or had there even been motion? It could have been a tree limb in the breeze reflecting off the glass.

Nothing happened. Nothing moved or made a sound. Still, an unease washed over Jay, and his hand reached back to touch the Beretta PXP holstered on his belt. He unclipped the holster, flipping the strap off the butt of the pistol, leaving it ready for him to draw it.

Trailer or boat? His gut told him to check the yacht first, but the little orange mobile home sat between where Jay waited and the vessel. The problem was, if someone was in the boat, they'd have a clear shot of him approaching the house. If, on the other hand, someone was in the trailer, there was a lot of open area between it and the old yacht for them to spot Jay.

Of course, they would need to be watching out the window to see him. He'd already scanned the vicinity for more trail cams. There'd been none, and he bet they were only on the outer edge of the property.

Jay came off his haunches in a hunched sprint. His boots crunched gravel as he ran. Even then, the noise was minimal.

He was halfway across the clearing when the ratcheting sound of a shell being pumped into the chamber reached him. Jay didn't turn, instead diving toward the crumpled remains of a BMW. The muzzle blast of the twelve-gauge barrel echoed through the scrapyard. A hole appeared in the bent rear panel of the mangled luxury sedan.

Jay rolled to the other side, drawing his Beretta. "I'm police! Put down your weapon!" he shouted.

In response, the shotgun chambered, sounding like it was right over Jay. He popped up, aiming in the sound's direction. No one was there.

Jay stepped toward the front of the Beemer, his Beretta sweeping in short arcs in front of him as he looked for the shooter. A figure moved to his far left, and Jay whipped around as the shotgun blasted again. The rear window of the BMW exploded, spewing Jay with pebbles of tempered glass and sending him sprawling across the grass.

31

Jay rolled to his side, spitting out a mouthful of dirt and grass. The *chunk-chunk* of another shell being jacked into the twelve-gauge chamber prompted him to move. Jay Delp belly-crawled like a snake under a Dodge Caravan. The minivan had no wheels, leaving only a few inches for him to squeeze beneath it. In the moment, he realized it wasn't the smallest space he'd ever fit into, but it was close.

He twisted around to see two boots approaching the Caravan. The Beretta lined up with the gunman's ankles. Jay stared down the sights at the feet. He could blow the man's legs out from under him and finish him with a clean head shot.

Of course, that wouldn't work. At this point, he and Towns were trespassing. While he'd announced he was a cop, he knew that might not be enough. What if this person, Paul Cooper, was innocent, and Jay violated his rights by illegally entering his property?

Where was Towns? He hoped she stayed hunkered down and wasn't moving on the gunshots. The feet crunched through the grass around the Dodge. Jay kept the barrel trained on the man's leather work boots. When they moved away, he wriggled out from under the front of the van.

He fumbled for his phone and texted Towns. *"Stay down."*

She didn't respond, and he hoped she saw the message.

Jay raised his head to peer through the busted back windows of the minivan. A lanky figure stalked three cars over. The man was in his thirties, and he appeared to be not just skinny but toned.

"Paul?" Jay called. "I'm with the police. Put down your weapon."

The gunman spun around, firing the shotgun at the Dodge. Jay felt the impact vibrate the junker.

"Last warning, Paul!" Jay shouted as Paul Cooper ejected the spent shell.

Jay peered through the windows, but the man was gone. With the Beretta stretched out in his grip, Jay straightened. On alert, he scanned the junkyard for movement.

"I have backup on the way, Paul," he called again. "This doesn't have to end badly."

"You're trespassing!" a deep voice shouted. The sound echoed through the lifeless vehicles, and Jay turned to locate the source.

"I just wanted to talk," Jay said loudly. His own words bounced around the scrap heap.

A muffled noise caught his ear, and he tried to identify where it came from. Jay took a single wary step. His Beretta swept in an arc in front of him.

"Paul, come out," he demanded.

An eerie silence bathed the junkyard. The shotgun blasts had sent any bird or squirrel that had been providing an ambient soundtrack scurrying away. Even the chirping crickets had ceased their calls.

Jay took one more step, his boots scraping against the clump of gamagrass. He strained to listen for any movement, worrying that his own footfalls were resounding through the metal graveyard.

Another muffled sound. It was shrill, but Jay was unable to pinpoint its origin. A sultry breeze blew off the leaves, rustling branches and signaling to the insects that things were back to normal. Patches of chirping started from the nearby trees.

Jay continued along the line of cars toward the direction the last shotgun blast came. Paul Cooper had taken refuge somewhere. Jay recognized that Cooper had the advantage. He knew the layout of the junk maze. It was his home turf.

In his gut, Jay trusted he had more combat skills. Or, at the minimum, he trusted in his field training. However, he'd been on missions with plenty of skilled Marines who hadn't made it back despite their conditioning.

He rounded a once yellow Pontiac Sunbird. The passenger door of the little coupe hung ajar. Jay pointed the Beretta into the empty vehicle as he stepped around it. Across the aisle sat a Ram Charger with a roof caved in by a rollover. Jay rotated the pistol to the cab of the Dodge. His eyes drifted to the ground, and he wondered if his prey could have retreated under the body of one of these dilapidated ruins.

A blue jay squawked in a tree, attracting Jay's gaze for a split second in the bird's direction. Something moved behind him, and Jay whirled about. His Beretta lined up on Towns, who stood next to the trailer with her own service weapon drawn. With two fingers, she pointed at her eyes, asking where to look. Jay shook his head and extended a palm, telling her to stay there.

"Paul! Let's talk this out. No one has to die here," Jay shouted.

The veteran Marine felt his heart thud in his chest. He didn't like being out here with an untested—at least to him—Towns. The thought verged on absurd. She'd shown herself to be an excellent police officer, but it unsettled him, nonetheless.

The trunk of a Cadillac sedan flew open to his left. Jay spun around as the barrel appeared in the gap, and the muzzle blasted as he threw himself back. The Pontiac Sunbird absorbed the slug, spewing Jay with plastic and glass shrapnel. He struck the ground, rolling clear of the blast and firing at the same time. Another shot sounded from the trailer as Towns returned fire.

"He's hit!" Towns shouted as Paul Cooper ran for the three cabin cruisers under the pines. Jay pushed himself to his feet. Blood trickled down his face, and he swiped it with his palm.

Cooper held what Jay recognized as a Mossberg. The man turned, scowling at the two officers.

"He should have two left!" he called to Towns.

"Roger," she replied.

"Stop, Paul!" Jay shouted, raising his Beretta.

Cooper raised the Mossberg toward Jay, and the chief fired the weapon. Behind him, Towns opened fire as well, shooting twice. Both of her rounds hit Cooper in the chest while Jay's bullet impacted him in the face.

Paul Cooper flinched, pulling the trigger long after he was already dead. The Mossberg bucked out of his grip, firing into the air as he dropped to the ground.

Jay moved forward, aiming the Beretta at the fallen form.

Towns caught up to him, still training her weapon on Cooper's body. With his toe, Jay kicked the Mossberg out of his reach. It seemed stupid, considering there was nothing left of the back of Cooper's head, but Jay did it, anyway.

"That was a cluster," Towns remarked.

"No kidding," Jay agreed.

"What's that?"

More muffled screams—now Jay recognized the sounds as such. "Help me!" they said.

"The boat," Jay said. "Stay on my six."

Towns agreed as Jay moved toward the three vessels. As he focused on the middle one, he saw more movement. His brain struggled to make sense of the motions. They weren't from someone walking around.

"I'm going up," he warned Towns. "Cover me."

She nodded, and Jay holstered his Beretta while he hoisted himself on the front deck. Even though he'd grown up on the coast and had some decent familiarity with boats of all sizes, he didn't recognize the make of this yacht. It was about forty feet long, give or take a foot, and resembled an older Hatteras-style cruiser. Although, given its age, he suspected it was a manufacturer that had long gone out of business.

His hands stuck to the layers of pine sap that covered the front deck as he pushed up. He got to his feet and pulled the Beretta. As he swept over the yard, Towns holstered her own weapon and climbed up.

"Help! Please!"

The cries were more audible now, no longer indistinguishable sounds. They were coming from inside the boat.

Towns drew her Beretta, and both officers moved toward the companionway. Jay pushed through the door, releasing a waft of mildew and mold into the air. Towns turned her head, burying her nose in her shoulder for a second as the scent of rot passed them.

Jay signaled he was entering. He stepped through the entrance into the salon of what had once been a nice yacht. Now the floors, made mostly of rotting plywood, looked like they couldn't hold weight. The remains of a rat-infested sofa reeked of rodent urine and must.

"Oh my," Towns uttered as she followed Jay into the cabin.

Dangling from leather straps was a naked form. It took Jay a second for his brain to register what he saw. The face pleading with him was Angel Haywood's. Her wrists and ankles were bound by restraints, holding her spread-eagled. A leather collar around her neck pulled her head up so that she could see out the windowed salon door. Someone had strung an old child's swing under her midsection, connecting it to the ceiling to support her weight.

Three video cameras sat on tripods in a triangle around the cabin. They all pointed at Angel.

"You're safe," Jay told her. "Is there anyone else here?"

Angel Haywood bawled as they came through the door. She tried to shake her head, but the collar didn't allow her to move her neck at all.

"We need to get her down," Jay told Towns. "Stay alert."

Towns swallowed hard and nodded as Jay holstered his Beretta. He pulled out a folding knife from his pocket.

"I'm going to remove the collar first," he warned the girl.

"'Kay," Angel mumbled.

Jay held her chin up as he cut the rope connecting the strap to the ceiling. As soon as the pressure vanished, Angel's head sank like a stone. She had been trapped in that position for over thirty-six hours. Her muscles couldn't lift her head.

"I need you to help, Shannon," he told Towns. "She can't hold herself up."

"Yes, sir," his officer said, slipping her Beretta in its holster as she approached the young woman. "We have you, Angel."

"Thank God," she rasped.

Jay stepped behind her. "I'm about to cut your feet free, and Officer Towns will help you down."

Towns locked eyes with Jay before casting her gaze at the wooden floor. Jay followed her stare to the brown stain beneath Angel. Blood.

Jay lifted Angel's right leg and cut the rope. He lowered it until her sole touched the plywood and then repeated the effort on the left side. As Shannon held the girl's weight, he freed her hands until they could slide her out of the swing onto the floor.

Jay unbuttoned his shirt, stripping down to his bare chest. He draped it over her shoulders.

"We need to get an ambulance here," he stated. "Why don't you sit with her while I call the station?"

Towns nodded as Jay moved out of the cabin. He retrieved his phone and dialed the department number. While he waited for Jennifer to pick up, he surveyed the vehicle graveyard and the prone figure of Paul Cooper.

32

—————

"His name isn't Paul Cooper," Lawson explained.

"Who is he?" Jay asked.

"We're running prints, but we are clueless," Lawson continued. "What we do know is that the real Paul Cooper was older than our unsub was, and unless he underwent a ton of facial reconstruction, he looked entirely different."

"Can we find Cooper?"

"So far, no. His last known address was outside Macon, Georgia. But Cooper's only family was Carl. He has an ex-wife, but she said they haven't spoken in three years. No kids, no siblings, no significant other."

"What about him?" Jay asked, pointing at the body now being carted off by Dr. Harley and his assistant.

"He has a driver's license from Utah that says he's Paul Cooper. Has credit cards in his name, too, although those might actually be Cooper's."

"I have a feeling we aren't going to find Paul Cooper," Jay suggested.

Lawson shook his head. "Tend to agree, boss."

"The question is, did he kill Cooper to get this lovely piece of property, or did it just work out?"

"Tim's working on Carl Cooper's friends. He was a bit of a hermit, in case this fine estate fooled you. But people were acquainted with him. From the pictures in the house, we are certain the person you and Towns shot wasn't Paul."

"Nothing like adding more questions," Jay said with a sigh.

"Towns said Angel Haywood confirmed he took her. He caught her as she ran by on Front Beach Drive. In broad daylight. We are not sure where yet. I'm sure that will be after Angel's out of the hospital."

"What does Shannon say about her?"

Lawson bowed his head. "It wasn't good. He raped and tortured her. The guy wanted her to see him coming. That's why he strapped her up the way he did, so when he came out of the house, she'd know what was about to happen."

Jay looked at the body bag on the gurney. "Jamie wasn't his first," he surmised. "Might be the first around here."

"There are several VHS tapes inside, along with a computer that is password-protected. Will have to get the tech guys to open it."

"The videotapes?"

"I only played one," Lawson admitted. "Had to turn it off."

Jay shook his head. "Don't want to imagine it."

Lawson pointed to a small garage. "Got a little center console, a Grady-White, in there. Registered to Carl Cooper, but it looks like it's been run recently. Guys are gonna hit it for DNA. Probably find some of Jamie's."

"He just slipped in and took over here?"

"According to the probate records, he proved he was Paul Cooper. Not sure how he did that. Since he was the executor of the will—or, rather, Paul Cooper was —no one batted an eye. The state didn't care as long as they got their taxes."

"I wonder if we're certain that Carl Cooper died of natural causes?"

Lawson shrugged. "What was left of the body left us little to decipher. I'd assume Harley knew enough."

"Let's hope," Jay agreed.

"We found Clay Miller's car, too," Lawson added. "The VIN Towns called in matched Jamie's CRV. Miller's Mitsubishi is parked over on the far side of the garage. Matched its VIN, too."

"Reach out to Warren in Slidell," Jay said. "Our suspect might be connected to the house where Clay was discovered."

Lawson nodded.

"I'm going to go to the hospital," Jay told Lawson. "I need to drive Towns's cruiser back, anyway, and pick her up from there."

"Roger that. Want me to stay here?"

"Yeah. I'd like to make sure we present an ironclad case against our John Doe."

"I don't think you have anything to worry about. The one video I watched clearly showed him in it. It wasn't here, though."

"We'll need to identify any other victims, too," Jay realized, wondering how many might be out there.

"Hey, Chief, the other thing," Lawson said. "All the trail cams were dead. Not sure when they went offline, but the batteries were all corroded."

Jay chuckled at his skirting around the cameras that hadn't been in use since Carl Cooper was alive. "It's insane," he considered. They had Jamie's killer in custody, yet his identity remained a mystery.

He left Lawson to oversee JD, Tomkins, and Felton, who volunteered to collect evidence. The Mississippi Bureau of Investigation had an agent on the way from Jackson, and Jay suspected the FBI would show up soon to dig around. Especially if the real Paul Cooper had been murdered in Georgia.

It took him ten minutes to hike to the road where he and Towns had left her police car. He drove to town, stopping at the hospital on Bienville Boulevard. News had already spread, and when he got out of the cruiser, a reporter and camera crew bombarded him.

"Chief Delp, we hear you've killed the individual responsible for Jamie Rene's murder. Is that true?" a blond woman with a microphone asked.

Jay looked at the camera. "There was a shooting earlier. One gunman is dead; however, we do not have a positive identification of the victim. We suspect that this is the murderer we have been hunting."

"Is it true you rescued Angel Haywood as well?" the female reporter asked.

"Currently, I cannot comment on that," he replied.

"Why are you at the hospital?" she queried.

It seemed a stupid game to play. The reporter knew Angel Haywood was brought here, or she wouldn't have been waiting to ambush Jay. Still, he wanted to share with Amanda Haywood that he found her daughter before the news did.

"No comment," he stated as he pushed past.

"Chief!" she called after him, but Jay left her on the sidewalk.

Shannon Towns sat outside the room in the emergency suite of the hospital. She glanced up as Jay approached.

"You doing okay, Shannon?" he inquired.

She nodded grimly without saying anything.

"Was that your first shooting?" he asked, settling in a chair beside her.

"Yes," she replied.

"I'm sure we have some counseling if you want it," he offered.

"It's not that," she told him. "I just don't believe someone would do that to another human."

"We as a people are often pretty terrible to each other," Jay acknowledged. "I'd like to tell you it gets better. But my experience has been that something worse will show up."

"I can't imagine," she mumbled.

"Best not to," he suggested. "Need to head home?"

"Thought I'd wait in case Angel needed me," she replied. "Plus, I already chased off that blond reporter."

"Good. Did Ms. Haywood get here?"

She nodded. "Angel called her from the ambulance."

Jay felt some relief at that.

"Chief, you should have your face looked at," Towns remarked.

He reached up and ran his fingertips over the cuts inflicted by the shattering glass and plastic bits. When he pulled his hand away, the ends of his fingers had sticky blood on them.

"Might not be bad. Let me talk with the Haywoods first," he said.

"While you do that, I'm going to get a doctor for you," she insisted. "What good is being chief if you can't skip the line in the ER?"

"At least there are some perks, right?"

Towns smiled. "Besides working with me?"

Jay returned her smile. "Shannon, you've been great on this. I think you have an investigator inside you."

Towns blushed as Jay knocked on the door.

"Come in," Amanda Haywood called, and Jay entered.

"Chief! Oh, thank God for you. You saved my baby!" she declared, leaping from the stiff chair beside Angel's bed and wrapping her arms around Jay's neck.

"Just glad we found her," Jay said.

Angel didn't say anything. She stared at the man who rescued her without expression. The shock was kicking in, and he couldn't blame her for retreating.

"I'm not staying," he promised both women. "Angel needs her rest. I'm going to have an officer here for the next few days. We will have to get your statement, Angel. But don't worry about it now."

"He's dead, though?" Amanda Haywood asked.

Jay nodded once.

"Good," the woman growled. "I hope he rots in hell."

Jay had never been sure about what the afterlife held, but he had to hope, like Amanda Haywood, that it wasn't good for the man who had stolen this girl. Ms. Haywood held him by the hands and squeezed his palms. Her eyes glistened, and she wiped away a tear before turning back to her daughter.

When Jay excused himself, he found Towns with a woman in scrubs. "Dr. Schaeffer said she'd fix you up," Towns explained to him.

"Thanks," he said as Dr. Schaeffer directed him to a bed behind a curtain.

33

J ay sat at a table on the patio of the Mosaic Restaurant, eating a Cuban panini. The courtyard atmosphere offered an appealing place for an after-work drink. For Jay, it served as a brief midday refuge from the chaos of the last few days.

Following the recent shooting, he and his staff became overrun with FBI, MBI, and state police from Mississippi and Georgia. They still had no ID on the John Doe. Georgia police now presumed Paul Cooper to be dead, and likely had been for at least a year.

The suspect had taken over the man's life, even posting on his social media. The posts largely displayed overt political themes. It occurred to Jay that this could have been a strategy to give the impression Paul Cooper was still living, though having no actual communication with associates.

John Doe's fingerprints got no hits, so whoever he was, he'd stayed off the books. That had proven a feat after they started cataloging the videos. John Doe had been killing for the better part of a decade. Right now, forensic techs were scouring the footage to identify victims. At present, the FBI had connected at least twelve missing persons to him.

He'd kept notes and journals, too. While he didn't name the victims, he referenced them with names from the seven dwarfs. Once he cycled through all seven, he started over with the names. The recent one referred to Angel Haywood as "Sneezy," though he referred to Jamie and Clay as "Doc" and "Dopey."

His internet searches showed him looking for rental property, including a brief conversation with the landlord of the house in Slidell. He'd used a fake profile and asked about the house. Once he determined it wouldn't be available until the end of the month, he must have decided to dump Clay Miller's body there.

That made little sense to Jay. While the videos showed the killer's sexual perversion, it seemed strange to have taken Clay's corpse so far. The scrapyard had ample space to bury him there.

It remained an unanswered question for them. Although they'd found footage of other murders on the property, they had not yet identified the women, nor had they discovered any remains. DNA, on the other hand, was abundant. The crime scene techs had found eight distinct biological samples that didn't belong to Jamie Rene or Angel Haywood.

"You look ragged," Rebecca noted as she sat across from him.

"Well, sleep is for the weak," he remarked. "You surprising me for lunch again?"

She smiled. "I already ate."

"The Cuban is pretty good."

"You should try the shrimp and grits."

"Next time."

"You're kinda the big hero, aren't you?" she commended him with a sly grin.

Rebecca wasn't wrong. Marcus Taylor had covered the *Sun Herald* with Jay's face and the story of a new chief who stopped a psychotic killer. Jay had fielded interviews with all the local stations, along with *The Today Show* and *Good Morning America*. He had another scheduled later today with *NBC Nightly News*. There was even talk of *Dateline* coming down to film a feature.

Personally, he wished it would all blow over.

"How is Angel?" Rebecca asked.

"I talked to her yesterday. She's holding up as best as one would expect."

"It's crazy. It was going on right here."

Jay didn't question the insanity of it. He'd seen the worst of humanity before. It clung to the underbelly of most places.

"You've shut down Tom," she remarked. "Quite a feat."

Jay shrugged. "I wasn't too concerned."

"He isn't sharing much with me lately," she admitted.

Big surprise, Jay thought. But he just gave a slight nod.

"Listen, Jay," she said. "I laid out my cards the other day, so I'm not going to beat around the bush. Would you like to go out with me?"

Jay cocked his head in bemusement. "Aren't we out now?"

"Don't be a smartass," she reprimanded. "Before you answer, I get it. We have a lot of history, but we also have a lot of history."

He bent forward, raising a hand to stop her. "Wait, Becs. I agree, but the last thing I want is this to end badly. Right now, you're my only friend in town."

"You have Sam," she corrected.

"He's family."

"Shannon?"

Jay rolled his eyes. "Work friends don't count as friends."

"Yes, they can," she told him.

He nodded. "Yes, but not after a week and a half."

"Fair. How about I promise we can be adults about this?"

He smiled. "I'd like that, then."

Rebecca grinned from ear to ear, and Jay couldn't help smiling back. She reached over and grabbed his hand, squeezing it.

"How about I take you to dinner tonight?" he suggested.

"Where would we go?"

"I was thinking we pick up a pizza and head to my place."

"Won't your dad be there?"

Jay nodded. "He's got to eat, too," he reminded her. "And he falls asleep by 8:30."

"Rebecca, Chief! I hadn't realized you were coming here," Tom Franklin stated as he exited the restaurant's dining room. "I was just leaving."

Trailing Franklin was an older white-haired man with sunglasses and a gray beard. He stopped behind the mayor as Franklin droned on in his politicized manner. Jay glanced past the mayor at the individual who suddenly struck him as familiar.

"You're Chief Delp, right?" the other man asked, extending a hand.

"Yes, sir."

"I was close to your folks," he explained. "Dale Collins. Nice to meet you."

Jay stared at the face of the man whose hand he was shaking. The face of the man he'd seen only once before in a Polaroid.

"I'm sorry," Jay said. "How do you know my parents?"

"Oh, we were real tight in the day," Dale answered. "Used to work with your dad way back. Spent a lot of time with him and your mom when you were little."

"What do you do now?" Jay asked.

"I'm something of a business owner," he replied. "I own a couple of hotels in Biloxi and some garages. Pretty much whatever I can put my hands on."

Jay nodded, retracting his hand. "Pleasure to meet you, Dale."

The mayor gave the pair a nod before he and Collins left the patio.

"Who was that?" Rebecca asked.

"You don't know him?"

She shook her head.

"I think he knows something about my mom," Jay said.

"Like what?"

He cocked his head from side to side. "I'm not sure yet."

"You didn't want to ask him?"

"In front of Franklin?"

"Good point."

"Also, he has that vibe," Jay added.

"Vibe?"

"Something about him doesn't fit," Jay said. "I need to know a little more about him and why my father denies knowing him."

"Your dad has dementia," she reminded Jay.

"It's more than that," Jay explained. "There's a secret he's hiding."

Rebecca sighed and reclined in her chair. "Can we go back to our plans tonight?"

"Pizza and beer?" he confirmed.

Rebecca grinned. "See, you had me at pizza."

.   .   .

Want a glimpse in Jay's past?
Revisit the tragic day in August 1994 when his sister
drowned
Scan the QR code or link here:
https://dl.bookfunnel.com/fhv82a1z2z

ALSO BY DOUGLAS PRATT

The Chase Gordon Tropical Thriller Series

Diamond Reef

Dark Cay

Deep Gold

Runaway Tide

Devil Water

White Coral

Shark Pass

Gator Alley

Havana Sunrise

Gulf Dreams

Red Light At Night

Green Flash

Dead Slow

The Corsair Novels

La Playa de Los Muertos

Midnight Dance

Guerrilla Gold

The Jay Delp Mystery Thriller Series

The Woman Under the Bridge

The Girl on the East Beach

The Rikki Talens Adventure Series

Crossbones

Lost Cause

The Greene/Wolfe Series

Missing in the Keys

Missing in Zanzibar

Missing in Hawaii

The Max Sawyer Mystery Thriller Series

Blood Remembered

Baptism of Blood

Blood Stained

Crimson Blood

Blood River

Blood and Roses

www.ingramcontent.com/pod-product-compliance
Lightning Source LLC
Chambersburg PA
CBHW061120310726
48974CB00002B/617